OPERATION WHITE ROSE

Deatri King-Bey

I0520107

King-Bey Productions

This is a work of fiction. All of the characters, events, incidents, names, organizations and places portrayed in this novel are either products of the author's imagination or are used fictitiously. Any resemblance to actual persons, living or dead, business establishments, events or locales is entirely coincidental.

OPERATION WHITE ROSE

A Note From The Author

Those of you who have been hanging out with me over the years know I've often said that my first published novel was originally a different book, but one of my characters kept trying to take over the novel. Ernesto wanted his story told and it wasn't quite the story I was writing. Sooooo, I wrote Caught Up (my first published novel) to make Ernesto happy.

But what happened to the original book? This is that book. If you've read Caught up, you'll notice similarities between the stories, yet they are still very different, so I suggest you let Caught Up go and read this for what it is: Operation White Rose. If you haven't read Caught Up, wha'cha waiting for? Grab a copy. It's a great book.

I did take artistic license a few times in this novel. For example the death penalty in New York, but I think it all works nicely.

I'd also like to take a second to thank each of you for continuing to ask for more and supporting me through the years. I couldn't have made it this far without God, my family and you.

Happy Reading

Deatri King-Bey
http://deatrikingbey.com

CHAPTER ONE

Frustrated with hitting another wall in their investigation, DEA agent Ashton Powell spread the mystery lady's correspondence across the coffee table. He re-read the last two letters. "I've missed something. What's she trying to tell me?"

Agent Leonard Rogers flopped back on the couch. "Wishful thinking. She doesn't even know we exist. We've run out of time." He closed his weary blue eyes.

They'd searched for the author over six months. In a few days their only tie to her would be executed by lethal injection.

Ashton smoothed his dark hand over his mustache. "I'm not ready to throw in the towel yet. She's written once a week for what, seven years? I can't believe she'll walk away now. She'll be somewhere close to the execution. We just have to find her."

"Damn, man. Do you know how many anti-death penalty demonstrators will be there?" Leonard hunched his shoulders. "We don't even know what she looks like. How will we pick her out?"

"The tone of her letters has changed. I think she'll contact Steven in person before the execution. She's telling him without actually coming out and saying it."

Ashton gathered the copied letters and stacked them neatly. He'd grown to know and admire the author. From everything he'd read, she was strong, intelligent, fun loving; and most importantly, loyal.

Leonard frowned. "I think you've read too much into her letters. She's eluded the agency for years and won't slip up now. We need to devise a new plan."

"Call the warden anyway. She may have contacted him again."

"I can't stand that jag-off. Why did it take him so long to tell us about Steven's lover? He's full of it." Leonard snatched the phone off the end table and dialed the warden.

"We have to work with him. We don't have a choice."

"Pepita." Santiago shook her gently and switched on the nightstand lamp. "Pepita."

She clutched her chest. "San... Santiago? You scared the bageebees out of me. Why are you here? How did you get into my room?" Three men stood in the darkened corner of the hotel room. She pulled her blanket up fully. "What's going on?"

He pointed to the closet. "Take the rest of her bags to the car," he ordered two men. The third man silently waited, ready to watch the show. "We have to leave for Colombia. Tonight. Tony just arrived in town." He tossed a jogging suit on the bed. "Get dressed."

"Go away and leave me alone. I'm not going to Colombia. I'm going to Florida. I'm not leaving now. I'm not going anywhere until tomorrow at a decent hour."

He cursed in Spanish, jerked her out of bed. "You're leaving tonight."

At five foot nine and in excellent condition, she was more than a match for Santiago. She folded her arms over her chest. "No—I'm—not." She glared at the man lurking in the corner. "Take one step toward me, and I'll give you a sex change for free," she warned.

The man chuckled in a sinister way. "*No hablo Ingles.*"

"We don't have time for this, Pepita. Tony's here in Atlanta."

She shrugged. "So. I'm leaving tomorrow anyway. And what's this mess about Colombia? I'm heading to Florida for the flower show. After my new identity's ready, I'll move on. I don't give a darn who's in town. I'm not changing my plans."

He massaged his temples with his chubby fingers. "You're turning me into an old man, Pepita. I feel my last few strands of black hair turning gray."

"You are an old man," she teased. "Please, Papi, don't make me go." She hugged her middle-aged godfather. "I have to give up everything from my business to my name. Don't take this from me also."

He patted her back. "I can't go to Florida with you." He motioned toward his guard. "I'll send Jose and another man with you, but you leave tonight. After the convention, they'll escort you to Colombia."

She winked at Jose. "He doesn't even speak English."

Jose stepped toward the beautiful black senorita. Santiago stopped him in his tracks. "I've killed for less," he growled. Jose looked down, stepped back.

ഏഏഏ

"Pepita, the smell of all these flowers makes me sick," Jose complained.

"It's a flower show. And I've told you to call me Diana." She led the men through the maze of flower-laden booths to the most odorous area of the convention hall. "Only my family calls me Pepita. My friends all call me Diana."

She hoped the exhibit she sponsored met her expectations. "Oh my goodness," she gasped. "I don't believe it." Feigning surprise, she rushed toward the exhibit.

Jose stopped a few yards in front of the humongous red monstrosity with white dots. "What the hell is that?"

Diana could barely contain her laughter but maintained a straight face. "It's called a Giant Rafflesia. It's the largest flower in the world. This type of lily can grow to three feet across." She fished her camera out of her bag and snapped pictures of the lily.

"Is it a man eating plant or something? What's that smell?" Jose covered his nose with his hand.

"It smells like rotting meat to attract flies."

"Hurry up so we can move on. Where do these things grow? I'm never going there."

She stepped to the left, snapped another picture. "Malaysia and Indonesia, and stop rushing me. I haven't been to one of these conventions in years. Who knows when I'll have a chance to attend another?"

Four hours later, Diana felt like throwing up yet pretended to enjoy every second they spent in the temporary green house. Jose and his partner were greener than many of the plants. "You two look awful. Why don't we call it a night? We can order room service and watch a movie or something."

Jose didn't wait for her to change her mind. He

grabbed her hand and rushed for their suite.

⚜ ⚜ ⚜

Diana finished her catfish dinner. "You two should eat something. We have a long day ahead of us tomorrow."

"I've lost my appetite." Jose flicked the remote to select a movie. "Please tell me we won't be sniffing flowers again tomorrow."

"Do you want me to lie to you?" She took out her itinerary. "Tomorrow I'm touring the world of the roses. I absolutely love the smell of roses. Don't you?"

"If it's a flower, no."

She laughed. "I'll tell you what, Jose. You two can stay in the room or tour Miami while I enjoy myself at the convention. If you don't tell, I won't tell."

Jose and his partner grinned at each other. "Now that sounds like a plan to me. Do you want to meet for lunch?"

"I want to hear the speaker at the luncheon banquet. You can come if you'd like."

"No thanks. We'll meet for dinner."

⚜ ⚜ ⚜

The next morning, Diana rushed out of the hotel to the airport at break neck speed. The plane she'd chartered sat on the runway waiting. She trotted up the steps and aboard. "Sorry I'm late. I got a little lost."

"No problem, ma'am." The co-pilot nodded a hello and handed her the cellphone she'd requested. "Strap in. We'll be off in five minutes."

"Thanks for doing this on such short notice." Dialing the warden's number, she walked to the rear of the small plane and took her seat. "I'm all ready," she called out as she fastened her seatbelt.

"Who is this?" the warden asked.

"I'm sorry, Warden Owens. I was speaking to the pilot. I'm calling about Steven Warren. I wanted to ensure arrangements were made for my visit."

"You know this is against the rules. I could lose my job."

"Warden," she sighed, "I'm paying you handsomely. If you're caught, you don't need the job. There's no reason you should be caught. After all, it is your facility. You're only allowing him a conjugal visit."

"Maybe you aren't aware," he spewed sarcastically, "but Steven is on death row. He's only allowed out of his cell for one hour a day for recreation. And he's never allowed contact visits, thus no conjugal visits..."

She watched out the window as the plane lifted off. *God, please take all obstacles out of my way.* She'd tried to see Steven over the years, but all attempts had failed.

Santiago Calderon, her godfather, was protecting her from the men who framed Steven. Calderon didn't physically lock her away, but she still felt captive. He'd had someone watching her at all times, preventing her from making any contact other than letters.

"Are you accepting my payment or not?"

"I've made the arrangements for you."

"Thank you, Warden Owens. I appreciate your assistance. I'll see you in a few hours." She disconnected. *Thank you, God.*

CHAPTER TWO

Warden Owens showed agents Ashton Powell and Leonard Rogers into his office. "Steven is being taken to her now." He turned on the monitor, displaying conjugal-visit room six.

The ocean and dessert had more in common than the agents, he ruminated. The differences went well beyond Agent Powell being black and Agent Rogers being white. Dressed nicely in a custom-made suit, Agent Powell's size made him an imposing figure, yet something about him exuded gentle giant. He carried himself like the consummate professional.

The short balding warden craned his thick neck back. "Damn you're a big one. Remind me to stay on your good side." A quick estimate of his height set Ashton at six four.

The warden pointed to the chairs beside his desk. The average height, slender Agent Rogers wore faded jeans and a New York Rangers hockey jersey that looked like it never saw an iron. His mannerisms and foul mouth yelled of his lack of professionalism.

The agents pulled two wing-backed chairs in front of the monitor for a closer view. In twelve hours, Steven Warren would be executed by lethal injection. This presented their last chance at gaining a lead on information he held on two of the largest drug lords in the world.

All three men watched Diana sit patiently with her fingers intertwined on her lap. Transfixed to the screen, Ashton stared at the monitor in a way that made the warden feel uneasy.

"I knew you'd be pleased I overlooked the rules for this one. You've been after him for years." The warden squinted at the screen. "Damn, he sure does like 'em young." The chair creaked from the warden's excess weight as he leaned back. "Yeah, we don't want him to die with the goods, do we boys?"

❧ ❧ ❧

Diana stood at the sound of the door's hinges

grinding. Her heart raced with anticipation, anxiety and fear. Eight years was such a long time. She brushed a few wrinkles out of her bright yellow sundress, drew in a deep cleansing breath and fought to appear calm.

Steven walked into the room. For a few moments, joy and sorrow viciously battled across his face. "Oh, baby," he sighed. "Why are you here? You shouldn't have come."

She crossed the room, hugging him, loving him. "Please don't make me leave. I'm already here now." Her eyes twinkled with devilment. "It's too late."

He lifted her chin with his knuckle. "You're a sneaky little devil." He took her by the hand and led her the few steps across the room to the bed.

"You'll never guess what I have." She grinned, pulled a deck of cards from under the pillow, then sat beside him on the twin bed. "Your deal or mine? If you deal, I pick the game."

Hours later, the warden complained, "I can't believe my guards left their post to play cards with that murderer. Here comes his last meal. Maybe we'll finally hear something."

The agents continued ignoring the warden's comments. Ashton stretched his long legs, then scooted the chair closer to the screen. "He must know we're recording them, Leonard. It's the only explanation."

"You have a point." Leonard sucked air through his teeth. "There's no way in hell if it's my last day on Earth I would spend it playing cards with my lover." He resituated himself in his seat. "Damn, man, after all this time, I don't think I'd care who watched. Look at her. She's only what, twenty-eight? Thirty tops. I'd take the blanket, cover us, turn out the light and get busy."

Ashton watched the monitor, admiring their relationship. Of all the places to find an example of true love, the penitentiary didn't come close to making the list. "He respects her too much to use her. I'm impressed. She's the only one of his lady friends who stayed in contact with him over the years. Then she arranged this special visit."

He shuffled through the copies of her correspondences to Steven. She wrote once a week without fail. All the while she never received a reply, never gave a clue to her location, never used her real name and always said she loved him. Ashton had read them a thousand times, marveling at her misplaced loyalty.

As the day gave way to night, Diana became more nervous. "That was a wonderful meal. Thanks for sharing with me." She released an anxiety laugh, hoping to maintain some semblance of composure. Soon they'd take him away from her forever. It wasn't fair. She couldn't prove it, but she knew in her heart he was innocent.

Steven pushed his plate away. "Did Santiago tell you I was baptized a few years ago?" He took her by the hands. "I'm scared, but I know I'll be fine. So will you." He caressed her face. "I'll always be with you."

"I love you."

He pulled her into his arms. "Let it out. Let it all out." She sobbed on his shoulder as he pat her back.

"I can't do this. I have to tell the warden." If she could somehow stall the proceedings, maybe Santiago could find the proof.

"No!" He softened his tone. "No, baby. You can't say anything. You shouldn't even be here."

"Do you know what you're asking me to do? You're innocent. You can't expect me to stand by and do nothing." Mind spinning out of control, she drew her hands through her thick, dark hair as she staggered to her seat. "It's just..." she trailed off.

He gently combed her hair behind her ears with his fingers. "I understand how hard this is for you."

She stared into his big brown eyes. Eyes that matched her own. How could he understand when she didn't fully understand herself? She couldn't lose him. She couldn't give up the chance at healing their relationship. Her nose stung, eyes burned, throat lumped. "Please don't make me do this."

"I'm not innocent." He displayed his palms. "I have blood on my hands."

"But—"

"No buts," he cut in. "You know how I've lived my life." He looked around the small room. The guard had left them alone. He bent forward, whispering, "I'm sorry I wasn't there for you, but I'm here now. We must do things my way. If I could change the past, I would."

How he could sell death and destruction one minute and be loving to her the next hurt her soul. She'd begged him to give it up the drug life. Visions of her, Steven, and Santiago sitting around the table playing cards filled her mind. She'd prayed they'd both change. When they refused, she moved on with her life, without them. Only eighteen at the time, she'd felt like she'd lost her whole world. Before she could hope, but now Steven was dying.

In her head she knew what they were and despised the path they had chosen, but in her heart she couldn't give up on them. They were her only family and she would always love them. "You can't change the past, but you don't have to throw away your future. Tell me what I need to know, and I'll go directly to the governor. I can't do this alone."

"I'm not throwing away my future." He held her hand close to his heart. "If you come forward, we'll both die. This is my world, not yours. Do as I say."

Disheartened, she withdrew her hand. He'd chosen death over her again. "I'll do as you say."

He lowered his voice. "Promise you'll do as Santiago says. He'll protect you."

"I promise."

"That's my girl."

Hinges creaked. They both turned and saw a guard waiting by the door.

"It's time, love. I have to leave now." Steven kissed her forehead. "Remember your promise, and I love you."

Diana stood on shaky legs. "I will." She watched him walk out with his head held high.

Three seconds.

It took an eternity of three seconds for the door to close and her world to crumble. The deafening silence of the room mirrored the feeling in the core of her soul. Burning tears flowed down her face. Engulfed by pain, she couldn't make a sound; she couldn't stand. She slumped to the floor, rocking.

One of the guards, from earlier, came into the room.

He stooped, trying to console. She softly chanted, "He didn't do it. He didn't do it. He didn't do it..."

He helped her stand. Grabbing his hand, she tugged him toward the door. "They're gonna murder him. You have to make them stop. He didn't do it. Make them stop."

He pulled her away from the door. She hit at him. "Let me go. You have to stop them."

"Steven told me you'd say something like this," Officer Mason said. He held her until she stopped struggling, then guided her to the bed. "Try to calm yourself. I'll stay with you."

"But he really didn't do it." She gazed into his sorrowful brown eyes. "You have to believe me. Please take me to the warden. I'll make him listen to me this time."

"Steven's last request was that I prevent you from stalling his execution. You have to let him go. Don't prolong things for him."

"How much is he paying you? I'll pay double—triple."

"I'm doing this for free," he lied.

She fell to the bed in tears. He'd actually chosen death over her.

"Turn it off." Ashton pushed past the warden who didn't move fast enough. "I said turn the damned thing off before I throw it out the window." He cut the monitor off.

"Shit, man. Have you ever seen anything like that? I sure the hell haven't." Leonard shook his head. "I'm feeling sorry for a bastard who murdered two of our own. Damn, man, what the hell is happening?"

"Could we have some privacy, Warden?" Ashton asked. "We need to discuss our next move."

"Sure. I have to be present for the execution." He nodded and left.

"Did they track her rental car yet?" Ashton paced the warden's office.

"She's using another bogus name. We'll put a tail on her when she leaves here." Leonard watched his large friend closely. They'd been best friends since pre-school and knew each other from tip to toe.

Ashton smoothed his hand down his face. "I'm sure he confided in her. We need to find out what she knows."

"Once we learn where she lives, I'll have your cover made. Do you think you can get close enough to her? She was really in love with him."

"You make my cover tight. I'll handle the rest. The execution should be in progress now." He turned the monitor on. The conjugal room was dark.

"There is no doubt about his guilt, right?" Leonard asked. "I mean, well hell, she sounds like she knows he's innocent."

"We've gone through the evidence a million times. He did it. I wish she'd gone to the trial, so she'd know her loyalties are misplaced."

Leonard kept his suspicions about Ashton's feelings for the mystery woman to himself. Ashton had always been one hundred percent business. He wouldn't allow anyone to interfere with work. "She sounds like her parents come from New York, but was raised in the deep-south or vise versa. Then again, sometimes she sounds like she has a Spanish accent. Do you think she's trying to throw us off?"

Ashton nodded his head in agreement. "She uses a lot of southern idioms in her letters but doesn't have much of a southern drawl. She either lives down south, or knew we were intercepting his mail and tried to throw us off. I don't know what to make of it. Look, Leonard, I need some fresh air."

Officer Mason exited conjugal room six, practically knocking Ashton over. "I'm sorry."

"I shouldn't be standing so close to the door. How is she doing?"

Mason eyed Ashton's visitor badge. "I'm shaken, so think of how she feels. She finally cried herself to sleep about an hour ago."

"Can I use your flashlight? I don't want to flood the room with light."

Instead of giving Ashton his heavy-duty flashlight, he handed him a small pocket flashlight from the end of his key chain. "This should do."

"Thanks." Ashton entered the room and closed the door behind himself. Leonard would kill him for this, but he couldn't leave her alone. Quickly, quietly, he crossed the room, took a seat on the edge of the bed, then doused the flashlight.

The bedspring's eerie creak woke Diana. "Mason?" she mumbled.

Ashton took her into his arms, gently rocked. "Umm-hmm."

She rested her head on his shoulder.

Ashton's soft hum lulled her into a deep slumber. What role did she play in this high-stakes game? Steven was visibly shaken when he saw her. Which drug lord did he protect her from: Santiago Calderon, who ranked number two? Robert Carter, who ranked number six? Or both? He didn't know what to do or how to proceed. All he new was someone needed to protect her.

What am I doing? She isn't my responsibility. I have a job to do, and she is the key to it. He released a sigh of loss. *She isn't mine to protect. She can never be mine. Just do your job, Ashton.*

He stroked her back. *She's his lover. She knew of his crimes yet stuck by his side. Even if she believed he was innocent of the murders, she knew he was a major player in the drug world. I don't want her. I'm just doing my job.* He embraced her closely. *I'm just doing my job.*

CHAPTER THREE

Ashton and Leonard continued their surveillance of Diana's room from the high-rise building across from her hotel. After leaving the penitentiary, she turned in her rental car and checked into the hotel under the alias Alex Walker. She entered her room, closed the shades and never came out.

"Shit, man. This is the third day. Do you think she killed herself? Hell, should I take the DO NOT DISTURB sign from the door, so the maid can find her?"

Ashton sorted through the surveillance pictures of Diana exiting the car rental agency. She wasn't a classic beauty, but attractive in a girl next-door sort of way. He ran a finger along the outline of her smooth caramel complexion. "She wouldn't kill herself. She needs time to mourn."

Leonard focused the telescope on the hotel entrance. "Mourn smourn. If she doesn't come out by morning, I'm goin' in my damn self. Somethin' ain't right."

"You know we can't. This is no time to be emotional. Just do your job."

"Forget that shit, man. Were you doing your job when you were all hugged up on her? Hell no. I know how you feel about her. You're my partner and best friend. Don't sit there acting like this shit doesn't affect you. This ain't that kind of party, *partner*."

Ashton pushed away from the desk. "What am I going to do?" He stared out the window at the busy street twelve stories below.

"We don't have a legitimate reason to drop this case. We'll be careful and do our job like you said. I've got your back." Leonard adjusted the telescope. "Oh shit! Calderon's entering the hotel. Why didn't someone call us?" He strapped on his holster. His cellphone rang. "Yeah," he answered. "Well it's too freakin' late now. He's already in."

Ashton checked his weapon.

Leonard held up his hand. "You can't come, man. If

they see you, your cover will be blown before I create it. Stay here. I can handle this."

"But..."

"No. You have to stay here. I won't let anything happen to her. Just stay the hell back." He ran out the room.

Ashton focused his binoculars on Diana's window. A short while later his heart leapt into his throat at the sight of Santiago opening the shades. "He's in her room. Hurry!" he said into the headset to Leonard.

"I'm on my way, man. Hold tight."

He fought to clear his mind. If he didn't separate from his feelings and treat this as a normal case, he'd get them all killed. "Don't do anything stupid, Leonard. Stay back and observe. I can see into the room. If he tries to kidnap her, be ready to intervene."

"I'm on it."

Santiago used his key to enter the room. "Pepita, it's Santiago." A small bit of light seeped around the blinds into the cold, silent room. He saw her curled on the bed wearing the same yellow sundress his informant from the prison described.

He crossed over to the window and opened the shades. He knew he shouldn't be there, but he had to console her.

"He's dead," she whispered.

He hugged her. "But you aren't. Take a shower, then we'll eat."

Barely shaking her head, she turned away. "I'm not hungry."

"Well you smell bad. Do you think Steven wants you carrying on this way? I know you've never had a loss like this, but trust me, love, you have to move on with your life. Steven will always be a part of us."

She rested her chin on his shoulder. "You're right. I know you're right. It's just so senseless. He didn't have to die."

"Stop torturing yourself, Pepita. We can't change the past. I'm not saying I know your pain, but he was my best friend, my brother and spying on Carter for me. It's my fault he was caught."

She shook her head, messy black hair flying every which way. "No it wasn't. You tried to save him."

"There's plenty of blame to spread around. In the end, none of it will bring him back." He smoothed down her shoulder length hair. "Now shower so we can have lunch." His face showed a grin his heart didn't feel. "You're always hungry."

Ashton kicked at the table in disgust. "Stand down, Leonard. She knows him."

"What's happening?"

"She's in the shower, and he's standing at the window talking on the phone. She's in this deep." After she checked in, Leonard had stalled her while Ashton planted bugs in her room.

"I'm sorry, man. I'm on my way back."

Santiago pointed to the center of the room. "Over there. Thanks"

His bodyguard put the small round dining table down. Other men set the table and brought in the food while Diana finished her shower and dressed.

"Wait outside the door. I need time with Pepita." The bodyguards followed Santiago's order.

"You were right." Diana exited the bathroom. "I smelled awful. How was the service?"

"Beautiful. You sent the roses didn't you?" The church was filled with white roses. He chuckled, thinking you could smell them a block away. White roses were Steven's favorite.

She grinned as she topped her baked potato with butter and sour cream. "I might have had a little something to do with it. I wish I could have been there."

"It was too dangerous. Everyone wants to locate you." He reached into his suit coat and pulled out a folded business envelope. "Here's your new identity and your plane ticket. Are you sure you want to move to San Diego? I can't protect you as well in his territory."

Sorting through the documentation, she grumbled, "You mean you can't snoop on me as well in his territory.

Don't you think California is the last place Carter will look?" She spent most of her life hiding from drug lords and was tired. She longed for freedom from the world that was hers, yet not hers.

He cut into his steak. "You have a point."

Diana examined the plane ticket. "Oh great. I have time to shop before I leave."

Santiago took out his money clip and counted out two thousand dollars. "Spend cash. You're Alex until you board the plane." He tried to hand her the money.

"No thanks, I have plenty of cash."

"Be careful when you check out. Someone could have followed you here. I can't believe you ditched my men."

"Don't blame them. I knew you'd show up eventually. I've been planning this for over a year. No one followed me. After I turned in the car, I had the taxi take the scenic route while I watched for someone following us. I also tipped the cabbie two hundred dollars and told him to remember me as a short, balding, white male."

Leonard hit at the table. "Damn, Ashton. That's sure what that bastard told me. I have a good mind to kick his ass."

They listened as Santiago and Diana finished their meal, had conversation the agents couldn't use, said their goodbyes and separated.

Ashton asked Leonard, "How long until my cover's ready?"

"It'll be final by the time you hit San Diego. I'll have agents in the airport to follow her when she arrives. The earliest flight is tonight. I'll join you in a few days. I've a little cleaning to do before I leave."

Ashton grabbed his keys. "Come on. She's on the move."

Diana stepped back to fully appreciate her handy work. She'd gone to Steven's grave and planted a floral arrangement of various white and red seasonal plants. Beneath the tribute were bulbs that would bloom in the spring with a special surprise. Her favorite touch was the arching trellis over his headstone. Someday the running white roses would bloom to their full magnificence.

Ashton readjusted his earpiece, then watched and listened to Diana while pretending to visit a friend's grave a hundred yards away from her location.

"Heads up, Ashton," Leonard warned. "Here comes Santiago. His men just gave me the third degree about waiting outside the cemetery. I told them I'm waiting on my mother."

"I see him now."

Limos pull behind Diana's taxi. Ashton couldn't tell if she didn't notice or didn't care. Two of Santiago's men walked to the taxi and spoke to the driver. They took her bags and placed them in a second limo. "This doesn't look good," Ashton commented.

"What? Shit, man, tell me what's happening."

"Santiago is headed for Diana and looks like one pissed drug lord." Ashton pressed his earpiece in tighter and listened.

"Pepita!"

Diana froze at the sound of Santiago's angry voice.

"I should turn you over my knee for this." He stood in front of her. "What in the hell do you think you're doing? He died to save you, yet you continually place yourself in harm's way! Did he die in vain?"

The truth within his words brought tears to her eyes. "I'm sorry. I just wanted to say goodbye. I'm sorry."

Cursing himself under his breath, he took her into his arms. "No. I'm sorry. I shouldn't blame you for his death. It was my fault, not yours. I had him infiltrate Carter's regime. My arrogance killed Steven, not your naiveté. I should have arranged to sneak you into the funeral so you could pay proper respects."

He glanced over his shoulder at the grave. "This is your best work yet." He turned them both to face it.

Tired of crying, she wiped the tears from her face. "Wait until spring when it's all settled and the bulbs bloom."

He rested his hand on her shoulder. "You can't return. You can't go anywhere associated with Steven."

"I know, but I've pictured it in my mind." She turned toward him. "I'm sorry you had to come after me... again. This was something I needed to do. I didn't think anyone would still be watching the graveyard. I didn't see any danger." She shook her head. "I haven't been thinking clearly since..." she trailed off.

"You have no reason to be sorry. Look, you need to clean yourself before the flight. I've hired someone to ensure you board the plane." He pointed to the second limo. "His name is Hernando. Don't give him a hard time, or I'm sending you to Colombia. I'll have my men straighten this mess."

"This was my last time disobeying you. I promise."

"Didn't you promise Steven you'd do as I say?" Her sheepish grin triggered his memories of her troubled teenaged years.

Instead of attending school, she'd skip to visit botanical gardens or anything outdoors. She'd been suspended on several occasions for her truancy, which set well by her. By the time she was fifteen, Steven had given up trying to make her stay in school. She passed her G.E.D. and started working for a lawn care company.

"Technically, you told me not to attend the funeral. You didn't say anything about visiting his gravesite."

"You knew exactly what I meant." He relaxed into a smile. "That's neither here nor there though. I'll call you tomorrow."

He gently pushed her toward the limo, then knelt beside the gravesite. "What am I going to do with her, old friend?"

CHAPTER FOUR

Ashton's shoulders slumped. Of all the flights to San Diego, of all the seats on the plane, how did he end up not only on the same flight, but seated next to his assignment? He stalked off the plane.

⸙⸙⸙⸙⸙⸙⸙⸙⸙

Diana caught a whiff of the cologne Officer Mason wore. She'd never smelt it before him and loved the masculine bouquet. The fragrance was so faint she hadn't even smelled it until the officer embraced her in her time of need. She turned her head away from the window to see who wore it. No one was there. She leaned her head against the window, ready to leave her old life behind for a new one.

A few minutes later, she felt someone slip into the seat next to her, then she saw a rose placed in her lap. Picking up the rose, she automatically drew it to her nose. Like Steven, white roses were her favorite. She turned to see who'd been so sweet. "Thank you, but why did you give me this?"

"You looked so sad," he said with a deep calming voice. "I was hoping to bring a smile to your face. I'm glad it worked."

Heat rushed to her face. "Sweet. Really sweet. Thanks." She snuck a peek at the man sitting beside her: short cropped hair, smooth chocolate skin, dark bedroom eyes, perfectly trimmed mustache, luscious lips.

"I guess the only proper thing to do is introduce myself. I'm Ashton. Ashton Powell."

"I'm Diana. Diana... Diana Josephine Warren."

He chuckled lightly. "For a second there, I thought you forgot your name."

She grinned. "For a second there, I did forget my name." His broad, bright smile encouraged her to continue the conversation. "Are you heading to or coming from?"

"Heading to, and you?"

"To." After the flight attendant completed the flight instructions, Diana watched the lift off. Once in the air, she closed her eyes, affectively ending the New York chapter of her life.

"You look at peace."

Accepting her past to ready for the future, she kept her eyes closed. "My parents died when I was young. It didn't seem real to me. I guess, in a way, I never lost anyone close to me until a few days ago. I went a little nuts for a while, but now I'm back."

Feeling an unusual kinship with the handsome stranger, she opened her eyes. "I knew he was dying. I thought I was ready, but when he passed, I couldn't hack it." She released the last bits of anxiety she held. "I'm glad he's free." *Now we're both free.*

"I'm sorry about your loss."

Head cocked to the side, she looked at him crosswise.

Shoulders hunched, he asked, "What?"

"What planet are you from?" Attractive, great sense of humor, sensitive, yet still masculine. No way did he come from Earth, she mused.

"Mars. Why? You have something against people from Mars?"

Thinking him too good to be true, she raised a brow. "The jury's still out on that."

"So where are you headed? I'm transferring to San Diego."

"Really? Me too. I mean, I'm not transferring, but I'm moving to San Diego. I'm starting a new life in a new place."

"What do you do?"

Brushing her hair behind her ears with her hands, she wished she'd styled it before the flight. "Landscaping."

"You cut people's grass?"

"If they need it." She always got a kick out of people's reactions to her profession. "Actually, I design and implement landscapes. One of the reasons I picked San Diego is the climate. What about you? What do you do?"

"I'm a defense attorney."

"Are you any good?"

Mouth rolled into a slow, sexy grin, he said, "I can hold my own."

After hours of engaging conversation, she fell asleep.

Always afraid her background would interfere with relationships, Diana shied away from men. She didn't want to shy away from Ashton, and wouldn't. For the first time in her life, she was free to live fully, and live was what she intended on doing.

Ashton drifted off a few times, battling with his conscious and past experience. He'd been married to the woman of his dreams once before. It turned out to be a nightmare.

Loving his job, he wouldn't jeopardize it for a woman of questionable background. Diana being the most stimulating person he'd ever met didn't matter. Her beauty increasing by the millisecond didn't matter. Her genuine interest in him didn't matter. Nothing mattered but finishing the job he set out to do.

Brushing her hair behind her ear, he wished he could do this when she was awake. The high pitch of the fasten seatbelts chime sounded. "Diana, we're landing," he whispered.

She stretched, yawned. "Too quick. I could use another hour or two." She rubbed her tired eyes with her fingers. "Thanks for the rose and the conversation. I enjoyed both." Her mood darkened. After their taxi dropped them off at their hotels, she may never see him again. She already missed him. She shook off her sorrow. It was silly to feel this way about a man she had just met.

"When can I bring you another rose?"

"You're a smooth one aren't you?" A few days ago she sat at the lowest point in her life. Now she flew high in a plane, joking with Mr. Right. Conflicting emotions swirled through her mind. She wanted him, but what about her drug ties? She pushed her worries away, reaffirming new state, new life, new freedom.

"Liked that didn't ya?" He winked.

To hide her expression, she dropped her head. "You have your moments." She wanted to kiss a man she'd just met. *How embarrassing.*

One second Ashton's flirting with the best of them, playing the game as he had so many times before. This time was different. This time there were emotions involved: emotions he refused to admit he harbored, emotions that attacked his defensive barriers, emotions that caused him to act out of instinct instead of duty.

He cupped her face into his hands, leaned in and kissed away his career as a DEA agent. He rested his forehead on hers, searching for the right words to say, lightly kissed her one last time, then regained his control. "I've changed my mind about the taxi."

She relaxed her head on his shoulder. Six seconds. It took an infinitesimally short six seconds for Diana's world to be rebuilt on a kiss. The passionate hum of his moan had mirrored the feeling in her heart. "Don't you want to share a taxi?"

He lifted her face, brushed his lips over hers. "The problem is I want to share a lot more than a taxi." He leaned back in his seat and willed the hardness throbbing against his pants zipper to calm. "Until a few seconds ago, I'd been the perfect gentleman." He peeked at her out of the corner of his eye. "You're ruining me woman."

Boy how he loved to hear her laugh. They continued their conversation and allowed the other passengers to exit first. "I don't have new business cards yet." He pulled out one of his old cards. "Call me once you're settled in a week or two." He wrote his new cell number on the back of the card.

⋇⋇⋇

"What's taking so damned long to find her? It's been five days," Robert Carter chastised into the receiver.

"Stop yelling at me or this conversation is over," came Tony's angry voice through the line. "I'm not a child, Dad."

The elder Carter propped the cordless phone between his ear and shoulder, then poured himself a brandy. "Did you go to Atlanta?" Drink in hand, he walked to his desk.

"Once I discovered her true identity, I went to Atlanta. She'd sold her house and business. I had my men track the moving truck—"

"And?" he interrupted before finishing his drink.

"And if you'd allow me to get more than two words out of my mouth, I'd tell you. Damn. The truck went to the airport. Santiago had one of his private jets flying all over the damned world with her stuff. There's no telling where he had it dropped off, or if he still has it."

Carter pointed his glass across the desk as if his son were in the room with him. "How did you lose her in New York? You should have taken her when you had the chance."

"We didn't have a chance. I had to convince the cabbie it was in his best interest to tell me where he dropped her. In exchange for his life, he tipped me off about the DEA closing in. I couldn't go within a mile of the hotel without one of Santiago's men tagging me. It was too risky to chance going in."

"What about the graveyard?"

"DEA was following her. I saw those sneaky bastards and backed off. Santiago had her taken to the airport, and we lost her."

"Santiago's been contacting people along my pipeline. You have to find her before he makes his move. Did you check into her family?"

"She's estranged from her family. They haven't spoken in at least fifteen years. Santiago is all she has left."

Carter threw his drink across the room. The glass shattered against the wall. "Could she be in Colombia?"

"Doubtful. I'm having all of Santiago's holds watched, and he knows it. I need more time."

"We don't have more time!"

"Well damn, Dad. It's not like I can look in the phonebook for Diana Pepita Johnson. Hell, she could be anywhere in the world. I don't know her name. I don't know if she's had plastic surgery. I don't know shit. If you hadn't framed Steven, Santiago wouldn't be after us. So get off my back, and let me do my job."

"Damn." Carter massaged his temples.

"I can agree with you there. Leave it to me. I'm the best. I'll find her. You know I have my contact inside the DEA working it."

"Can he be trusted? We haven't used him in years."

"Not only am I paying him a friggen' mint to keep his eyes and ears open, I also hold incriminating evidence of his extra curricular activity with extremely young boys. He's a straight up pervert, Dad. I had him transfer to the Atlanta office. If she returns to Atlanta, she's ours."

"I'm leaving it in your hands. I don't know what

Santiago has planned. You know we can't stop him without her."

"I'm doing everything humanly possible. The man has an unlimited amount of money and connections all over the planet. Why'd you pick a fight with the meanest dog in the pound?"

"My fight was with Steven, not Santiago!"

"Come on, Dad. They were like brothers. I told you not to believe that bogus fight of theirs. Steven wouldn't betray Santiago, so you let him die. Now Santiago's after us with a vengeance." He sighed. "This isn't getting us anywhere. I'm heading to New York. Maybe I missed something."

CHAPTER FIVE

Ashton opened the file on his first client and scanned through the pages. *I can't believe I kissed Diana.* A week later, thoughts of their career-ending kiss still haunted him. Memories of her soft laugh and the sparkle in her big mahogany eyes warmed his heart.

He lowered his head into his hands. *She isn't loyal. Her longtime lover died, a few days later she's kissing on a new man, acting like Steven didn't exist. She's as two faced as any other woman.*

Loyal to his money is what she is. He reached under his desk for his briefcase, unlocked it and searched for her financial statement. He stared at the total as if it might have decreased since morning. *Over seven million dollars. That's a lot of grass cutting.* He tossed the statement in the case and slammed the case shut. *I would have written every day for seven million.*

He heard a knock at the door. "Come in." He quickly placed the briefcase under his desk.

Leonard strutted in and closed the door. "What's up?" He rested in one of the leather chairs that sat in front of Ashton's desk as he craned his neck to look around the opulent office.

One wall was taken by built in bookshelves that housed Ashton's law library. A sixth floor view could be seen through the shaded fiberglass back wall. Leonard's eyes narrowed on the wet bar off to the side. "Damn, man. This shit is sweet." He ran his hand along the antique oak desk. "I guess I should have gone to law school."

"You can always go."

"No thanks. I like being the go to man too much. I'd go crazy doing all the reading and writing you do. Now the goin' to court shit I can handle." He stood slightly and took a set of keys out of his pants pocket. "Here are the keys to your new home. It's in an upper-middle class neighborhood. The *movers* are there now setting up the surveillance." He tossed the keys.

"What's she up to." Ashton caught the keys and set

them to the side.

"Doin' yard work and keeping that old lady company. Diana really likes dogs. It's the only thing she stops for. I'm buying you a dog."

"No dogs, Leonard. You know I hate dogs."

He waved Ashton off. "Well she loves them, and it'll give you two a common interest."

"Did you hear me? I hate dogs."

"Stop whining. You two can take the dog on walks after work. It's the perfect excuse to be together without *being together*. She takes a walk every night."

"No." Ashton regretted telling him about their kiss. Now he'd never hear the end of it.

Leonard sucked air through his teeth. "You know I'm right. Stop being a jerk. You're at work most of the day. You'd only have to be with it what, an hour? With the way she acts around dogs, she'll take over. Trust me on this. I know what I'm talking about."

"Get me one of those small dogs. You know—the ones that eat tacos."

Leonard contorted his face as if he smelled something offensive. "There's no way in hell I'm buying you a Chihuahua. What's wrong with you? Don't tell me mister big and bad is afraid of dogs." He searched Ashton's stern face. "Oh hell naw. You're afraid of dogs!"

Ashton straightened his already neat desk. "Just because I don't like dogs, doesn't mean I'm afraid of them." He tapped a stack of papers on the desk to align them neatly. "It means I don't like the way they smell, the way they tear up the house, the way they dig holes all over the yard, or all the noise they make when they bark, and don't get me started on their crapping all over the place. Small dog, small noise, small mess."

Leonard didn't believe a word. Thinking back to their childhood, Ashton never liked dogs. He held up his hands in defeat. "Okay. You win. A small dog it is. But forget about getting one of those freakin' toy dogs. That ain't gonna happen." He reached over Ashton's desk for the file. "What's this, your new case?"

Ashton gently took the file from him. "You know you can't read these files. And yes, it's my new case."

"You be crackin' me up with all your lawyer mumbo-jumbo. You really like this stuff, don't you? Why don't you just switch all the way over?"

He placed the file in the top drawer. "I like the cloak and dagger I can't have as your everyday, run of the mill lawyer." The firms Ashton worked for provided legitimate covers in exchange for his working pro-bono cases. Though his paycheck came from the company, his real employer was the United States Government. Ashton and Leonard were on a special task force within the DEA. They were considered the new secret weapon against drug lords and given more freedom to get the job done.

"But you're good. You could make so much more on the outside."

"You know it's not about the money."

When Ashton was in law school, his sister died of a heroin overdose. Before her death, he wanted to be a defense attorney. After her death, he needed to fight against men like Santiago Calderon and Robert Carter. The kind of men Diana fell in love with. Now he found himself doing his job because he knew nothing else, nothing but a spark within him ignited by Diana.

He failed to shake away the memories of the passion they shared. He wondered why everything always led back to Diana. "Is Santiago still in town?"

Leonard's cellphone sounded. "Wha'cha got for me. Cool. Thanks." He disconnected and slid the phone onto his belt clip. "Speak of the devil. Guess who just gave our little flower girl a visit?"

"I knew he'd show eventually."

⚜⚜⚜

"Won't you take a break, honey?" Norma asked. "Come on, you've been out here all morning."

Resting on the shovel, Diana wiped the sweat from her brow with her hand, leaving a dirt smudge. "Once I finish the holes along the walk, I'll quit for a bit. I promise. Why don't you pull up a chair and keep me company." She continued digging twelve-inch diameter holes along her walk, starting from the front steps, spaced three feet apart. "I only have four to go."

"Oh my goodness." Norma pointed at the stretch limo

pulling in front of the house. "Do you know who this could be?"

Diana glanced over her shoulder. "Santiago!" She dropped her shovel and ran for him.

He exited the car and opened his arms. "I had to see my baby girl's new home."

She introduced him to Norma O'Connor, her neighbor, then entered the house. "Please take a seat. I'm so glad you came. I didn't expect you." She continued standing to keep the white furniture clean.

"I have to move on," Norma said. "I need to start lunch. Will you be staying long, Santiago?"

"No, señora. I just dropped by to see how Diana was coming on."

"Well it was nice meeting you. I'll show myself out, honey."

He watched the older lady leave. "So she's your nosey neighbor."

"Don't call her nosey. She's just friendly. I can't believe you're here. Do you want to go out for dinner?"

"I'd love to, but I have to leave before DEA locates me. Do you like it here?"

"So far so good." The three-bedroom ranch house was a little large for one person, but she loved the location, quiet neighborhood and huge back yard.

"Have you heard from Ashton?"

She sat on the edge of the coffee table. "I knew you were up to something. You're checking on me. I've been fine for the past twelve years on my own. I'll be fine."

"Give me his last name."

"He's just a man I met on the plane," she dragged out.

"He isn't *just* a man. He's a man you're interested in."

"I'm not marrying him, so what's the problem? Are you planning on giving the third degree to every person I meet."

"Yes," he stated calmly. "You're my responsibility now. Steven allowed you to cut us off. I'm not having it."

Knowing there was no use in arguing, she crossed her arms over her chest.

He continued. "Did you know Brian O'Connor is retired FBI?"

"Yes I did. Shall we waste the rest of our time on this silliness?"

"Are you sure you don't want to move to Colombia for a while?"

"What are you up to, Santiago? You're afraid he's coming after me again, aren't you?" She'd been hiding from faceless drug lords her whole life. All she wanted was freedom to be. *No more hiding.*

"He is. I can't leave men in town or he'll find you. The only contact we can have is phone. That's why I'm here. I don't know when I'll be able to see you again."

She looked away. "Why won't you leave Carter alone? I'm not running again, Santiago. I want a life."

"I know you don't understand, but I can't drop this." He gently turned her chin to face him. "Carter's responsible for the death of my brother." He stopped to compose himself. They weren't blood brothers, but brothers in the most important way, the heart.

"It wasn't enough to frame Steven. No, he took after you. Why, Pepita?" He caressed her face, stroking a few strangling hairs into her ponytail. "What have you done? I know I've earned a spot in Hell when I die, but I have never gone after the innocent. Besides helping raise you, that's the only decent thing I've ever done. When he came after you, he started a war I intend on finishing."

"When will it end?"

"When you first cut us out of your life, I was hurt and angry. But now I understand. You did the right thing, baby. Now try to understand that I must do this my way." He took her hands into his. "I don't like leaving you without protection. When you were in Atlanta, things were different. The DEA didn't know about you. I want you to move to Colombia." She didn't even know what Tony or any of Carter's men looked like. Santiago was always afraid if she recognized one of them, she'd go after them for framing Steven.

"Don't worry about me. I'm thirty years old. I'll manage." Her eyes lit up along with a half-hearted smile. "Hey, my next door neighbor's retired-FBI. I'm in the safest place in America."

"I'm afraid it's time for me to leave." He kissed her

cheek lightly. "Keep a low profile. Carter's son is looking for you in Atlanta. If I stay away, there's no way he'll ever find you."

"I'll go to Colombia if you come with me. We can both start a new life of freedom."

"I'll never be free." He stood. "I must leave. Do not contact anyone from your past and you'll never be found. You are free."

"Love you." She showed him out, leaned against the doorframe and watched the limo drive off. He'd chosen the drug world over her again. Just as when she was eighteen. She wished his choice had been a shock. Attempting to bury her feelings of abandonment, she returned to the yard and dug holes. For once she wanted someone to choose her.

Ashton let Benji out the back sliding door, then went to answer the front door. "Hello." He saw Diana across the street kneeling beside her front stoop, filling a pot with dirt. Even in baggy black sweats, she looked beautiful.

Norma's eyes followed the path of Ashton's stare to Diana. "Welcome to the neighborhood. I'm your neighbor from across the street, Norma O'Connor. Just call me Norma. I hope it isn't too late. I saw your light on."

"I'm Ashton Powell. Would you like to come in?"

"Why thank you." She followed him into the house.

"I'd offer you a seat, but everything's a little unorganized. I was just about to feed my dog." He headed for the kitchen.

Norma followed through the living room, down the hallway, into the kitchen. "When does the rest of your family arrive?"

He glanced up from opening the dog food bag, flashed a million dollar smile. "I'm single." He took a small dog food bowl out of a grocery sack, filled it with kibble.

She watched the large man fumble with the puppy, thinking he and Diana would make a handsome couple. "What do you do for a living? I'm a fulltime grandmother."

"I'm an attorney. I don't know why he won't eat." He put Benji out, then read the ingredients on the dog food bag. "This is supposed to be the good stuff."

"Why don't you take him on a walk to work up his appetite?" She grabbed Benji's leash off the table. "Here you go."

He raised a brow in consideration. He'd worried about Diana becoming suspicious of him living across the street. The only other house available for long term was two miles away. "I guess he could use a walk." This way Norma could break the ice.

"Great. I'll introduce you to the other neighbors."

Diana set the last pot at the end of the walk and stretched her back.

"Diana, I want to introduce you to our new neighbor."

Diana glanced over her shoulder, took a double take, smiled. "I can't believe this. Ashton Powell." She shook her head. "This is too unbelievable."

He stepped forward with open arms. "And me without a rose." They hugged.

Norma scratched her head. "You two already know each other? Of course you do. Let me get in the house before Brian comes for me. It was nice meeting you, Ashton." She nodded and left.

"You, too, Norma."

Diana stooped to pet the puppy behind his ears. "Who is this adorable little fellow?"

Sick of the mongrel, he answered, "Benji."

Diana stood and stared at Ashton a few seconds. She'd thought about him constantly and couldn't believe her eyes. "Want to sit on the porch for a bit."

"Sure." He followed, dragging Benji along. "Would you come on?" Benji stopped and smelled every other blade of grass. Ashton lifted the dog and carried him the remaining distance.

Diana giggled at the pair. "How long have you had Benji?"

He settled beside her on the porch swing, placed the leash in her outstretched hand and eyeballed his watch. "I'd say a good three hours. Or bad depending on where you're looking from." He watched her play with the puppy. Longings of family stirred within him. Raised in a large family, he wanted one of his own. He buried his feelings.

She was part of the drug world. Not wife material.

"Why did you name him Benji?"

"Full of questions today, aren't you? How about I tell you everything about him?"

"I'm being rude, aren't I? I'm sorry. I've been around Norma too long."

"She is a bit much, isn't she?" He stretched his long legs out and leaned against the back of the swing. "I found Benji in our parking lot at work a few days ago. I told the dog pound to call me if no one claimed him. I wanted to make sure he wasn't put to sleep."

She gently clutched her heart, and her face softened. "Awe, that's the sweetest thing I've ever heard." She watched Benji nibble on his foot.

Ashton smiled. She ate Leonard's story up. He could hardly wait to tell how he selected the name. "I named him after the dog on those old movies. I guess he's so skinny from being on the streets. Once I fatten him up, he'll look just like Benji's cousin."

She giggled. He became worried. He'd never seen a Benji movie and had no idea what the dog looked like. He just repeated what Leonard told him. "What?"

"You really don't know anything about dogs, do you?"

"No. Not really." The puppy chewed on the leash. "Stop it, Benji." He gently tugged at the thin leather leash. "He wouldn't eat his dinner, but he wants to chew everything else in sight."

"Ashton." His powerful, dark gaze held her captive. She'd always dreamt of freedom, but relished in this new form of captivity.

He reached out for her. "Diana?"

Recomposing herself, she mentally shook lose. "I'm sorry. What type of dog is Benji?"

He cocked his head to the side. "A mutt. He's about two."

"Two what?"

"Two years." He frowned. "What's this about?"

Hoping to contain her laugh, she held her hands over her mouth. "I'm sorry." Tears of joy filled her eyes and were pushed out by the laughter. "I'm really sorry. This is too funny." She wiped the tears from her eyes. "They should have told you this at the pound."

"What's wrong? Does he have rabies or something?"

"Let's just say the name Benji fits him now, but it won't fit him a year from now."

Eyes zoomed in on the scraggly mutt, he tried to figure out what she was talking about. Leonard had given him all the information he needed.

"I've always wanted a dog like Benji." She rubbed the puppies back.

He relaxed considerably. For a second there he thought Leonard had set him up.

"Benji isn't a mutt. He's a very expensive breed."

He stared at the bony mass of fur. "I'm glad I didn't pay."

"Benji is an Irish Wolfhound."

He knew more about quantum physics than dogs. "Is there anything special I should know about his care? It looks like you know more than I do." He had to give it to Leonard. He knew his stuff. This would be perfect.

"For starters, he's a lot closer to two months old than two years. When he's full grown, he'll stand about three feet tall and weigh around 145 pounds. His breed is the tallest breed there is."

Leonard is a dead man. He raised his eyes from the puppy to hers. "You're serious, aren't you?"

"I'm afraid so." She pulled Benji onto the seat. "He'll grow and grow and..."

"That's enough, Diana. I get it." He dropped his head into his palms. "He's a puppy."

"Heck, I know lots about dogs, and a dog that size could be intimidating to me. They should have told you at the pound. I can't believe they allowed you to take him home without any information. What kind of establishment are they running?"

"He's a puppy?"

"If you don't want him, I'll take him. I'll even pay."

"Thanks, Diana, but I'll keep him."

"What will you do with him while you're at work?"

"My back yard is fenced."

"Six or eight foot?"

"Four."

"You need at least a six foot privacy fence. Why don't I watch him during the day while you're at work? I could use the company."

"I would never impose on you. I'll take him to a kennel or something."

She took his hand into hers. "You let a complete stranger cry on your shoulder, but you won't allow your friend to watch your puppy. I don't understand you."

"You really don't mind?"

"Ashton, listen to me. I want to watch Benji."

"Wolfgang."

Her face scrunched. "Excuse me?"

"I've changed his name to Wolfgang. He can't go through life with a name like Benji."

"Shall we take *Wolfgang* for a walk?"

"Sure." He held his hand out for her. "Thanks for helping me with him. I'll pay you."

"I won't take your money, but thanks for offering. Just drop him off in the mornings."

Hand in hand, they continued their stroll through the neighborhood: Wolfgang discovered he liked to eat grasshoppers and other various insects, Ashton fought the urge to drag Diana home and make love until he died from exhaustion, and Diana's mind internally rambled through one of her many conversations with Norma.

In this conversation Norma had told her she was glad Diana wasn't against marriage like most single people of her generation. When she explained to Norma that just because she wanted marriage someday didn't mean she actively sought a husband, Norma's reply hit close to home.

She glanced at Ashton, then leaned her head on his shoulder. Norma had told her she'd find her Mr. Right because she wasn't looking.

CHAPTER SIX

After a quick home-cooked meal, Ashton and Diana sat on her front stoop and allowed Wolfgang to run around the yard dragging his leash.

"Your yard looks fantastic. I can't believe how much you've done in a week."

"If I had the proper equipment, I'd be done by now. The men aren't building my tool shed and fence until tomorrow. After they finish, I'll order equipment. By next week I'll have everything I need to work."

He looked at the shrubs, flowers, young trees, and rock formations then compared them to his yard—grass, lightly sprinkled with dandelions and clover. "Are you sure you don't have the proper tools?"

Usually oblivious to compliments, his sent her heart soaring and temperature rising. "Thanks. It took me five days to do what I could have done in two if I had the proper equipment."

He stood, walked around the yard and examined it closely. "You actually did all of this?"

"I told you I design landscapes."

He settled on porch swing. "This is really great. I'm not an expert or anything, but if you did this without the proper tools, what can you do with them?"

"You're embarrassing me." Feeling flush, she looked away. "After I finish my yard, I'll start on Norma's. I'm thinking low maintenance yet pretty. She say's my yard makes hers look like the junk heap."

"She's right. You make everyone in the neighborhood look bad."

"How about I do your yard after Norma's?"

"You're already taking care of Wolfgang for me. I can't ask you to do my yard, too."

"I love yard work. It's relaxing. And you didn't ask, I volunteered."

"I'll pay you."

"If you must, pay for the plants, but the labor is free. Deal?"

"Deal."

She ran into the house without warning. Wolfgang jumped onto the stoop and barked at the door. She peeked out a few seconds later. "Scoot back, baby." She gently opened the door, moving Wolfgang out of the way. "I wanted to show you this." She handed Ashton a blue binder that said *Residences* on the side.

"What's this?"

She flipped the yellow porch light on. "Examples of my work to help you decide how you want your yard. Pick a few designs. I'll choose the correct plants for this region. I know you're not interested in drawing butterflies or hummingbirds, so these should be fine."

He opened the binder. "You just happened to have this sitting around?" Her luscious lips curled into a grin. Memories of their passion-filled kiss flooded his mind. He quickly dropped his gaze and paged through the binder. *I have a job to do. She's part of the drug world. She isn't wife material.* He used the binder to help cover his hardening state.

"I unpacked my binders and books first. They were the easiest."

Hundreds of yards, each having its own appeal, yet still shining through showcasing her artistic signature. Amazed he asked, "Did you do all of these?"

"I designed them, but I had people working with me to help implement them. I've been scanning pictures all week. I'm creating electronic galleries on my iPad to replace the binders"

He flipped through the photos. "You had your own business landscaping?"

"I told you I do landscapes."

His eyes traveled from the binder to her expressive mahogany eyes. "I'm sorry. I know you did. These are magnificent. How long have you had your own business?"

"I started out when I was fifteen with the small stuff. You know—cutting grass, trimming trees, shaping bushes, pulling weeds. When I was eighteen, I moved to implementing designs I'd created for people whose yards I used to care for. Eventually, I had a pretty good business. I've even done international sites."

She prided herself in never accepting a penny of drug money and making it on her own, unlike her siblings. She couldn't select who her family was, but she did have a choice not to accept their behavior. It hurt her deeply and was hard to cut off Steven and Santiago, but she didn't see an alternative. Now Santiago wouldn't allow her to leave again. And honestly, she couldn't let him go right now. She needed more time to grieve and sort out her feelings. Plus, she needed his protection. She couldn't trust the government to keep her safe from Carter.

Am I free? She buried her feelings of being trapped. This was her new life, and she'd create a new kind of freedom.

Truly impressed, Ashton asked, "Do you have any binders of your international work?"

She cocked her head to the side. "You want to see my work? You don't have to do this."

"I'd love to see your work," he replied truthfully. Her face lit up, causing his heart to skip a beat.

"I'll be right back." She exited the house a short time later with the international binder. "Here you go."

He thumbed through the pages. "How many people worked for you?" She'd done major campuses around the world, and they were just as spectacular as the individual yards.

"Fifteen full time. Since we implemented designs all over the world, we subcontract the vast majority of the labor. My people designed and supervised the jobs. I personally don't do much work for companies. I design; my team implements. I prefer working on smaller jobs."

"Companies must pay a pretty penny for this."

"They do pay better, but it's not as rewarding. Seeing Norma's genuine smile when I finished her flower bed was worth more than the two hundred thousand I charged Hughes Corporation."

He couldn't believe his ears. His ex-wife would have followed the money.

"Most people figure a yard is a yard, but they're wrong. It's kind of like how you prefer working pro-bono cases. You just find them more rewarding." She chased Wolfgang across the yard and wrestled with him.

His case against her crumbled quickly. Somehow he'd known Diana had earned the seven million legally. The way she carried herself, her outlook on life, her everything was opposite of the drug world. He couldn't fathom why she chose to remain a part of it. He watched her play with Wolfgang, wondering why she had to be perfect. "I believe it's time for us to leave."

"Sure. Do you have a blanket for the puppy?"

"He has on a fur coat. I don't think he'll be cold."

A smile flashed across her face as she approached him. "You can keep the residence binder for a while to help decide what you want. Come, Wolfgang. Let's get a blanket."

He followed her into the house. "Thanks for the binder. I'll return it tomorrow."

"No hurry." She pulled several blankets out of the linen closet and compared them.

"What are you doing?"

"Wolfgang needs two beds. One for here." Wolfgang tugged on one of the blankets. "I guess he's decided on one of his beds." She took the blanket from the puppy, folded it, then set it on the floor. Wolfgang stepped onto the blanket, did several circles, then plopped down.

"He's really tired isn't he," Ashton commented.

"Let me grab one more blanket so you can take your sleepy puppy home." She stuffed the left over blankets in the closet. "I have an old rug in the kitchen. I'll be right back." She raced off to the kitchen.

Ashton glanced from the sleeping puppy toward the kitchen. *It's time to leave before I do something stupid.* The whole evening worked against his common sense. He loved everything about her, felt she'd stick by him through thick and thin.

He headed for the kitchen, thinking about her belief in him. On their walk he'd explained how his client looked guilty of murdering a cop. She had told him she thought the man was innocent. He asked her why; she had said because she knew he wouldn't defend a cop killer.

Her blind faith in him touched him more than anything. "Diana don't worry about—" He bumped into the rushing Diana, knocking her and the rug to the floor.

He knelt beside her. "Are you all right?" Her lighthearted grin lifted his spirits and tickled his already amorous libido.

"I'll survive." She pushed herself up and rested her hands behind her. "Did you need something?"

She asked in all innocence, but being only a few inches away from her mouth tempted him to taste. "Yes I did." He closed the distance between them along with his eyes and mind to his work and followed his heart.

This is what she'd been nervously anticipating all evening. His kisses sent sensual waves through her, crippling her self-control. She wrapped her arms around his neck, allowing him to lift and carry her off.

Ashton set her on the bed. Continuing his shower of kisses, he slowly stripped her. Under her sweats and baggie cotton shirt laid a body it should be illegal to cover. He ran his hand along her long torso, traveling past her six-pack to her ample breast. "Don't ever wear that outfit again."

He descended on her breasts suckling, savoring, licking her into frenzy. He so moved her she could barely work her fingers to unfasten his shirt and remove it from his shoulders.

She kissed his chest, kneaded it with her tongue, filling him with the pleasure he'd given her.

He backed away slightly, needing to slow the pace to keep from ravaging her. He stripped to his briefs. "Turn over. Let me massage you."

She rolled over to oblige. He caressed her shoulders. The days of manual digging left her muscles weary and body aching. She melted under his touch. He kissed lightly along her spine, adding a degree of sensuality to the already high heat.

The hallway phone rang. She ignored it. He lay on her back, gently grinding behind her. "The phone," he whispered.

She pressed against him, forcing the grind deeper. "There's a reason I don't have a phone in here."

The answering machine picked up. "Pepita, Alice will be in San Diego for the next week. If you see her, you know what not to do. Love you."

Diana had tuned everything out except Ashton. She

didn't hear or care about the message. On the other hand, the sound of Santiago's voice slapped Ashton across the face, knocking him out of the ecstasy-laced fog. *Love you. Alice is his wife. Is he afraid she'll cause a scene?* He rested his head beside Diana's and his hand on her waist.

She turned in his arms. "Is something wrong, Ashton?"

He stared into her eyes. He had to stop. He'd almost destroyed everything he'd worked so hard to gain for a drug lord's lover.

She kissed him lightly on the lips. "Ashton."

Fighting the truth, he closed his eyes. *She's as crooked as the day is long. She's my link to Santiago and Carter.* One of those two would be coming down. If he played his cards correctly, he might be able to bring both of their reigns to an end.

He kissed her. "I'm sorry, Diana. I don't want to make the same mistake twice. I'd never use you. I respect and value our friendship too much. I shouldn't have allowed things to go so far."

A pang nipped her heart. In a way she felt flattered he respected her, but she wanted him to trust her enough to accept her, to choose her. "I understand."

He caught a glimpse of her sorrow before she shut him out. "It's not you, Diana. It's me." He caressed her face. "If we ever make love, it will be as husband and wife. I can't give you marriage. I don't want to mess up what we could have." He kissed her forehead, turned and exited the bed to dress.

She looked so sad, lonely. He couldn't leave her like this. Two choices: make love as he wanted, or do his job. "Do you have any ice?"

She released a hesitant yes, covered herself with a sheet and watched him dress.

The warmth of her dark gaze glided over his body. "If you don't mind, I'd like to take some home. I'll be needing it for my bath." Her genuine belly laugh signaled he hadn't screwed things too royally.

Still tickled, she hugged her pillow. "Serves you right. Why don't you just leave Wolfgang here tonight? I'm sure he's out cold by now."

CHAPTER SEVEN

Norma pulled a lawn chair behind Diana. "He did the right thing. You shouldn't be mad."

Diana tossed over her shoulder, "I'm not mad. I'm horny. That man *flustrates* me in ways I've never been flustered before." She yanked weeds out of the garage flower garden.

"*Flustrates*?" Stifling her grin, Norma leaned back in the lawn chair. "You young people today are a mess. I know you think I'm a crazy old bat, but I know what I'm talking about. You want marriage with Ashton. Don't cheat yourself by settling for a shallow sexual relationship."

"But he doesn't want marriage."

"So you plan on settling. Haven't you ever heard, 'Why buy the cow when the milk is free?' Of course he doesn't want marriage, what man does? It's your job to show him he does."

"Normally, I'd agree with you, but this case is different."

"Why? Because it's about you?"

"No, Norma. It's his ex-wife. He'll never marry again. I'm comfortable with things as they are. I'm tired of fighting for acceptance. I'm tired of fighting. I'm tired..." she trailed off, drew her knees in and stretched her back. "I can't believe how I acted last night. I've never been so fast."

Norma knew of Diana's disappointments and understood her apprehension. "You've already fallen in love with him, so you're taking what you can get. Don't settle. He'll come around if you give him time."

"I'm not in love with him," she said with confidence she didn't feel. She sighed. "I won't sleep with him, but I am settling." Norma cocked her head to the side. "I'm settling for friendship. It's all he has to offer. I won't disrespect myself trying to seduce him. I deserve to be chosen."

Norma tipped her peach tea toward Diana. "I recognized the look in his eyes when he saw you. It confused me at first because I didn't know you knew each other. He is a man falling in love." She swirled the tea. "It's your duty as a woman to make him see it." They both laughed.

"You don't understand. He thought he was in love with the perfect woman when he married the first time. He told me last night he won't make the same mistake twice." She shrugged. "He won't pursue a relationship with me."

"What happened with his wife?"

"They married when he was in law school. After he finished, he took a job with the state as a prosecutor. He was ready to start their family, but Lori changed her mind, saying they didn't make enough money. She tried to convince him to take a higher paying job with a firm, but he liked what he was doing."

"What type of work did Lori do?"

"A junior high science teacher. She kept after him about moving to a higher paying job, but he wouldn't budge. She quit her job saying she hated it. He thought she'd find another easily, but she didn't. After a year, their savings was almost totally depleted."

Norma's nose scrunched. "She was a teacher, why couldn't she find another position?"

Diana offered a smile instead of an answer. "He loved his job, but quit to take a higher paying one with a firm so he could cover their living expenses and pay off her student loans. She found a job a month later."

"Little manipulator."

"Only the tip of the iceberg. With both of them working, he wanted to start having babies. She brought up the money issue again. He made a considerable amount more by working for a private firm, but his chances for advancement were slowed because he preferred taking their pro-bono cases. He showed her on paper they could afford a baby. Can you guess what happened next?"

"She quit her job again didn't she?"

Diana opened her eyes wide and displayed jazz fingers. "Ding, ding, ding. Norma O'Connor wins the prize." Norma laughed. "To make a long story short, Lori kept manipulating him and eventually asked for a divorce. He wanted counseling, but she didn't. He gave her the divorce."

"He was lucky she didn't want children. It was all for the best. I know she was a manipulator, but at least she had the good sense to end it."

"I think if it had just ended he could have taken it. Two weeks after their divorce, she married one of the senior partners in his firm."

Norma dropped her peach tea on the ground. "Hold it. Wait a second." She picked up the empty glass. "She was cheating on him?"

"Oh yeah," Diana drawled out slowly. "He gave up his career for her. She rewarded him by sleeping with his boss. She lived the high life. Had a baby."

"Oh no she didn't."

"Yes. But you know what goes around comes around. Her new husband divorced her while she was pregnant. Thanks to the prenuptial agreement, he left her with nothing. He even received custody of the baby."

Norma shook her head. "This is more complicated than I thought." She sat back thinking.

"Come here, Wolfgang," Diana called. He came loping along. "How's my little boy doing?" He flopped on the ground. She rubbed his belly.

"Do you want to marry Ashton?"

"I don't know. I see him as a definite possibility, but I won't make a fool of myself chasing after him. I'm also afraid he won't understand my life." She stroked the puppy's fur. "I've been running through things since he left last night. I was deluding myself. I'll never be free. I can't take away his freedom."

"Explain everything to him, Diana. Give him the chance to decide for himself."

"His sister died from a drug overdose." She hunched her shoulders. "How can I tell him about Santiago? I don't want to endanger him. You know—I can't remember a time when I wasn't in this crazy unseen danger."

Norma could see Diana physically withdraw. "Santiago says you're safe. You're just not used to freedom yet. It's time for you to start living your life. Do as I say. Continue being everything you are. Follow Ashton's rule of no sex. He's in love with you. His will power is only so strong. He'll crack."

Diana giggled. "You are too much, Norma. You're telling me to hold out on sex to win a man. You sound crazy."

Norma's graying brows arched. "I'm telling you to keep your legs closed. Get to know each other. You kids today are too quick to jump in the sack. Go buy some sex toys, but stay away from Ashton."

Diana laughed loud and hard. Totally tickled, she fell over. Wolfgang licked her face. "Ewww." She gently pushed him away. "Does Brian know about your dirty mind?"

Norma blushed. "Well, as a matter of fact, he does. This may take a while, but it'll work if he's the one for you. Otherwise, you two will grow tired of each other and drift apart. I'm just telling you to make sure it isn't only physical."

"I will." She hugged Norma. "Thanks."

❧❧❧

"Damn, man, that was too close," Leonard said.

"You're telling me." Ashton couldn't believe his loss of control. "If Santiago hadn't called, I would have blown this whole thing. His voice was a much needed reality check."

"I never thought I'd say this, but thank God for Santiago." He continued perusing the binder. "She just let you have this."

"She earned the seven million, Leonard. I've gone through those pictures over and over. I don't think they're in New York."

Leonard nodded in agreement. "These are great. Did you look on-line?"

He turned the computer monitor around to face Leonard. "I've been searching all morning. I think her real name is Josephine. Santiago called her Pepita again, and the middle name she goes by now is Josephine."

"What's that got to do with anything?"

"Pepita is Spanish for Josephine. It really doesn't matter what her real name is or where she's from. It won't get us any closer to Carter or Santiago."

"I'm just nosey and want to know." Leonard flipped the page. "Did she tell you she was from New York?"

"No." He pressed speaker on the phone. "I just assumed she was. That's where Steven's from." He dialed her cell number.

"Hello, Ashton. How was your bath?"

He chuckled. "Extremely cold and lonely. What are you up to?"

"I'm at the pet store trying to convince Wolfgang he wants the ugly squeaky stuffed animal with ropes for arms and legs instead of the cat looking stuffed animal. Make sure you bring your checkbook tonight. This dog is expensive. He's gotten his shots and had a much needed bath."

"While you're there, buy two dog houses."

"No problem. Did you call to check on your baby?"

Leonard and Ashton stared at each other, both deciding if she referred to Wolfgang or herself. "I was looking through the photos you gave me. These pictures don't look like they're in New York."

Leonard smiled his approval of the side step Ashton took.

"They aren't. I was born in New York, but moved to Atlanta when my mother died. You don't have to worry about the climate. I can still create the look you want. I'll switch to plants for this region."

"Sounds great. Do you want to eat out for dinner tonight?" Ashton ignored Leonard's arched brows.

"What time will you be around?"

He tapped on the stack of cases piled on his desk awaiting his review. "I'm thinking by nine."

"I'd starve before nine. How about when you pick Wolfgang up tonight, you eat what I've prepared for dinner. I'll keep you company then you take your puppy home. I'm horrible with leftovers and even worse at cooking small enough portions for one."

"You don't have to cook for me, Diana."

"I'm not cooking for you, Mr. Arrogance. I cook because when I'm hungry I like to eat."

Pointing at Ashton, Leonard quietly chuckled.

"I'd rather you eat the leftovers than throw them away. The vet said not to feed Wolfgang table scraps like we did last night."

"If you're sure. I have to run. I'll see you tonight."

"See ya."

He disconnected. "Atlanta Georgia."

"Damn, man. You are so full of yourself." Leonard sat straight up in his seat, mocking Ashton's stuffy mannerisms. "You don't have to cook for me, Diana." He slapped the desk. "I really like her. Mr. Arrogance. After this is over, I may look her up."

"That's enough, Leonard." Ashton used his search engine to locate landscapers in Atlanta, Georgia.

"How will you stay away from her?" Leonard moved his chair around for a better view of the monitor. "Look at you. Her voice gives you a boner."

Ashton resituated himself in the chair. "Shut up, Leonard." He scrolled through the list of sites, hoping something would catch his eyes. "That's it. Josephine's." He clicked on the link. "Nope. False alarm. Look at those drab lawns."

"Go to the search page and check out that *Diana's Landscapes* place."

Ashton backed out to the search page, then clicked on the Diana's link.

> *Sorry. Diana's has closed its doors. I have decided to take an early retirement...*
>
> *My business has been split into two smaller companies that will each be able to supply your needs...*
>
> *My associates...*

"This is it. Diana Pepita Johnson. Get everything you can on her. If I remember correctly, her mother died when she was twelve." Ashton searched through the site. The images all contained her artistic style.

"I'm on it," Leonard said.

"Make sure to avoid DEA channels. What if Steven was framed?" Their special unit was technically under the DEA, yet had more leeway to use other resources.

"He was guilty; she was his lover. Remember those facts, and your life will be a lot easier. I've got to run. I'll let you know what I find."

"I have a meeting with my client today. I should be done with him by two."

Leonard replaced the chair. "Do not sleep with her, Ashton."

"I won't. I can control myself."

"I'm not accusing you. I just want you to think about something for me." Leonard locked his big blues onto Ashton's big browns. "How much pain will you cause when she finds out who you are? She'll already feel used and betrayed. How will she feel if you make love to her, tell her how much you love her and then she finds out who you are?"

"I know. I know. I'm just doing the job." Ashton turned away from the truth of Leonard's words.

"Then don't get physical. What if she falls in love with you? I'd have no problem playing her, but you aren't like me. It would tear you apart." He headed for the door. "I'll see you at two."

CHAPTER EIGHT

Tact and Leonard were mortal enemies, but he was usually correct. Doom was the only place their relationship could lead. Ashton knew he could love her, but wouldn't allow his emotions to interfere with the job for both of their sakes.

He'd let emotions and attractions influence him before and wouldn't be a fool again. His mission now was to cause as little damage to Diana as possible yet still obtain the information he needed.

"Hey, man." Leonard closed the office door, then took his seat. "Are you ready for this?"

"As ready as I'll ever be. Does her money have any drug connections?" He braced himself for the answer.

"Allow me to give you the whole story. I think they had a relationship before she came of age. When her mother died, Steven moved her to Atlanta. As you know, his base was in New York."

"What did her father say?"

"This is why she's estranged from her family. Steven must have paid her father off. Her father died from cancer a year or so later."

"How much?"

"He paid a cool million for an eleven-year-old child. Steven set her up in an apartment in Atlanta with a nanny of sorts. When she was sixteen, she started her business with money from her parents' life insurance."

Leonard handed the tax returns to Ashton. "As you see, he's the person who prepared her taxes. Once she was eighteen, she began having H&R Block prepare them. By then she had almost three hundred thousand in the bank. She grew her business into a multi million-dollar venture that supported fifteen full-time employees. When she left Atlanta, she split the business and divided the equipment among the employees."

"She took his last name."

"Well damn, he was old enough to be her father. Nasty assed pervert. The law should have gone after her father for letting that bastard have her."

His eyes traveled from the tax forms to Leonard. Something didn't feel right about this whole scenario. "What about the rest of her family?"

"She's the baby. She has two sisters and a brother. Steven paid for their college educations and Lord knows what else."

"They turned their backs on her." Leaving the tax forms, he pushed away from the desk.

"That's what it looks like." Leonard gathered the tax paperwork. "Let it go, Ashton. She isn't your problem. We have a job to do. None of this matters. Carter is our problem, and she has the solution. Stay focused."

"I guess she's so devoted because her family gave up on her."

"I don't know any psychological bull. What did she tell you about her family?"

He leaned against the window and watched the busy street below. "When her mother died, she had a dispute with her siblings. Basically, they didn't agree with the company she kept. When she told me, I agreed since the company was Santiago and Steven, but now..." He shook his head. "I'm disgusted. How could they sell her then disown her? They left her on her own." The more he spoke the angrier he became.

"Hold up, Ashton. You're getting all worked up."

He stuffed his hands into his slacks and paced between the wet bar and bookshelves. "This just pisses me off. Why didn't her father protect her? None of this makes sense."

"Let's change the subject. Alice was spotted at the airport."

He stopped pacing a second. "Why does Santiago bother getting married? Which wife number is this?"

Leonard smiled. "I think she's number eight. I couldn't find any tie between her and Diana. I found out Diana came up missing during Steven's trial. Santiago had her taken to Colombia until it was over. That's when Carter first started looking for her. From what I could tell, everything cooled down until Steven's execution."

"You look worried."

"Hell, we're more than partners. We're like brothers." He glanced at his white skin, stiffened his back. "I'm the handsome one."

"I can do this."

"I know you will. You know me. I'm about keeping it real. Back in the day, when I was messing up, you knocked sense into me. If it hadn't been for you, I'd be working for someone like Santiago. I know you want to save her, but she's in too deep."

"I'm not trying to save her."

"She's a good person, and you're falling in love with her. She was taken advantage of as a child. Now we're taking advantage of her. It's eating at you. Our options are limited. We can pull out completely, or do our job. If you just up and leave, she'll be hurt and confused. Another agent won't be able to get as close as you have. It's you or Carter goes free."

"I've already decided to continue with Operation White Rose. I'm not falling in love with her. I'm intrigued. She's sexy and interesting. I'm not in love. Anyway, once she finds out the truth, she'll hate me."

Leonard leaned back in his seat, calculating a way to help Ashton. "Give me a few seconds. I'll work something out."

"It's a lost cause." He surfed the web. "We don't have a snowball's chance in Hell. I won't throw away my career for nothing."

"You are interrupting my train of thought with your whining. *Shhh.*"

"I don't whine. I'll work this case like any other. In a month or so, she'll be ready to introduce me to Santiago."

Leonard threw up his hands. "Could a brotha get thirteen seconds of peace? Damn!"

As usual, he ignored Leonard's outburst. They'd grown up together in the same poor inner city neighborhood. "We're gonna bring down two of the largest drug lords in the world. That's what I'm in love with."

"Where is the information Steven stole from Carter?" Leonard asked.

"Santiago has it. My way to Santiago is Diana."

"Why hasn't he used it against Carter?" Anxious to

reveal his thoughts, he scooted his chair close to the desk. "What if there was no information? What if Carter thinks Steven copied his network, but he didn't?"

"Steven had a copy." Ashton opened his briefcase, pulled out a file. "The two DEA agents Steven murdered knew about the stolen information. One was in Carter's camp, the other in Santiago's. They both reported the theft was real. They both caught a glimpse of the information then were murdered by Steven before they could obtain copies."

Ashton set the files on the desk for Leonard to review. "That's how we know Steven copied Carter's pipeline, contacts and connections. Steven was able to do in three months what the agency couldn't accomplish in three years. The evidence on those files would bring Carter and a whole lot of others down."

Leonard tipped his head forward. "Exactly. So again, I say, where are they? If Santiago had them, he would have sent Diana into hiding years ago and used them against Carter."

Finally getting the picture, Ashton grinned. "You think Diana has the files."

"Yep, and I doubt she'd give them to Santiago. She'd never start a war between the two families. If you convince her to give you the files..."

"I'll be taking down Carter."

"Now you're with me. It'll take months for you to find out where she's hidden the files, which is actually in your favor. By then she'll be hopelessly in love with you."

"I was with you for a second, Leonard, but this won't work. Once she finds out that I lied from the beginning, I'm through."

Leonard's facial features twisted into a sarcastic grin of confusion. "What have you lied about?"

"How about my motives?"

"Don't get technical on me. You have nothing to lose. If you go after Carter, she might forgive you. Briggs and Norton are supposed to be working on Santiago. Let them do their job."

"How did you find out who's working the Santiago case? No one is supposed to know."

"Because no one gets anything over on me. Don't worry, no one will ever find out who you are. I know how to cover tracks."

"She's sleeping with Santiago."

Leonard laughed. "I don't think so. Neither do you. You're justifying distancing yourself from her."

"You called Steven a pervert."

"I'm an asshole. You saw how Santiago treated her at the hotel and graveyard. He loves her in more of a fatherly way, if you get what I mean. Even looking at her letters. I forced her lover roll because that's what the warden told us, and I could see you starting to fall for her. The letters don't have the tone or content of love letters. She's talking about the places she's visited and plants. Nothing lovey-dovey."

"You're right about the letters, but wrong about my feelings for Diana. We're friends. I'll just keep being as real as I can."

Leonard leaned in his seat. "That's the spirit." He narrowed his eyes on Ashton. "You still can't sleep with her."

He chuckled. "I'm putting my stuff on ice until further notice."

CHAPTER NINE

Six months later...

"**M**r. Carter on line one."

Santiago took pleasure in watching Carter's empire crumble. He leaned back in his executive chair. "What do you want, Carter?" He'd been methodically encroaching on Carter's territory.

"I'm giving you fair warning to keep your men in check and stop peddling your goods in my territory." They both knew the DEA tapped Santiago's landline phone. Carter couldn't risk an attempt on his life by meeting Santiago in person. Calling was his only resort. He'd just have to be careful what he revealed.

"I'm a businessman and venture where the market dictates. If you'd stop selling inferior products, your customers wouldn't switch over to me," Santiago said.

"So you have nothing to do with my shipments not arriving in a timely manner?"

"If some of your shipments were lost along the way, it had nothing to do with me; blame your poor management. Next week I have an appointment with Edward Douglas." Edward was Carter's main west coast distributor.

"Stay out of California, Santiago."

The tension in Carter's voice delighted Santiago. "I'm a grown man and go wherever I damn well please. It's time for you to retire."

"Go to hell, Santiago!"

Santiago's robust laugh filled the line. "Did you need anything else? I'm feeling generous today. You can work for me. I'll allow Tony to run the region you think you control for a small percentage. Let's say fifty-fifty for now."

"I'm not giving up."

"Fifty percent is better than nothing you ungrateful piece of shit." He could have had him killed. Under the circumstances, he thought himself quite generous. Diana always affected him this way. "I'll give you one month to decide to accept my offer. In thirty days I pull out all the stops and take over your territory. You need to decide if you want fifty percent of the action or nothing."

"All of this over Steven? You're making this personal. How many of my men have you killed for less than what Steven did?"

The angrier Santiago became, the thicker his Spanish accent became. "Your begging won't help. Steven was my brother and knew the rules of the game. Business is business. But you made this shit personal."

"Steven was business! Why are you attacking me? You've taken this too far. I won't go down without a fight, Santiago."

He cursed in Spanish then remembered his attacks were lost on Carter. "What about Pepita you son-of-a-bitch? You attack me by going after my godchild. How the hell can I let that slide? You couldn't beat me in the business arena, so you take after my family. Hell yeah, I take that shit personal. You can fight all you want, but the results will be the same. You're ass is mine." He slammed the phone onto its cradle.

"Shit, shit, shit." Santiago hadn't meant to become so emotional. The agents would have a great time listening to his loss of control and know his weak point. "Shit."

He dialed Diana's number using his cellphone, confident that no one would ever find her. "Hello, Pepita."

"What's up?"

"I'm just checking on my baby girl. How's your mutt doing?"

"Huge. I'm doing pretty well myself. I love the spring."

"Has Ashton asked you to marry him yet?"

"Oh no. Not again. No he hasn't. We're just friends."

He leaned back in his seat. "Um-hum. So why are you acting like his wife?"

"I'm not sleeping with him."

"Is he gay?"

"Santiago!"

"Listen to me, Pepita. I know what I'm talking about. It's been months. He must be gay or... I have to go. I'll call next week." He hung up the line. *That bastard's government. Shit.* He pressed the intercom. "Hugo, get down here now. Pepita's in trouble."

Hugo, Santiago's right hand man, rushed into the office minutes later. "What's wrong?"

"I need you to check out Ashton. His house is across from Diana's, so start there. I want to know everything about him by end of business today. Be discreet"

⚜⚜⚜

"What are you doing here, Tony? Get out and find that bitch before Santiago takes everything," Robert Carter chastised.

"I told you, I'm not going on a wild goose chase. She's gone, Dad."

"She has to be somewhere. People don't just disappear."

Tony poured himself a brandy. "Hell. I make people disappear all the time."

"This is no time for joking. Do you know what's happened over the past six months?" He took the drink from Tony, motioning around the executive office. "This'll all be yours someday. Santiago is attacking you, and you're acting like you don't care."

"He isn't attacking me. This is your empire, not mine."

"Where's your loyalty?"

"I've spent my whole life doing your dirty work, yet I'm not loyal because I won't continue a friggin' lost cause. How many men have I killed for you without asking questions? I'm here for you, Dad, but I can't perform miracles. I've followed every avenue there is. Santiago planned this perfectly. The only way we'll find her is if she returns to Atlanta or New York. Do you honestly think Santiago will allow that? You need to kill Santiago and Hugo and forget about her."

"I've tried. They're too well protected. Hell. I can't even keep track of Santiago anymore."

"You should consider his offer." Tony poured himself a second drink.

"I'm not giving him my empire," Carter tossed over his shoulder as he stalked to his desk.

"He doesn't have anyone to leave the cartel to. I can work from the inside. Even take over someday. By joining forces, we'll have the largest cartel."

"I'm not giving him my empire. I'll make him pay."

"You aren't listening, Dad." Tony sat on one of the bar stools.

"He will never leave anything to a Carter. Hugo or one of his other top men will take over when Santiago dies. Try your contact in Atlanta. He might be holding out."

"He isn't, but I'll try again anyway."

CHAPTER TEN

Nelson Stein, senior partner at the firm, entered Ashton's office. "Don't get up. I just wanted to speak with you briefly."

"Have a seat."

Nelson was usually even-tempered and calm. Today he seemed jittery and nervous. He took the seat offered. "You've been doing an excellent job, Ashton." He fidgeted with the papers on the edge of Ashton's desk.

"Thank you. Is there something wrong?"

"You see, we have a tiny situation brewing that I need to make you aware of."

"Just give it to me straight."

Nelson released an anxiety-laced laugh. "The problem is, you've been doing an excellent job. When I agreed to this arrangement, I didn't think you'd actually work so hard on these cases." He stumbled over his wording. "The other partners have been pressuring me to promote you to full partner and raise your salary accordingly."

Ashton released a sigh of relief. "I thought there was something wrong. I haven't been here long enough to make partner. Use that as your argument against the promotion. You can site jealousy of the other associate partners that have more tenure."

"I've tried." He twiddled his fingers, straightened his posture. "Ashton, you are the best litigator in the firm. Everyone knows this except you. I thought your record was false. I didn't do the research because I didn't think you'd actually work for us. I gave you your first case knowing we couldn't win, yet you did. I gave you case after case we didn't expect to win. You pulled them off. You've earned the promotion, but I'm not allowed to pay you more than associate partner pay. If I give you the promotion without the salary increase, your cover will be blown. If I continue fighting against your promotion, I'm not promoting you because you're black. I'm proud of the way my attorneys are sticking up for you, but I'm stuck."

Ashton's robust laugh filled the room. "I never

thought of anything like this in my life. I wondered why everyone's been extra friendly lately."

"Have you considered leaving the DEA? I'll hire you outright. I'm willing to buy out their contract."

"I'm not under contract. I can quit whenever I want."

"You love the work you do here, and what about Diana? Don't you want to settle down and marry? If you accept my offer, your travel will be limited. You can continue doing pro-bono work. You're giving our firm a good name and bringing us business."

"I'm not sure. I need time to think." Nelson didn't know Diana was his case. Nelson had met her a few times when Ashton brought her on business dinners. "How much longer can you stall them?"

"Not long." He tapped his fingers on the arm of the chair. "This is what we'll do. I'll give you the promotion and the raise in salary. The DEA doesn't have to reimburse me for the difference. If they say anything, I'll explain that your cover would have been blown otherwise."

"Thanks you."

Nelson rose and held out his hand to shake. "No. Thank you. Have a great day." He turned to leave. "Your friend is waiting outside for you. I needed to speak with you first. If you'd like to switch over, the job is yours." He walked out.

Leonard strutted in with recording on his cellphone. He played it for Ashton and brought him up to date on Carter's activities.

"So he's her godfather," Ashton said. "After her mother died, Santiago finished raising her because her father was ill."

"That's what it looks like. I'll forward this to your phone for your future enjoyment."

"Then she cut him out of her life when she was eighteen."

"As soon as she was legal she severed ties until Steven was arrested for murder."

"What took them so long to give us the recording?"

"Those stingy bastards had no intention of turning over the recording. I pitched a fit until the big boss man gave me what I wanted to shut me up." Leonard leaned back in his seat. "Santiago had you checked out the same day he had this conversation with Carter."

"Why? There must be some connection." He didn't worry about his cover being blown. His only government checks came when he was a prosecutor. When he joined the DEA, after his divorce, his idea to work for legitimate law firms and be paid by them was considered ingenious. The DEA agreed to keep his name out of all of their employee databases and form a team around him.

"Did you hear the recording? He loves her to death. I'm shocked he didn't have it done sooner. She's his weak link. That's why those bastards tried to hide the call. They want to use her to catch Santiago."

"But they don't know where she is."

"Of course not." Leonard flashed a sly grin. "I'm a stingy bastard. How are things going with you two?"

"I absolutely hate cold baths."

"That good, huh." He chuckled. "Well you need to find the information Steven copied from Carter so you can marry her."

"I'm never marrying again. Diana and I are friends. I think I'll snoop around Atlanta."

"For what?"

"I saw a picture of Steven on her dresser." He wished he'd asked her about the picture, but at the time she was so sad he couldn't bring himself to ask.

Leonard raised a brow. "You were in her bedroom?"

"I was umm… chasing Wolfgang through the house. Anyway, she only had it up for one day. His birthday."

"No shit."

"It makes me think that maybe they were lovers after all. I want to help her get over him, so she can move on. Something isn't right. The answers to their relationship are in Atlanta."

"But the letters don't sound like a lover's letters."

"Maybe she was trying to throw us off. I don't know."

"Well, it was only one day. She obviously loved him. You can't expect for his birthday to pass without her being affected."

"I'm not jealous. I want her to share everything with me. I can't ask her about Steven until she mentions his name at least once, or I'll blow my cover. Since I can't mention him, I'll go to Atlanta and try to figure out what he did to her."

"All right, man. I'll make the arrangements."

Ashton checked the time on his watch.

Leonard shook his head and smirked.

"What?" Ashton picked up the phone.

"You are whipped. You can deny your feelings for Diana night and day, but I know better."

"I'm not whipped." He pressed speed dial. "Hey, baby, what ya doin'?"

"I'm deciding how much to charge Mrs. Foley to redo her flower garden," Diana replied. "I'd do the work for free, but it's a complete mess. If I charge, maybe she'll take better care of it."

"Where's my boy?"

"Worrying Mrs. Foley's German Shepard to death. One of these days he's gonna get his tail kicked."

The sound of her warm, cheerful voice always brightened his day. "I'm coming home at a decent hour tonight. Want me to bring take-out for dinner."

"I've already planned dinner. We can eat in."

"Anything for my baby." He threw a pencil at Leonard. "By the way, Leonard says I'm whipped." He had told her Leonard was his investigator.

"Is he in the office with you?"

"Yes. He's making stupid faces."

"Put it on speaker."

He switched over to speaker.

"You'd better stop teasing Ashton before I come over there and kick your butt," she joked.

"Well damn. You make him call you everyday at one sharp."

"I don't make him do anything. He has his own mind. When will you find a woman of your own and stop harassing Ashton?"

"I'll have you know, I have several I keep very well satisfied. Thank you very much." They both laughed.

"So when are you coming over for dinner. I'm a great cook. I want to see what you look like."

"You'd better stop coming onto me."

"Avoiding the question again, I see. I'll let it slide this time, but this is the last time. Goodbye."

"Bye."

Ashton took the phone off speaker. "What's this I hear about you hitting on my best friend?"

"I guess I'm busted. What time will you be home?"

"Five. I have work to do."

"Love ya." She hung up.

"How will you explain your trip to Atlanta?"

"I'll figure out something." He tapped his desk with his pen.

"Why don't you just say what's on your mind?"

"We've been through a lot together. I wanted to thank you for helping me with Diana." He hunched his shoulders. "You know, keeping me focused on what needs to be done."

"We'll always be partners."

"That's it. You see, after this case I'm quitting."

Leonard leaned back in his seat. "You think I didn't know? Damn, man. I'm crude, not stupid. Hell, I'll bet you even bought a ring."

Ashton's lips slowly curled up. "I'm not marrying again. I learn from my mistakes. I don't repeat them."

"You are in such denial. Reality check time. Why are you giving up your career with the agency?"

Ashton sat straight, smoothed his suit coat. "I have the types of cases I like. I've been offered a good position."

"You're in love with Diana. Hell, man, I knew we were in trouble back at the penitentiary when you snuck into her room."

A sly grin oozed from Ashton's lips. "I was afraid you'd never let me forget it. She's been great, but the fact still remains, she is part of the drug world. She isn't a child anymore and has a choice. She hasn't mentioned Santiago to me at all, yet I know she talks to him at least once a week. She's holding out. What else isn't she telling me?"

"There you go. Making trouble where none exists. Why are you flying to Atlanta? It won't help us catch Carter. You're flying across the country to learn more about Diana and Steven's relationship."

"I'm going to Atlanta to find a lead on the information

Steven stole. While there, I'll help *my friend*."

Leonard started ticking off points with his fingers. "Why do you call her everyday? I know you make more than the one o'clock *love ya* call. Who cooks your meals? Who cleans your house? Who do you call baby? Where do you call home? Who do you dream about making love to? Who is the only person you take off for? Who are you flying across country for? Who are you giving up your career for? Stop lying to yourself."

"You're wrong this time. I'll admit we're close, but that's it. I dream about making love with her because she's a beautiful woman. I haven't made love to her because when this is over, I want to continue being her friend. I'm quitting because this case has turned me off the agency. I can't deceive people like Diana anymore. I don't have the stomach for it. I took off because she needed me. It's my job to get close to Diana and obtain the information to sink Carter."

"I can't make you admit your feelings. I just hope you realize them before it's too late. You are in love with Diana." He pushed away from the desk. "I'll see you later."

CHAPTER ELEVEN

Ashton knocked on Diana's front door. Leonard's words flowed through his mind. Her house did feel like home. He hated leaving after Wolfgang's walks.

She didn't answer. He rang the bell. She still didn't answer. He unlocked the door with his key and stepped in. "Diana, where are you?"

"I'm out back," she called. He followed her voice toward the kitchen, finally finding her in the back yard playing tug-of-war with Wolfgang.

A crew was building Wolfgang a larger pen. Ashton settled in a lawn chair to relax. Watching Diana and Wolfgang play always warmed his heart. He closed his eyes to the images of the family he wanted with her. He had a job to do. She hid her drug ties from him. She didn't trust him because she shouldn't be trusted.

Wolfgang did one last mighty tug, then released the rope. Diana fell on her butt. The oversized puppy immediately pounced, licked and stepped all over her. She laughed. "Don't just sit there. Save me." She rolled Wolfgang over, wrestling him to the ground.

Ashton hesitated a few seconds before running to her aid. He pulled her off Wolfgang.

"Hey, what are you doing? I've almost got him down." She pushed at Ashton trying to catch Wolfgang.

"Come here, boy." He quickly penned her to the ground, straddled her and allowed Wolfgang to lick all he wanted.

"Get off me you... Ewww, he licked my face." She struggled beneath him.

"Will you stop being mean to my puppy?"

She shook her head yelling, "Never!" She bucked her body, laughing while Wolfgang barked and jumped.

"Looks like I have to take drastic measures." He tickled her.

"Oh my God. Stop it. Stop it. I give. I give. Let me up. Get off me."

He grinned. "I repeat. Will you stop being mean to my

puppy?" She closed her eyes. "Diana?"

She cracked open one eye. "I'm deciding." He tickled her again. "Okay, all right. You win." He released her. "I'll remember this, Mr. Powell." She crawled away.

"Just get my dinner ready before I tickle you again."

She knelt up to his ear whispering, "You'd best watch yourself. I like that freaky stuff." She laughed at his astonished look and stalked off.

Leaning on his hands, he watched her enter the house through the back sliding door. It always felt good being home. Wolfgang dropped his brush in Ashton's lap. "You're spoiled." He brushed the puppy's fur.

One of the workers approached Ashton. "You have a very lovely wife. You're a lucky man."

Ashton's gaze focused on the sliding door. "Yes I am. Thanks."

"We're all done." He handed Ashton the work order.

Ashton signed then handed the order back to the man. "Come on, Wolfgang. You might as well test your new pen." He locked the gate behind Wolfgang. "How do you like it?" He pet the now humungous puppy through the fence and laughed at himself for originally naming him Benji.

⚜⚜⚜

"As usual, dinner was excellent." Ashton resituated himself on the couch and held his hands out for Diana to sit with him. "Just don't touch the stomach, baby."

Over dinner she'd begun opening up. She told him she wanted him to meet her godfather Santiago. His heart burned with love for her, but he squelched the fire. Once he obtained the information on Carter, she'd learn his true identity and hate him.

She sat across his lap, hugged him. He hadn't said much of anything since arriving home. She could sense something was wrong, but waited patiently, loving him, hoping he'd confide in her.

He held her closely, taking all she offered yet trying not to cross the line he wanted nothing more than to cross. "I was promoted at work. I'm a full partner now."

She pulled back, taking in the full view of his worried face. She frowned. "I'm glad you were promoted, but will you still be allowed to do your pro-bono work. I thought you loved it."

He grinned. She was completely different than his ex-wife. "Yes I will." He gently guided her head to rest on his shoulder. "I've had a hard day."

Wanting to shut out his feelings for her, he closed his eyes. She couldn't be his. It wouldn't work. How long before she went back to the drug world? She chose it over her family before. Would she choose it over him once she found out the full truth of his identity?

"I'm going to Savannah for a few days. I need to interview a few people about my new client."

"When do you leave?"

"Tomorrow morning. I'll only be away four, five days tops."

"I'll take you to the airport and pick you up."

"I can take a taxi. You already put yourself out too much for me."

"Don't insult me just because you've had a bad day." She snuggled closely, enjoying the rumble of his deep voice, his cologne, his loving embrace.

"Baby, we need to talk about why you left Atlanta." He could feel her stiffen in his arms.

"That part of my life is over now."

"I want to be here for you, Diana. Not to toot my own horn, but I'm an excellent lawyer. If you're in trouble, let me help." He lifted her chin. "You had a very successful business you loved and walked away from without looking back. Won't you trust me enough to confide in me? I'd never do anything to hurt you." He could see her withdrawing.

 He rested his forehead on hers. "I'm sorry, baby. This has been bothering me since day one." He allowed her to lean on his shoulder as he continued to caress her arms, truly sorry he caused her pain. "I'm trying to help. Why won't you talk to your family? Why did you give up your life? If things get rough here, will you'll leave..." he stopped himself and acknowledged the fear that kept him from giving his all to her.

After a long pause, she drew in a deep breath and closed her eyes. "Mama had me late in life. She didn't think she could get pregnant, but I'm living proof she could. When I was ten, she lost her battle with breast cancer. My siblings came home for her funeral understandably upset. I can't go into details, but they didn't like all of the guests who attended."

"Your godfather, Santiago?" *and Steven. Come on, baby. Say his name. You gave me Santiago. You can do it.*

"Yes, and a few others. I defended their right to be there. When Mom was sick, Santiago paid her medical expenses. They didn't know. He didn't want them to. Her funeral was not the proper place to have the fight. I told them as much. They stopped arguing until we went home.

"After our guests left, my siblings tore into me saying I betrayed them, Mom, and Dad by defending Santiago. I reminded them who these people were to me, but they didn't care. They said I was young and stupid. They told me I disrespected our father. I blew up. I'd just lost my mother, and they were attacking me. I saw her die slowly. I heard her beg to be put out of her misery. I saw Dad cry. I told them all to go to hell and walked out."

"You were all emotional. It's been years. I think you should contact them."

"There's more. They all carried on with their lives, leaving Dad and me behind. He hadn't told us he had cancer. I noticed his weight loss." She pulled away.

"It's all right." He gently kissed the tear she so bravely tried not to shed. "I'm here with you."

"He didn't want me to see him die." She choked on her words. "I moved to Atlanta to live with the only people I considered my family with my Dad's blessing. My siblings all lived in New York. Dad wanted me to leave. If I moved in with one of them, I'd see him die just as I'd seen my mother die."

"Why didn't you tell them?"

"They wouldn't listen to anything I had to say. They said Dad was sick and talking crazy. Then they told me to make a choice I shouldn't have had to make. After I moved to Atlanta, I tried to stay in contact with them. They wouldn't return my calls or answer my letters. My Dad died a little under a year later. They didn't even tell me. I found out because I spoke to him weekly on the phone. He didn't answer one day. I called his doctor who told me he'd passed the previous day. They wouldn't even allow me to ride in the family car for the funeral. They said I turned my back on him, and he wasn't my father, so I didn't have a right to be in the family car. I didn't want to argue at the funeral, so I rode with my real family, the ones who stood by me when my mother died."

"So you didn't tell them when you changed from Diana Johnson to Diana Warren?"

"They wouldn't care. I grew tired of trying years ago. They turned their backs on me. I know we were all hurting, but I was a child."

Relieved she didn't catch his slip of saying her real name, he worried about pressing her further. He needed her to say Steven's full name. Then he could truly help her. He knew her family disowned her because of Steven and Santiago. Her siblings were trying to show tough love. Her father must have been too sick to think rationally. "Why did you leave Atlanta?"

"I wish I could tell you everything, but I can't. Not because I don't trust you, because I do. Someone I loved dearly died because of me. If anything were to happen to you because I couldn't keep my mouth shut..." She shook her head. "I don't know what I'd do. I have to protect you from the truth. I can't take away your freedom." She rested her head on him.

The fires of love he held for her burned so fierce he couldn't extinguish them. She was protecting, not withholding. *Pull yourself together. You almost have the information you need. Get the job done, Ashton. Don't make the same mistake twice.* "I can take care of myself."

She placed her hand on his lips, delved deep into his eyes, reached for his soul. "Don't you understand? I love you and wouldn't risk your life to satisfy your curiosity. The people who are looking for me are in the drug world. They'd kill you without batting an eye. What would that accomplish? They can't find me. For the first time in my life, I'm free. Please, just let it go."

Wanting to protect her, he held her tightly. "I will." He knew she'd never tell him about Steven.

CHAPTER TWELVE

Norma sipped her coffee. "What time are you leaving?"

Diana checked the clock above the stove. "I'm thinking eight. He's packing now." She poured herself a cup of coffee, drew it to her nose, inhaled deeply. "This smells delicious."

"I'm so happy for you."

"Thanks. But why?" She sat on a stool at the counter next to Norma.

"He'll ask you to marry him any day now. Probably after this Georgia trip."

"He won't marry again. Especially someone with an unknown past that has ties to the drug world." She poured a tad bit of cream into her coffee.

"He's in love with you, Diana. He's been running from it for months now."

"No, Norma. I won't to do this to myself. I know he loves me, but he'll never accept it. Do you know what I mean? His wounds are too deep. I see him battling his feelings, and it hurts me to be the cause of his pain. I'd have to confide everything for him to accept his feelings. I don't know what to do about this."

"Just keep being yourself. He'll come around. Don't give up."

"I want to share my life with Ashton. I want to tell him everything. I thought I had freedom." She hunched her shoulders. "I'm still trapped."

Norma looked up from her coffee. "You're right. You can't tell him. I've been thinking about this. He's a man and believes he can solve everything. He'll make matters worse."

"It's a no win situation." She stirred her coffee with her spoon. "If I told him everything, he'd give himself to me completely, but confront Carter and get killed." She paused to inhale the rich fullness of the Colombian coffee and sort out her feelings. "If I don't tell him, he'll always have doubts about me and won't give himself to me. I'd rather he be safe than mine." She'd told Norma everything months ago, knowing she'd keep her secret.

"He'll ask you to marry him soon. I know the signs. You don't actually think he's flying to Georgia for a case do you?"

Thoughts of his lame excuse had her giggling. "He's checking up on me. I'm not worried though. I'm sure Tony gave up on Atlanta months ago, and I don't have any ties to my old life."

"Of course he's checking on you. He wants to know who you were in Georgia. He wants to know who he's marrying. You can't tell him, so he'll find out on his own. He's a man. You can't change him. He's marking his territory. Let him. You'll see I'm right."

Norma rose to pour herself another cup of coffee. "Santiago and Steven made sure you were never linked to them. He won't find anything except your business. He'll see you're the same person here as you were there. You just changed your name." Norma checked her watch, hoping Brian had enough time to give Ashton a good man-to-man talk. She hadn't told Brian anything about Diana's history. He knew the couple well enough to be able to give much needed advice.

She was shocked he actually agreed to speak with Ashton. He usually told her to mind her own business. Thoughts of her husband brought a smile to her face. *Such a good man.*

Watching himself in the mirror, Brian stretched, then brushed what was left of his short gray hair with his hands. He sat in a chair out of Ashton's way. "Are you DEA, FBI, CIA, or what?"

Ashton stopped mid-stride. "I do not work for the government." When Brian first asked him the same question, ten minutes ago, it threw him. But now he was in control again. He wanted a relationship with Diana, but how much of a relationship? Marriage was out of the question. He'd tried marriage before and it ended in disaster.

"Like you'd tell me. Did I ever tell you I'm retired FBI? I can smell an agent from fifty paces." He grinned. "I know you can't admit it, but I'll tell you what gave you away."

Ashton had never blown his cover and thought he was doing a damn good job this time. "I am not a part of any agency. You're wrong." He placed four T-shirts in his suitcase then searched the closet for shirts and slacks.

"How much is your water bill?"

He glanced over his shoulder, narrowing his gaze on his neighbor. "Excuse me?"

"You heard me. It must be awfully high with all the cold showers and baths you take. Do you use ice?"

Ashton laughed. "You're wrong about me, Brian. I'm just a lawyer who doesn't want to become involved with his neighbor. We're only friends."

"You won't admit you're agency, which I admire. But what you're doing to Diana is wrong. Why are you leading her on, for Santiago? Then what? You leave her broken hearted?" Ashton raised a brow, Brian continued, "I told you I'm retired FBI. Agents aren't the only ones I smell fifty paces off. That nosy wife of mine is holding out on me. If you haven't noticed, she can't keep her mouth shut. Diana was in trouble. Santiago saved her. That's all I know."

"I would never hurt Diana." He selected five dress shirts.

"Yes you will. When she finds out you used her for Santiago, she'll be hurt, and you know it. That's why you're keeping your distance. You're protecting yourself while leaving her high and dry."

"You don't understand. I can't go back." He placed the shirts in the garment bag, then returned to the closet and selected slacks.

"You have to pick a side. You're cheating the agency, yourself and Diana. Continue on this path and everyone loses. While in Atlanta, ask yourself what's most important to you, fight for it and forget everything else."

Brian didn't give Ashton a chance to reply, he headed out. "One last thing." He stopped in the doorway. "I know you aren't an agent, but I met Norma while on assignment. She forgave me."

Ashton pulled into one of the parking lots outside of

the airport to catch the shuttle. Diana scooted over to his seat as he stepped out. Wolfgang jumped into the front passenger seat.

Ashton stooped down and rested his arm on the back of her seat for balance. Brian's talk spoke louder than anything and everyone.

"Is something wrong, Ashton?"

He lowered his head. *I have to pick a side. It's only fair.* He lifted his gaze to her. "I'll just miss," he glanced over her shoulder at Wolfgang, grinned, "my dog."

She hit at him. "Your dog?"

"Come on, baby, you know you can't come between a man and his dog." He grabbed her hands, stopping her frisky attack. "You know I'm playing."

She calmed. "Be careful in Savannah."

He rested his forehead on hers. "I'm in love with you and don't know what to do about it." He kissed her lightly. "When I come home, we need to have a serious discussion about where our relationship is going."

She grinned, thinking Norma was right again. "So you tell me you love me, then hop on a plane across the country. This has got to fall under the category of cruel and unusual punishment, counselor?"

"I guess my timing is a little off. I just didn't want to tell you over the phone for the first time."

"You are a hopeless romantic."

"Yes I am." He reached in the backseat, grabbed one of the white roses he'd given her earlier, then handed it to her. "I'll call you after I check in." He kissed her one last time. "Everything will work out. You'll see."

CHAPTER THIRTEEN

"**A**gent Barns speaking." He propped the phone between his shoulder and ear.

"This is Olivia Springfield. Do you remember me? You told me to call if anyone came snooping around for Diana Johnson. I'm so glad she's in protective custody. I'm still having a hard time believing she witnessed a murder. She must have been terrified."

Finally. A lead. Tony is crazy. "Yes, I remember you. She's safe for now." He reached for his pad and pencil. "In order for her to remain safe, we're asking her friends to help us. I'll need to know who was looking for her and when."

"Today this man came by. His name was Ashton Powell. He acted like her friend, but I knew all of her friends, and she didn't know him."

"Can you give me a description?"

"He's a fine as hell black man, around thirty-five, six three, muscular and the deepest, darkest bedroom eyes I've ever seen. He also visited the other site."

"Is this all the information you have, ma'am? Try to remember everything. Even the smallest detail would be helpful."

A long pause preceded her answer. "He isn't from around here. When I asked him out, he said he was heading home in a few days."

He couldn't believe this stupid woman thought Ashton wanted to harm her friend, yet she asked him on a date. "Thank you very much for your help, Miss Springfield. If you hear anything else, please let me know."

"I will."

He flipped through the yellow pages in search of hotels. He had a lot of calling to do before Tony arrived. If things worked out, he would know where and whom Ashton Powell was before Tony asked.

⚜⚜⚜

Ashton hung up with Diana to open the door.

"Are you Ashton Powell?"

"Excuse me, but you didn't introduce yourself."

"My apologies." He whipped out his badge as if to intimidate Ashton. "DEA Agent Barns. I need to ask Mr. Powell a few questions. May I come in?"

"Sure." Ashton stepped to the side and allowed the agent in. "How may I be of assistance, Agent Barns?"

"I have a few questions about an associate of yours. You are Ashton Powell aren't you?"

"Yes I am. Who would you like to know about?" He offered the agent a seat, then sat on the edge of the bed.

"A young woman by the name of Diana Johnson."

"Is she in trouble? She doesn't seem like the type to be involved with the DEA."

"We need to question her about one of her associates."

"I haven't seen her in over a month."

Agent Barns scooted to the edge of his seat. "A month. Where?"

"She visited me the last time she was in New York. I was in the neighborhood and decided to return the favor. Her associates told me she's moved."

"What's your relationship with Miss. Johnson?"

"We enjoy each others company from time to time. Why?"

"Do you think she'll be in contact with you in the near future? It's very important we speak with her. She could be in danger."

"Why don't you give me your card? If she comes by, I'll forward it to her."

Barns dug in his wallet for a card. "Thanks." He handed Ashton the card. "If I have further questions, where may I reach you?"

"I'll be in town until the end of the week." Ashton searched through his wallet for one of his old business cards.

Barns rose from his seat as he took the card. "This is a life and death situation, Mr. Powell. I know I can count on you to help your friend."

"Good evening, Agent Barns." He showed the agent out, then rushed to the cellphone and called Leonard. "A DEA agent came by here asking about Diana Johnson.

How long before he finds out who I am?" He sat on the edge of the bed.

"Damn, man. Where's your freakin' phone etiquette? What if you had the wrong number or some shit like that. I'm the asshole. You're supposed to be the sophisticated one, remember?"

Unable to deal with Leonard's jokes, Ashton drew in a deep breath. "You're right. I apologize."

"They'll never discover your true identity. You haven't worked for the Gov-meant on paper since your early years. Did you throw them off any?"

"I lead them to New York."

"If they're good, two days; if not, five. If they were me, I'd have your ass by the end of the day. But no one is that good. Once they find you, they'll check your work associates, friends, neighbors. That's when they'll find Diana."

He kicked at the imaginary image of himself. "I lead the Santiago team straight to her. Shit."

"Don't sweat it, Ashton. Ever since I pitched that fit for the tape, they've been trying to locate me. Once they located me, they would have her location anyway. They'll find my ass in another two, maybe three months. You didn't think I'd allow a trip to Atlanta without having all the bases covered, did you? Hell. I knew those sneaky bastards would have someone watching her old hangouts. I put precautions in motion to slow them."

"I should have known also." He paced the room. "Brian is right. I'm being careless."

"Brian? The old fart who lives across from you?"

"He pegged me for DEA. He thinks I'm cheating the agency and Diana. He said I had to pick a side."

"So what did you pick?"

"I told Diana I love her."

"That's my boy! Don't worry about those agents, man. We knew they'd come into the picture eventually. Tell her the truth before they locate her."

"I won't warn her they're after Santiago. I'd give my life for Diana, but I wouldn't blink an eye for Santiago."

"I know. Shit, what the hell do you think I am? I just don't want them pissing in your Kool-Aid. Carter will crack soon. He's been flying all over the place, and he's increased his arsenal."

"If he takes on Santiago, he'll lose."

"Duh. He won't go down without a fight. I wonder what Santiago's done to hype him up."

"You heard the call. Santiago's gunning after Carter if he doesn't turn over everything."

"But Santiago sounded so calm," Leonard pointed out. "What does he have on Carter? How is he pulling this off so easily?"

"He hates Carter and has had years to plan. I'm flying up to see my parents in the morning, then I'm heading back home. Don't tell Diana."

"I'll see you in San Diego. Peace brother."

"Peace."

Tony pinched the bridge of his nose. "What do you mean you don't know where he is? You spoke to him last night and lost him already. Damn. No wonder my dad can run amuck."

"He checked out of the hotel late last night?"

"Why didn't you have a tail on him? Shit, Barns. I can't be every damn where at once. Find him."

"It'll take time. I can't use DEA channels without drawing attention to myself. Even if I could, I'm not authorized to—"

Tony placed his nine-millimeter on Barns' temple. "I don't give a damn what you're authorized to do. You have seventy-two hours to hand me his correct address. Do you understand me? Don't fail me again."

"Y-yes, sir."

Tony stalked out the room speed dialing his father. "Hey, Dad."

"Do you have her?"

"If everything works out, I'll have her in a few days. I'll need a place to keep her. It can't be one of our holds."

"I've already taken care of it. I don't know who to trust anymore. You just find her."

"Consider it done."

Wolfgang greeted Ashton at the door by jumping up

on his chest. "Whoa, boy." He gently set the oversized puppy's front paws on the floor. "You almost knocked me down. No jumping." He rubbed him behind his ears. "That's my boy."

The site of Diana in her nightshirt sleeping in the lounge chair stopped Ashton. She'd wake with a crick in her neck if he didn't change her positioning. He turned off the television, then knelt beside her. "Diana, I'm home." Making love would have to wait until he told her the whole truth.

She cracked open her eyes. "Did I forget to pick you up?"

He kissed her forehead. "No, love. I came home early. Put your arms around me." She rested her head on his shoulder and wrapped her arms around his neck. He carried her toward her bedroom.

Unable to wake fully she whispered, "Did you find what you were looking for?"

He set her on the bed. "Yes, baby." He covered her, undressed himself, lay in bed and cuddled.

"What time is it?"

He peeked over her shoulder at the clock. "Three-seventeen." Wanting to make love, he pulled her close. "Go to sleep. I'm home and not going anywhere."

"I love you, Ashton."

"I love you, too." *Snow capped mountains, the Artic, Frosty the Snowman...*

Ashton woke early the next morning with Diana still in his arms. *I won't lose you.* He rolled her onto her back for a closer look. When he'd first seen her in New York, though he was drawn to her, but he didn't think her very attractive. Her caramel complexion was lighter than his taste ran. Her thick black hair reached past her shoulders. She was too tall, and her breasts were too large. Now he could see clearly and couldn't believe he'd thought her anything less than gorgeous.

He lightly brushed his lips over her shoulder while caressing her waist. Solid but not so hard she lost her femininity. His hand traveled to her breast, eliciting a moan from her.

He kissed her breast through the thin cotton

nightshirt. "You like that, love." She moved into his massaging hands. "I'll wake you moaning every morning." Wishing he'd never started down this dangerous road, he suckled along her neck.

Emotions and hormones running on high pushed his common sense out of the picture. He feather kissed along her jaw line, chin, mouth. Memories of the sensations that rushed through his body when they shared their first kiss on the plane enveloped him. Looking back, he knew he was sunk.

If this were a dream, Diana didn't want it to end. She felt more pressure to her lips. She opened freely for the man she loved. This couldn't be a dream. A dream couldn't be this sweet. She opened her eyes and heart to him.

"I thought you'd never wake," he whispered in her ear. She stretched in his hands, allowing him to slowly caress her thighs, hips, taking up her shirt above her waist, torso, chest, traveling on over her head and dropped her shirt to the floor.

No going back. He couldn't stop now if he wanted to, and he definitely didn't want to. She lowered her panties.

"Let me get those." He pulled them down, kissing and licking along the way. He lay beside her. "You know what this means? I want you to be my wife." He tasted her sweet lips. "I love you, Diana."

"I love you, Ashton."

He pulled her closer. "I can't stand another cold shower, bath or anything associated with cold." He hadn't been with a woman since they'd met, and being around her kept him highly aroused. He reached for his pants, which were on the floor beside the bed. After protecting them both, he returned to kissing her.

She maneuvered herself fully underneath him, pulled his face down to hers, kissed. Shocked by her strength, he hesitated. "Is something wrong?" she asked.

She was strong in more ways than one. "For the first time in a long time, everything is right." He descended on her mouth, kissing her while entering her heat.

He fought against the urge to plunder her fertile valley. This was the woman he loved, he respected, he wanted children with. He would be slow and gentle if it killed him.

Diana thought she was one of those women who would never have a sexual climax. Thought. "Oh, Ashton." She wrapped her powerful legs around his thighs, forcing him deeper, harder. He didn't need to be asked twice. He stroked with everything he had, sending them both over the edge.

Exhausted and sated, he pulled her into his body worried about what she'd do when she learned the whole truth. Someday soon, he would be able to give his whole self to her. They cleansed each other then returned to bed.

A few hours later, she stirred. "Ashton, wake up."

He kissed her lightly. "I'm up."

"Wolfgang is sitting at the foot of the bed looking like he'll bust a gut at any second. Let me go so I can take care of him."

Ready for a second round of lovemaking, he grinned. "You stay here. I'll take care of him this morning."

"I need a shower."

"Make it hot. I'll be right back."

After Wolfgang's walk, they made love again then lay in bed together. "If you don't like the rings, we can go shopping tomorrow. I'm not leaving this room today."

She reached for the small gold wedding bands. "Are you kidding me? They're beautiful. More so because they belonged to your parents. The ring is perfect, my hand is just too big."

He kissed her fingers. "Your hands are perfect."

Fond memories of him giving her the initial white rose brought a smile to her face. He'd given her a single white rose every day since they reestablished their connection.

"What's so funny?" he asked.

"I know where your romantic streak from. I wish my family was half as nice." Every five years his parents bought a new set of rings. They gave each of their six children their own set. Being the fifth child, this was his set.

"Let's go to New York next week so you can meet everyone. I'm sure the O'Connors won't mind watching Wolfgang for us. We'll find your family to if you'd like."

"I'd love to meet your family." She rested her head on his shoulder, enjoying his masculine scent.

But what about your family? "I need you to promise me something."

"I promise to love you forever."

He knew she meant it, but would she once she knew the truth? "I've been hiding a part of my life from you. I can't tell you yet, but I will shortly."

She stared into his dark eyes. "Tell me now. I want to know."

"I love you, but I can't. In New York we'll tell each other the whole truth. I mean everything. No more secrets."

Her heart leapt into her throat. "But I can't."

"Yes you can. I'll love you no matter what. Do you believe me? Do you believe that no matter what you hear, or see, my love for you has always been real?"

"I believe." She fumbled the sheet through her fingers. "I'm afraid you'll be hurt."

"No one will hurt me. I'm not flying off halfcocked. I need to know what we're against so I can be prepared."

"I need time to think." She closed her eyes. "I'm sorry. I can't let them hurt you."

"I won't turn my back on you." He could feel her trembling. Her family abandoned her because of Santiago and Steven, but he wouldn't. Tears fell from her eyes. "Don't cry." He wiped the tears away. "You don't have to tell me. It doesn't matter. Nothing matters except the love I have for you." He pulled her close to his body. "I love you. I'll take care of everything. You just plan the wedding."

CHAPTER FOURTEEN

Leonard pulled his chair around to Ashton's desk. "I think you should wait until after she knows who you are before you marry. Remember, she'll be pissed for a while." He started sorting through a box of Carter case files.

"How can I forget?" Ashton continued sorting through a second box. "I've been rethinking telling her about my agency ties. I'm giving my notice in a few days whether we have Carter or not. No one knows I'm agency except you and the senior partners I've worked for. Once we hand over these files, I won't exist as an agent anymore."

Leonard shook his head. "Bad idea. There are a few who know you're agency. They know what case we're on. After you marry her, the powers that be will come after you."

He pushed the box away. "How will I tell her, Leonard? I've been putting this off for two days."

"I don't think you have any choice but tell her. By now the Santiago team knows you live in San Diego. How long do you think it will take them to tie in that your neighbor Diana Josephine Warren is actually Diana Pepita Johnson?"

He lowered his head into the palms of his hands. "You're right." He released a long drawn out sigh. "I'm heading home to tell her."

Leonard's cellphone rang. "Hold up a second." He answered his phone. "Yeah." He hit at the desk. "Well what the hell took you so long? Shit." He disconnected. "Santiago is with her now. He snuck in somehow. The only reason we know he's there is from the surveillance camera's we put at your place."

Ashton hit speaker, then speed dialed Diana.

"Hello," Diana answered.

"Hello, baby."

"I'm glad you called. Are you busy? I was hoping you could come home for lunch today."

Leonard smiled mouthing, "This is it, man."

"We must be on the same wavelength. I was calling to

make sure you were home before I left."

"Great. I have someone here I want you to meet."

"I'll see you shortly. Love you." He disconnected.

Leonard hopped out of his seat. "Shit, man. She's about to introduce you to Santiago. Damn this is sweet as hell. You played it cool. I would have been all anxious and shit."

Ashton stood to leave. "I'm only meeting her godfather. Nothing more." He grabbed his suit coat. "We're after Carter, remember?"

"Hell yeah, but you know this means she trusts you. If she has the files, they'll be yours by the end of the day."

❦❦❦❦❦

"Pepita, stop pacing and sit down. You're driving me crazy." Santiago flipped the channel with the remote control.

"You're not listening to me. He'll recognize who you are."

He hunched his shoulders. "I'm not seeing the problem. You didn't think you could tell me you're getting married without me meeting the man did you? You should be thanking your lucky stars Hugo didn't come."

"I'm just afraid he won't understand." She straightened the magazines on the coffee table. "My own family left me. What if he does the same?"

"If he does, he isn't as good a man as I thought. You know I checked him out, don't you? I thought he had to be gay or government."

She stopped cleaning the spotless living room. "Gay or government?"

"He wasn't sleeping with you. What red-blooded man could hold off this long?"

"Santiago, your mind is too dirty. He loves me." She sat on the couch next to him.

"Yes he does. He won't hold your family against you. Stop worrying over nothing. He doesn't know it, but he actually defended one of my men in New York. I'd left the jerk hanging for fu..." he paused, cleared this throat, "... for messing up a job. I thought a little time in jail would do him some good. Your man got him off."

Releasing her childhood fears, she leaned her head on

his shoulder. Ashton had chosen her.

He stroked her hair behind her ears. "Try not to fret, Pepita."

She heard Ashton's car stop in front of the house, her heart raced. "He's here. Come on, Wolfgang. Out back." She ran through the kitchen and put the puppy out. "How do I look?" She straightened her cream linen pant suit as she re-entered the room.

Santiago stood. "More beautiful than your mother." He hugged her. "You know I'm not a monster. He'll learn the same."

Ashton walked into the house and instantly felt sorry for Diana. She looked so worried. She stepped forward, kissed him on the cheek. "This is my godfather, Santiago Calderon."

Santiago held his hand out. "Hello, Ashton. I've heard a lot about you."

He took Santiago's hand, shook firmly. "And I you. I'm glad to finally meet. Diana's been worried over nothing." He pulled her close to comfort her.

Santiago gave an understanding nod. "My baby girl had a hard life full of people letting her down, turning on her. I'm not able to visit as much as I'd like, but I'm sure you can keep her occupied."

Diana shook her head and shrugged away. "This is just too weird." She pointed at Ashton. "Would you two please stop talking in code? I'm not stupid."

Both men laughed. "No you aren't, Pepita. Would you mind giving me a few minutes alone with Ashton?"

She reluctantly replied, "I guess not. I'll be with Wolfgang." She left the two alone.

Ashton watched Santiago carefully shuffle through a black briefcase.

"Take a seat," Santiago said.

Ashton walked around the coffee table, choosing to sit beside Santiago. "I know who you are."

"Of course you do. Any defense attorney worth a grain of salt knows who I am." He pulled out a file. "Knowing who I am, you also know I'm out of my territory and have the DEA snooping around trying to find me, so I'm in a hurry."

"Why is Carter after Diana?"

"Straight and to the point. I like that. She's my weak link, and he knows it. I put her in hiding to give her a chance at a normal life. Steven and I have had to hide her since she was a child." He opened the file. "I'd show these to Pepita, but I don't want to worry her. We've always protected her. I need your help to keep her safe." He placed a photo on the coffee table. "This is Tony Carter. He's looking for Pepita. If you see him, or any of the men in these photos, contact me immediately. Don't play hero." He wrote all of his numbers down for Ashton. "I can't leave any of the men I trust in the area or he'll find her. You are her only defense."

"Is it true Steven Warren obtained a copy of Carter's pipeline?"

"Don't tip into other areas. Just protect Pepita. In a few weeks, Carter will be out of the picture, and Pepita will be safe again."

Ashton sorted through the photos and dossiers of Carter's men. "How deep is Diana involved?"

"She isn't. She walked out of our lives when she was a legal adult, and she'd walk out now if I'd let her, but that's not going to happen."

"We should go to the authorities."

Santiago's laugh echoed against the wall. "You're joking, right? Do you know how many of the authorities are on my payroll?"

"You're right," Ashton reluctantly admitted.

"Carter is after her because of me. I couldn't stop him from killing Steven, but I'll be damned if I let him hurt Pepita. Call me if you see anything suspicious."

"I will."

"What do you mean you didn't ask for the files?" Leonard demanded. "Damn, man. You're blowing it."

"She doesn't have them, Santiago does."

Thoroughly disgusted, Leonard plopped into his seat. "How do you know? Hell. We have a job to do."

"I'm doing it. Look at these." He laid out the photos Santiago had given him. "These are Carter's men. He gave me the names, numbers, addresses, hangouts of each of them and other useful intelligence." He picked up one of the pictures. "This guy's on the FBI's most wanted list. The information in this folder will give you enough busts to last a lifetime and cripple Carter."

"You really don't believe she has the information on Carter?"

"No, I don't. If the files exist, Santiago has them. He's moving on Carter in the next week or so."

"How do you know?"

"He strongly recommended I take her to visit my family sooner than later. He said he'd pay for a trip to anywhere we want as an early wedding gift. I asked him why, and he said he didn't like her being alone at all. Especially in the coming weeks."

Leonard tossed the folder onto Ashton's desk. "He just handed Carter over on a gold platter lined with diamonds, rubies and pearls."

"I know. Now I have to take Diana out of town before the storm hits."

"You'd best tell her you work for the agency before the Santiago team catches up with you. You'd better watch your back. They may already have an agent working in on you two."

"I doubt that."

"I was just shittin' you. You do need to tell her soon thought."

"I'll tell her when we're in New York. I booked our flight for tomorrow night."

"Why don't you leave now? You're cutting it awfully close."

"I don't know how long I'll be gone. I have to turn over my case load to the other partners before I leave."

"Will they take you back? You're about to ditch them for lord knows how long."

"I'll have a job when we return. If not, I'll find another. You know I'll need an investigator."

"I think I'll stay in for a while longer. Someone has to watch your back. Once things die down, I'll take you up on your offer. You realize what we're about to do don't you?"

"I'm in love, Leonard."

Ashton hid his hands behind his back. "I have something for you."

Diana stopped stirring her home made spaghetti in meat sauce, looked over her shoulder and smiled. "Does it have a green stem, white petals, and smell glorious?"

"Nope." He grinned. "Dinner smells delicious."

She took the wooden spoon out of the pot and tasted the tip. "Umm." She held the spoon out. "Want some?"

He leaned forward, and she fed him. He closed his eyes, savoring the tomato and perfect mix of herbs. "Are you sure you aren't Italian."

"I'll be if you tell me what's behind your back."

"Let's go in the back yard. Grab your shovel." He used his hip to nudge her forward.

"Pushy today aren't we."

He followed her though the kitchen and out the sliding door. "The back west corner should do."

"Do what?"

"A few more seconds." They stopped in the corner. "Close your eyes."

"You are dragging along on purpose, you tease." She closed her eyes.

He chuckled, placed the gift to the side, quickly dug a hole, then hid the gift behind his back. "You can open your eyes now."

She looked into the hole he'd dug. "Umm, darling. I like a good hole as well as the next guy but..." He handed her two young vines. "Grapes! Oh my god. How did you know?" She kissed him, stooped and planted her new vines.

"Norma talks a lot." He crouched beside her and watched her plant the vines. "I spoke to Brian earlier. They agreed to watch Wolfgang for us while we're away."

"Sounds great. I can hardly wait to meet your family." She surrounded the tender young roots with fertile soil, packed them down.

"I'd like to leave tomorrow. I've already booked our flight. I just need to drop by the office in the morning and finish clearing my schedule."

"I thought we were leaving this weekend?" She watered the plants.

"I want you to meet my family, and I still have something I need to tell you about."

She backed away and looked at the linked fence Ashton had put up a week ago. She thought it strange to have only twenty feet of fence forming a ninety-degree angle. And why place it three feet inside the privacy fence? Now she knew what he was up to. "These vines will be beautiful."

They ate their dinner, took Wolfgang for his walk and enjoyed each other's company. "Do you have time to pack?" She pulled her suitcase out of her bedroom closet.

"Probably not." He embraced her from behind.

For the first time in her life, she felt totally free to love and be loved. "I want to plant a few roses in the front. When I'm done I can pack for you."

"You don't have to."

"I know. I want to." She leaned back, enjoying his embrace, his distinct aroma, his everything. "I was afraid you'd turn on me like my family did."

He turned her in his arms and rested his forehead on hers. "I love you, Diana." He bent, brushing his lips over hers, sending sensual waves though her body. "I'll never leave you. Do you believe me?"

Believing in him, she hugged him tightly.

❦❦❦

Making love had a tendency to lull Diana. "Do we have to get out of bed, Ashton?"

He kissed her breast. "You can stay in bed all day, but I must go to the office for a few hours." He grinned. "In New York we can make love until we faint."

She pushed him away. "Get out of this bed, you tease."

"I'm leaving. I'm leaving." A half hour later, he exited the restroom ready for work. "I have time to take care of Wolfgang before I leave. Why don't you stay in bed a while longer."

She rolled over, hugging her pillow. "That sounds like an excellent idea. Some crazed maniac tried to sex me to death last night. I'm beat."

He kissed her lightly. "I'll see you this afternoon."

She watched the empty doorway for a while before she moved. Moving to San Diego was the best decision she'd ever made. "Get up lazy bones. You have breakfast to eat and roses to plant."

She quickly showered and put on her work jeans and T-shirt. The phone rang. "Hello."

"Pepita."

"You miss me already. What's up?"

"Ashton isn't what he say's."

She grabbed her tennis, slipped her feet into them. Santiago would never approve of anyone. "What are you talking about? Of course he is. You had him checked out."

"I don't know how they did it, but he isn't what he seems. I didn't catch on until a little while ago."

She sat on the bed to brace herself. "Catch on to what, Santiago? Tell me what's going on."

"He knew Steven copied the information on Carter's pipeline. The bastard asked me about it yesterday. I can't believe I didn't catch on immediately. No one knows about that except…"

"What pipeline? Wait a minute, Ashton's DEA, isn't he?" She held back her tears.

"I'm sorry, baby. I thought he was legit. Hugo is on his way. I'm sending you to Colombia. Without Ashton, you'll have no protection."

"No. Don't. I'm not running away from him. He told me he had something to tell me. He wants to marry me."

"Ashton's an agent and using you for Carter's pipeline. You can't believe what he's told you."

"He loves me, Santiago."

"You are only a case to him. Hugo is on his way."

"No, please don't. I just need to figure things out for myself."

"Hugo is on his way. You don't have a choice in this. Pack for Colombia and don't make me have to search for you."

CHAPTER FIFTEEN

Brian leaned on his brick mailbox-housing unit. "I'm glad you finally asked her to marry you. I was beginning to think I'd have to take you to the justice of the peace at gunpoint."

Smiling, Ashton reached down and rubbed Wolfgang behind the ears. "We're leaving for New York tonight. Can you watch Wolfgang for us? Something's about to go down. I need Diana out of town. I'm not sure how long we'll be gone."

"She'll blow when she finds out the truth."

"That's why I'm taking her to my family. They'll help convince her I'm not a complete jerk."

Brian looked past Ashton. "Oh oh." Diana approached them quickly, loaded for bear. "I'm going in. Stand your ground." He pointed to Diana.

Ashton turned slowly and readied for the day of reckoning. "Diana."

"Wolfgang, let's go." Wolfgang ran to her. "Let's go home."

Ashton ran toward her. "Diana, wait."

"Go to hell, Ashton, or whatever your name is. I just came for my dog."

He followed her. "Diana, let me explain."

She turned hotly. "There's nothing to explain, you murderer." She slammed the door in his face.

He took out his key, unlocked the door and let himself in. "Diana."

"Stop repeating my name." She threw a vase of assorted flowers across the room, barely missing his head. It crashed against the wall and shattered. "I thought you had to work. Holding two jobs must be hard." Tears pouring down her face, she ran into her bedroom.

Wolfgang jumped about agitated. Ashton calmly took him by the collar and let him out back. "I'll fix this, big boy."

Diana lay in her bed, hugging her pillow and a framed picture. "They murdered him," she mumbled.

Ashton knelt beside the bed. "I'm sorry I didn't tell you sooner. Please forgive me."

She lifted her puffy eyes, locked onto his gaze. "You killed him." She hugged the picture close and rocked.

Wanting to console, he sat on the bed. "I love you." He reached to hold her.

She slapped at his hands. "Get away from me. You don't love me. I'm your case." She choked on her words. "Just go away."

It was like she was in the penitentiary when they took Steven away to be executed. Ashton didn't understand why Steven's death was still affecting her so harshly, but he'd help her through. "I'm not giving up, Diana. I love you. I'll never abandon you."

She shook her head. "No you don't. You used me to catch Santiago."

"I'm after Carter, not Santiago." He was jealous of the pain she felt for Steven. This was the devotion he wanted. "Diana, let me hold you. I'm here for you." He held out his hand.

"You're here to catch Carter and you, Mr. Straight-And-Narrow, will let Santiago go? Sure, I believe that," she spit out sarcastically. "I'm just your means to an end. You murdered him." She handed him a picture of her, Santiago, Hugo, and Steven standing on a small wooden bridge.

He gently took the picture, thinking she was distraught and talking crazy. "I didn't have anything to do with Steven until the warden contacted us. I've been after Carter for two years."

"Your kind murdered him."

He set the picture on the nightstand. "I'm sorry, love, but all of the evidence pointed to his guilt. Leonard and I were given the Carter case because of our special skills."

"You knew and you let them kill him. You know evidence is almost as bad a statistics. You defended Ezel Booker when we first arrived in San Diego. All of the evidence pointed to him, but in the end, you proved he was innocent. People are set up every day."

"Are you saying the DEA framed Steven?" Memories of Santiago's eerie laugh after Ashton suggested telling the authorities pricked at him.

"They knew he was innocent and let him die. You're DEA, you let him die."

A nervous sensation jumped about his stomach. "You aren't making sense. What are you saying?"

"He was working with the DEA." She wiped the tears away. "They knew he didn't commit the murders, but because he wouldn't give them what they wanted, they let him die. You are just as guilty as Carter."

He held his hands out, gesturing. "Hold up. Wait a second. Steven wasn't working for the DEA. I didn't read anything about him being an informer."

"Are you calling me a liar?"

"No." He tried to calm his shaky voice. One of the reasons his squad was created was because of crooked agents. "Of course not. I just need to know everything." He'd have to wade through her grief filled words to obtain the truth.

"He didn't kill them." She fell to the bed crying. "He didn't deserve to die."

He wiped the tears from her face caressing, soothing her. "How do you know, Diana?" A gut feeling told him to brace himself for the answer.

She cried out, "Because Steven was with me in Texas the night before he supposedly killed those agents. There's no way in hell he left me, then flew to New York to commit murder. He was set up." She rolled into a ball.

He ran his hands over his face. They'd killed an innocent man. "Oh my God." He rose, pulling her into his arms and wouldn't permit her to escape, instead allowing her to cry and beat at him.

Diana finally calmed and went limp in his arms whispering, "Santiago looked for the proof, but Carter covered his tracks. He has DEA agents working for him. With their help, they framed Steven."

Unable to imagine her pain, he rocked her in his arms.

"Just in case Carter's men found out about me being with Steven, Santiago sent me to Colombia until after the trial. When I returned to Atlanta, Santiago's men were sent to protect me. I wasn't allowed to contact Steven. I couldn't even speak with him. I could only write and Santiago would have the letter posted from various locations." She shook her head. "They knew. They knew, and they killed him."

He continued rocking her gently, as he'd done at the penitentiary. She was so upset she wasn't making sense. Her pain pushed out his feelings of jealousy. "I wish I could have changed things. I'm so sorry." He caressed her back. "I'm truly sorry." He stroked her disheveled hair. "What agents knew, love? I'll make sure they pay."

She shook her head into his chest. "They killed him."

"Let me help. Please, Diana, let me help." He didn't want to hear this, but she needed to vent. "Tell me about Steven."

She stared at him. "You were at the prison the day of his execution, weren't you? I remember your cologne." She sighed. "Distinctly Ashton. Why didn't I catch on?"

He peered into her tear filled eyes. "Until today, that was the hardest day of my life. I wanted to hold you and tell you everything would be all right. I shouldn't have gone to you," he caressed her face, "but I was drawn to you. I couldn't stay away."

Unable to digest more of his lies, she pulled away and rested on the bed. "You were using me all of this time. I gave you my heart. You gave me lies and betrayal. I don't know who you are."

He rubbed her back. "The only lie between us is I work for the DEA, and they are the reason we met. I fell in love with you. I've already written my letter of resignation. I've already taken a full time position at the firm. I love you. I want you to marry me."

"You had no plans of telling me, did you?"

"I've been afraid to tell you." He drew her into his arms. "I love you, Diana, and I didn't want to lose you. I kept putting off telling you the whole truth."

"I don't know what to believe."

"Do you love me?"

"I love the man I thought I met on a plane to my new life."

"I am that man." He sat up straight. "Allow me to do one last thing as a DEA agent. I'll make sure the people who framed Steven pay. It's the least I can do."

She wiped her eyes. "You believe he was innocent?"

"You said he is. I believe you, so he must be innocent."

She cocked her head to the side in consideration, leaned over her bed, pulled out several shoeboxes and a shirt box, then handed the shirt box to him.

He opened the shirt box, took out a large mailing envelope. He lifted the unsealed flap and poured out the contents. A jump drive and some documentation fell onto the bed. He looked at the jump drive. The information he'd been searching for was literally right under his nose the whole time. "What is on this?"

"An electronic paper trail to a bunch of people I don't know. Santiago just said something about a pipeline. I couldn't trust the authorities for help, so I thought I could find a lead to prove that Steven was framed with them, then go to the press. But I couldn't. Those papers are everything I could find and the name of the agent Steven was the informant for. Carter has a lot of agents in his pocket. Are you sure you can get the dirty agent."

"Just give me his name." A spark of hope lit in her eyes, lifting his spirit. "I'll sick Leonard on him."

"I have every thing written about him that I could think of at the time. I couldn't tell Santiago the agent's name or he would have killed him, and I wouldn't have any tie between the DEA and Steven. I just couldn't figure out a way to use the information against him without Santiago finding out. His name is Barns."

Barns? Barns. Shoot! "I'm sorry to have to ask this, but did you meet Steven through Santiago?"

"What are you talking about?"

"I know you were deeply in love with Steven. You and Santiago are the only people who stayed in contact with him throughout—"

"I don't believe this. You thought we were lovers, didn't you?"

"The warden told us you were his lover. Why else would you stay in contact with him?"

"Steven Warren was my father."

"Your what?" he spewed.

"You heard right. Santiago is my godfather. Santiago and Steven were best friends. Closer than brothers."

"But Steven didn't have any children."

"No legitimate children." She held her arms out to her sides. "He obviously had children though. My mother cheated with him, producing me. After she died, my half sisters and brothers told me I shouldn't stay in contact with him any longer out of respect for the man who raised me. I refused and they disowned me."

"But the letters?"

"I couldn't let the agents Santiago said would read my *private mail* know he had a daughter, so I threw in misleading lines."

He pulled her into his arms. "I'll make them pay. I promise I'll make them pay."

"Can you prosecute Barns for murder? He as good as hired a hit man to kill my father. And I know others had to know. They all need to be taken down."

"He will pay. They all will pay." He looked at the clock setting on the nightstand. "Let's say I take the day off. We can spend it together. I'll get Leonard to start working on the jump drive. We'll fly to New York tonight and work through this together."

She pulled away and sank into the bed. "I don't want you to stay with me. I'm not going to New York. I'm hurt and confused. Just leave me alone. I need time to think."

"I don't want to leave you like this."

"If you loved me, you'd leave me alone to sort out my feelings."

He started putting the documentation and jump drive into the envelope. "I love you and will call you later. I'll work on these."

"Don't call me, Ashton. Just leave me alone. I know your number."

He kissed her lightly. "Everything I told you about my life and family is true. Everything I said to you is true. I have never spoken a lie to you. You know I love you and you love me. I'd wait forever for you." He took the information with him as he left for the O'Connor's.

Brian looked into Ashton's beaten face and shook his head. "She found out, didn't she?"

Ashton plopped onto the couch, ignoring Brian for

being right. "Would you mind keeping an eye on her, Norma. She wants to be alone, but I'm worried."

Norma pointed an accusing finger at him. "I ought to turn you over my knee and take a switch to your tail, Ashton Powell. What were you thinking?"

"Leave the man alone, Norma. He had a job to do."

"Job smob. People with the same job killed her father."

"You knew?" Ashton asked.

"I've known since the day after she moved in." She angrily paced the room. "I'm not a big time agent, so I don't know all of the tricks of the trade you agent and ex-agent types use to find out information, so I asked and she told me. You, with all your cloak and dagger, could have asked that first day on the plane, but you didn't. Now look at where you are. He says you're quitting."

"Yes, ma'am."

"Good." She stalked out.

CHAPTER SIXTEEN

After speaking with Brian, Ashton rushed to his office to ask Nelson Stein, senior partner, for help in having Barns prosecuted. Upon completing the consultation, he went through the jump drive storage device while waiting on Leonard to arrive.

"Hey, man. I have the goods on Barns." Leonard walked over to the wet bar. "The bastard was transferred to Atlanta last fall and put in a request for transfer to San Diego a few days ago. He's onto you."

"It won't take him long to find out who Diana is. I have to convince her to leave, if not with me, with Santiago. Hand me his picture."

Leonard tossed the photo package across the room from the wet bar. Ashton caught, opened it and looked through the employee files. "He's the one who questioned me. Did you find out if he's working on the Santiago case?"

"He isn't, man. Never was. To protect Diana, Steven never said anything about Diana seeing him the previous day, so Barns didn't pop up when we were researching the case."

"Shit, he's still working for Carter." Panicked, he rose from his desk. "He knows she's in San Diego. I have to reach Diana." He rushed out the office with Leonard close behind.

"I'll drive, man. You won't be killing me today."

Diana was sitting on the front stoop reading when a limo drove up. Thinking Hugo must have been closer than Santiago indicated, she stood to greet him when her cellphone rang. "Hello."

"Love, it's Ashton. Listen to me..."

She turned her back away from Hugo's car. "I told you to leave me alone. Don't call me again." She disconnected, then turned to greet Hugo. She wouldn't go to Colombia, Argentina, New York or anywhere and was prepared for the fight.

The man walking toward her wasn't Hugo but a very

handsome, young Latino with whisky eyes and a million dollar smile. She nodded a greeting, thinking he had Santiago's eyes and proud walk. She figured he must be one of his nephew's she didn't know.

"Hello, I'm Tony." He held his hand out to her. "Did you do these yards?"

She shook his hand, but he didn't release. "Yes I did as a matter of fact." She gently pulled her hand away. "I'm Diana." Her cellphone rang again. She held a finger up to Tony. "Please accept my apologies. I need to go off on someone."

She turned her back on him to answer the phone. Under her breath she admonished, "What on Earth is your problem? Don't you understand English?"

"Pepita, run." She froze at the sound of Santiago's voice. "Tony knows where you are. Hugo will find you. Just get out."

Wolfgang sensed her change in mood, growled softly, and stood at her side.

"Hang up the phone, Diana. It's time to leave."

She closed her eyes, praying for help. "I'm not going anywhere with you, Antonio Carter." Though she felt like she'd faint, she squared off her shoulders, held her chin high and looked straight into his eyes.

He stretched his hand out. She backed away. Wolfgang's growl grew louder. He dropped his hand. "Give me the phone." She handed him the phone, then slowly inched toward the front door.

"I'll take good care of your little girl, Santiago." He disconnected, then reached for her.

She ran for the house. Wolfgang attacked Tony. She pulled the front door open, ready to slam it behind her, when she heard a shot and Wolfgang yelp. Knowing she couldn't help Wolfgang, she slammed the door closed and ran for the cordless phone.

"Ashton! Help me. He's here!" She stared at the door, wishing her would be abductors away. The doorbell rang repeatedly. "Ashton!" They beat at the door. "Oh my God. They're busting down the door." She searched the living room for something to use as a weapon.

"I'm almost there, baby. Run. Hide. I'll find you."

Diana's front door crashed in. "Oh shit, shit." She ran into the kitchen, then dropped the phone for a butcher knife. "Get out. Get out. Get out!"

Three large men filled her doorway. "Come with us, and you won't be hurt."

"Go to hell." She backed up to the sliding door to leave. Tony pushed Norma into the room. Diana froze. Tony smiled sweetly at her. "Put down the knife and come with us now or Ma and Pa Kettle die."

She glared at him, set down the knife.

Norma cried out, "Run, Diana, run!"

"Shut up, bitch." He slapped Norma, and she fell to the ground.

Diana ran to Norma's side and tried to help her stand.

"Don't worry about me, honey, just get away," Norma said.

"Let's go. Rex, make sure there aren't any fingerprints left behind," Tony ordered. "This old biddy won't say a word if she wishes to live another day."

Mortified Tony struck Norma, Diana turned and narrowed her gaze on him. Rage had replaced her fear. "You son-of-a-bitch." Barely able to hold onto her control, she stood toe-to-toe with him.

He smirked. "Yeah."

Snap.

She grabbed him around the neck and threw her knee into his groin with all of her strength. His breath rushed out of him. His gun dropped to the floor.

Norma gasped, cupping her mouth with her hands. His three goons grabbed themselves with sympathy pains. The pain knocked Tony's breath out of him, shooting a searing ripping sensation from his groin up through his eyes, yet he managed to hold onto Diana, keeping her from escaping.

Tony fell to the floor, using Diana as his cushion, knocking her wind out. "You're going to pay for this," he breathlessly eked out.

Still lying on her, he drew in several breaths. "You are out of your mind, aren't you?" He gingerly propped himself on his elbows. "I could have accidentally shot you."

She pushed him off her. "You hit a defenseless old

woman and have the gall to say I'm out of my mind. Why don't you pick on someone your own size, sex and age you coward."

He lifted himself, leaning on his hands and knees. "We don't have time for this shit. Take her to the car." His men drug her off.

He regained his breath slowly. "I absolutely love a woman with fight. Did you see the way she took after me?" He brushed himself off as he stood.

Norma rose, using the back of the chair to steady herself. "Santiago will kill you and everyone stupid enough to associate with you if you harm one hair on her head."

His eerie laugh filled the room. "I'll bet you were something in your day, old girl." He walked out.

Norma, still a little disoriented from her fall, looked around for the kitchen phone. She took it off the base, dialing for 911.

"Hey! Stop hitting those damn buttons and talk to me."

She fumbled the phone, almost dropping it from the shock of a male voice. "Ashton? Oh God, Ashton, they took Diana." She paced, biting her nails.

"Take a deep breath, Norma. Go into the living room. Try to see the license plate of the car before they leave. I'm only one minute away." She headed for the living room. "Do not go outside, Norma. It's too dangerous. Do you hear me?"

"Yes, yes." As she reached the living room window, Brian entered the house. "Oh no they're gone already."

Brian reached for the phone. "Is that the police?" She handed him the phone. "This is Brian O'Connor... A new white Lincoln stretch limo license plates... South." He watched out the window as Ashton's car sped by. "Be careful."

He tossed the phone to the side, then opened his arms for his wife. "He'll bring her back. We need to do what we can for Wolfgang."

"Get in the damn car, Diana." Tony pushed her into the back seat of the Maxima, then scooted in beside her. "Move with the flow of traffic," he barked at the driver.

Diana ground her teeth as she watched the limo speed out of the filling station parking lot. She faced Tony. "I have never hated anyone as much as I hate you." She slouched in her seat, crossing her arms. *Sandwiched between two jerks.*

Tony laughed at her pouting. "You're just mad because I outsmarted Santiago. Do you know how long I've been looking for you? Hiding you in our backyard was ingenious. I always admired Santiago."

The Maxima pulled onto the highway. Ashton and Santiago would be looking for the limo. *I can't let them get me alone.* Diana stared at Tony. He smiled. She looked at the man to her left. *How can I get out of here?* She watched as they went along with the traffic.

"Don't get any ideas, Diana. You're outnumbered three to one."

"Thank you for the helpful advice, Oprah."

The driver and man to her left chuckled. Tony snarled. "Call me what you want, but heed my words."

"I didn't call you anything except a son-of-a-bitch, but that's a compliment, so I take it back."

He cocked his head to the side. "Whatever."

She closed her eyes, calculating. *It's now or never.* With all of her might, she flung her body through the crack between the front seats, then grabbed and turned the steering wheel sharply to the right.

The car spun out of control. The driver fought to straighten it. Tony worked to pull her back. Years of hauling seventy-pound bags had paid off. She didn't budge until cars banged into them, knocking them all over the road.

Her body was flung around, injuring her side, but she accomplished her goal. Now they couldn't take her away.

"Shit," Tony said. The driver was seriously injured. "James, are you all right? Shit." Tony grabbed Diana, pulling her arm behind her back. "Stop fooling around and get up."

"My side hurts. I can't."

"Of course it hurts. You wrecked the car you crazy bitch." He pulled out his gun. "We need to move before the cops arrive."

All traffic had stopped on their side of the highway. The opposite side quickly became congested with onlookers. He snarled at Diana. "Listen to me. You will come along peacefully, or I will shoot the next person I see. I don't give a damn if it's a man, woman or child. You think about that before you pull more of this shit. Now get out of the damn car."

He stuffed his gun into his waistband and covered it with his shirt, then held out his hand. "Hold onto my hand. Act like we're together." She placed her hand into his and went peacefully.

After seeing the accident in their rear view mirror, a couple stopped to offer assistance. Tony and Diana approached them. "Oh my God, that was awful. Sit down and wait for the ambulance. My husband already called 911."

Tony held up his gun and pointed it between the woman's eyes. The woman's eyes grew wide with fear as she trembled. Her husband froze in place.

"We'll be taking the car. Get in, Diana, before I get angry." She complied.

He pulled off, driving away from the multi-car pile up Diana had caused. A few miles away, he laughed. "Where the hell did you get that idea from? You really are out of your mind, aren't you?" Ignoring him, she continued watching out the window. "You will behave."

"Don't talk to me." One of the rare times she'd seen Oprah, they were discussing what to do if you were abducted. Rule number one was to keep your abductor from moving you to a second location. Your chances of survival decreased drastically upon changing locations. One of the suggestions was to wreck the automobile.

CHAPTER SEVENTEEN

Leonard shoved the two Carter thugs who were in the decoy limo onto the dinning room floor. "We need more rope, Ashton." He'd been able to tie their hands behind their backs but didn't have enough rope for their feet.

Ashton went to the garage and returned a short time later with more rope. Leonard made the two men sit in chairs.

"Have they told you where he's taken her?"

Leonard secured their feet. "Not yet, but they will. Santiago just called. He'll be here—"

Santiago and Hugo burst into the house and made a b-line for the men in the chairs. Santiago pulled out his nine-millimeter, attached the silencer, then pointed the gun at the temple of one of the now terrified thugs. "Where the hell is she?"

Thug one closed his eyes tightly. "I s-swear we don't know. Tony wouldn't tell us. We were only a decoy. I swear we don't know. We don't know." Santiago shot the man's foot. The second thug echoed his partner's sentiments.

Leonard stood, impressed. Ashton remained quiet and looked like he'd throw up at any second. This was the world these men chose to live in. Santiago was his only hope at saving Diana. He found it ironic that he actually needed Santiago.

Thug one cried out in pain. "I swear we don't know." Santiago slowly lifted the gun to thug two's knee and shot.

"Oh God, we really don't know. Please..."

Santiago moved the gun to the thug one's waist. "No. I can't shoot there. You wouldn't be able to talk. I'll shoot off every limb until you tell me what I want to know or die from the shock. Either way, I'll feel better. What about you, Leonard?"

Leonard smiled broadly. "I'm with you, man." He pulled out his piece.

"I'm begging you. We really don't know. Please just kill me."

Santiago and Leonard both cursed. "Shit, they don't

know."

"Hugo, call a clean up crew to take care of this mess." Santiago turned on his heals. "You two come with me."

Leonard and Ashton sat in the back seat of the limo across from Santiago. "I intended on having you killed, but you called me for help. And now this." Santiago looked back at the house they'd held Carter's men at. "You are helping me. Why?"

"I love Diana. I want her safe." Sorry for his deceptions, he trailed off. "Even if she never wants to see me again."

Santiago motioned his head toward Leonard. "What's your story?"

"He's my Siamese twin. If he's in the shit, I'm right there with him smellin' like shit."

Santiago chuckled. "That's how Steven and I were. We're going to Los Angeles and pay Robert Carter a visit. I'm sending you in to speak for me, Leonard. Don't take any crap off him. Let him know I will not negotiate—"

"But he'll hurt Diana," Ashton interjected as the limo merged onto a main thorough fair.

Santiago held up a hand. "Wait a second. Let him know I won't negotiate where Pepita is concerned. I won't speak to him until I know she isn't being harmed. If I'm not satisfied with the proof, I'll turn over the pipeline to you, then come after his ass."

Leonard smirked. "I already have a copy."

"Tell me something I don't know, asshole." He smacked Leonard on the side of the head. Ashton released a nervous laugh.

"Shit, man. That wasn't funny, Ashton."

"Pay attention. He doesn't know you already have them. You'll be a distraction while Ashton finds Diana."

"Oh shit yeah. I got it." Leonard punched his fist. "We'll get her back, man."

Santiago continued, "Stall him. Eventually he'll try to pay you off for the information. I've been needling him for months. He's at the end of his rope."

"That's what's worrying me. He might act out and hurt Diana."

Straining to calm himself, Santiago relaxed in his seat.

"Ashton, I love Pepita. I've lost my children to the lifestyle. I won't let it take Petita."

"I know you love her, but you said it yourself—Carter isn't thinking clearly."

Santiago fixed his weary eyes on Ashton's. "We can't go into his holds with guns blazing. We have to wait for him to make a mistake. We have to stall until she tells us where she is. Pepita is a lion in sheep's clothing. She's been dealing in this world her whole life. She knows how to handle herself."

He lowered his head in despair. "I know you're right."

Leonard's gaze traveled from his broken friend and locked on Santiago. "I'll do whatever needs to be done to get her back."

Santiago nodded in understanding. Leonard was so like him and Ashton like Steven. He rested his head back for much needed sleep.

"Santiago, why did Diana move to Atlanta when her mother died? She told me because her father was dying. Why did Carter go after her?"

"Pepita is the result of an affair her mother had with Steven when she was temporarily separated from her husband. Dorothy and Owen Johnson raised Pepita; but Steven and I were allowed to have a large role in her life. Steven wasn't listed on her birth certificate to keep Pepita safe.

"After Dorothy passed, Pepita's siblings treated her horribly for spending time with us. They called her a traitor, saying she betrayed the man who raised her in his hour of need. Those spoiled brats didn't care when Steven's money paid for almost all of their luxuries. He wanted his only child to have everything but didn't want the others to be jealous, so he paid for everyone in Owen's name.

"When Owen's cancer returned, he didn't want Diana seeing him die. Her siblings had disowned her, so Steven made arrangements for her to move to Atlanta. He hired an older woman to stay with her until she reached eighteen." The car veered onto the expressway entrance.

"When she first moved from her adoptive father, she wanted to live with us, but she didn't know what we did.

We couldn't allow our world to know she existed, or they would use her against us. As she grew older, she figured out what we were and tried hard to save us. She begged us to leave the life." He chuckled. "I can't tell you how many times she popped up unannounced, trying to convert us. We'd let her stay with us a few days, then send her back to Atlanta. Once her business started taking off, we didn't have to worry about her surprise appearances as much. Then when she was eighteen, she cut us off."

"Diana had distanced herself from you all. How did she end up with Steven the night before the murders of the agents?" Ashton asked.

"The DEA had agents in both my and Carter's organizations. Carter is a real pain in the ass. I wanted to rid myself of him. Steven and I pretended to have a fight. He crossed over to Carter's camp. The Carter DEA agent wanted Steven's help. Steven used him to obtain the information on Carter. Once Carter found out, he had the agents killed and framed Steven for it. Steven wouldn't tell Carter what he took, so he went after Pepita to make him talk."

"How did Carter find out about Diana? The DEA didn't know"

"Pepita was attending a flower show in Texas when she found out Steven was in the area. She gave him a surprise visit on the night before he was supposedly killing those two DEA agents. Pepita was caught in the middle of the setup. You see, Tony Carter paid a DEA agent to keep Steven busy so he wouldn't have an alibi. Pepita showed up and met the agent. The agent wasn't smart enough to tell Carter about Diana until Steven was brought up on charges."

Leonard chimed in, "They went after her to keep Steven quiet and hurt you. And Diana didn't show up in our records because the agent never told the agency about her."

"Correct. After Steven's execution, they continued looking for her to keep me in line. That's why I changed her identity." He paused. "Pepita is a fighter, Ashton. She'll find a way to contact us. We'll get Leonard on the inside and work this from both angles."

Robert Carter sat behind the large oak desk, fidgeting his cellphone nervously. "Where is she now?"

Tony rolled his eyes. "In the kitchen terrorizing the staff I assume."

"This is no time for joking, Tony."

"We're in southern Mexico." He motioned around the study. "This is a totally new spot, the staff doesn't speak English, and she barely speaks Spanish. She's stuck. Relax, Dad." He plopped onto the armchair.

"I can't relax. Santiago was taking over too quickly. I had to do something."

"No need to explain to me."

"I'm returning to the states. You stay here and make sure she doesn't escape. Do not harm her, or she won't be any good to us. Remember the staff isn't broken in yet."

Tony quickly rose from his seat. "I'm not staying here with her. I've told you all the shit she's pulled. I don't even have any real men to help."

"Dammit, Tony, she's only one woman! You can think of something. I'll leave Baxter and Leon with you."

"I'm not a baby sitter, Dad."

Carter pushed away from the desk. "You are staying here with her. Get her under control. I don't care how you do it, just do it without killing or bruising her. I want Santiago to see we haven't harmed her." He pointed his phone at his son. "Do you understand me, Tony?" He hit speed dial for his pilot.

"Just figure something out fast. She isn't the docile flower child we bargained for."

Carter held the phone to his ear. "I'll call Santiago tomorrow. He'll be frantic and ready to deal." He spoke into his phone. "Get the plane ready. I'm leaving soon." He hung up. "Santiago won't attack while we have his child."

Diana was too angry and scared to think straight. "Maria, may I please have some water." Maria was the only English-speaking servant in the house.

The middle-aged woman rounded the kitchen table with the water. "You should eat, darling," Maria said, her Spanish accent thick yet easily understandable for Diana.

"No thank you." She rubbed her lower waist. "I'll need a few things. If I make a list, can someone go into town for me?"

"Of course." Maria took out a pad and pencil, then handed them to Diana.

"Thank you." She wrote her list thinking guns, bullets, grenades, but writing what she'd actually need like clothes. "I'd prefer a female fill it."

Tony walked into the room. "Is the lasagna finished yet? I'm hungry."

"I'll serve dinner in five minutes," Maria answered.

He held out his hand for Diana. "I know you're hungry. Let's eat."

She pushed away from the table, handed Maria her list, then walked out. She'd never been so hungry in her life, but would rather starve than share a table with Tony.

"Diana, come back here."

She didn't bat an eye but continued on her path.

Tony clinched his teeth. "What did she give to you?" He thought shooting above the crowd at the airport would scare her into submission, but that didn't work. If the note was a trick, he'd kill Maria in front of Diana to straighten her out. He quickly shrugged that idea off; he didn't speak Spanish.

"I'll send Angela in the morning to fill it," Maria said.

He read through the list. "Hand me a sheet of paper and pen. I have a few changes to make." She hadn't made any unreasonable request, but he still didn't like the list. He'd told her to tell him what she needed, yet she went to the cook instead. He changed the list, making sure Diana would know he was in control, and she depended on him for everything.

❧❧❧

Baxter leaned on the dining table. "You'd better get her under control fast."

Ignoring Baxter, Tony finished his lasagna.

"How will you do it?"

Tony took a sip of wine. "I'll make her fear and respect me."

"But you can't mark her, or Santiago will retaliate." He poured more red wine, shaking his head. "I'm glad I'm not you."

"I don't need to mark." Tony turned his head. "Maria!"

A few seconds later, she ran into the room. "Yes."

"Where's Diana?"

"I believe she's retired for the evening."

❦❦❦

Diana looked in the dresser mirror at her reflection. "You need a good night's sleep so you can plan the great escape." She brushed her hair back in preparation for her shower. Santiago being ruthless would play in her favor. They wouldn't harm her in fear of angering him even more.

She locked her bedroom door, then headed for the shower. "How will I get away?" She turned on the water. She couldn't imagine what Ashton and Santiago would go through to find her. She allowed the water to flow over her hands until the temperature felt right, then she stepped into the tub.

The hot water pounding on her back felt wonderful. The events of the day rushed through her mind as she turned to face the downpour. She'd give anything to see Ashton again, but this was no time to feel sorry for herself. She pushed the sorrow away in exchange for the shampoo.

Tony stepped in the shower behind her. She quickly faced and pushed at him. "Get out of here."

He trapped her between the wall and his body. "Stop hitting at me." He held her hands beside her body. "Be still. I just want to help you shower."

Refusing to cry or show fear, she shook her head. "Get away from me, Tony. I'm a big girl. I know how to shower myself."

Wrapping his arms around her, he closed his eyes. "Umm, you're trembling."

She turned her head to keep him from kissing her. "Please leave me alone."

"The magic word. I'll leave you alone after our shower." He lathered up the soap, then began washing her waist. "Will you behave?"

The shower washed away her tears. "Please let me shower myself," she requested stiffly.

He grinned, kissing her neck for not saying she'd behave. "I love showers. What size cup do you wear?" She stepped away from his hands, meeting only the wall. "I'd say a least a D." He bent, trying to kiss her nipple.

She punched him in the side of the head before she realized what she was doing. He slipped and fell onto the tub floor.

He rose and pulled her back onto his body, the red mark of her fist marred his ear. "I'll have Maria send your dinner up. You will eat all of your food and go to bed or we'll finish this." He walked out, taking her clothes with him.

Diana dropped to the floor of the shower, weeping for Ashton to save her.

CHAPTER EIGHTEEN

Tony lay beside Diana, watching her sleep. He'd wanted to whip her within an inch of her life for punching him. He'd shown more restraint than he'd known he possessed. The thought of her determination brought a smile to his face. He'd assumed by taking her clothes she wouldn't leave the room. After she ate, she snuck out of her room and roamed the house wearing only a blanket. He barely caught her before she used a phone.

He chuckled, remembering her indignant expression when he snatched the phone and broke it. Needless to say, he had all the phones in the house removed and no cellphones were allowed, except his.

He finally resorted to spiking her drink, guaranteeing him a peaceful night's sleep. He opened her robe for a better view. He'd told her to behave. Her hard head would make her stay with them more enjoyable than he'd previously thought.

Time for punishment.

Diana knew she was dreaming, but didn't care. She missed Ashton's touch. His caressing her body, licking, massaging and suckling sent sensual shock waves along her skin. When he took her breast into his mouth, it took everything she had not to wake and ruin everything.

"Open up, baby."

He descended on her mouth, but it didn't feel right. She relaxed, trying to adjust. It just wasn't right. Her head continued spinning, but her memory trickled back. She'd been drugged. The dream ended, yet she still felt the suckling on her body.

She opened her eyes and saw Tony. "What are you doing?" Horrified, she scooted away, covering herself with her blanket. "Get away from me, you sicko."

Edging closer to her, he said, "That's not what you were moaning a few seconds ago."

She kicked at him. "You son-of-a-bitch. I hate you."

He batted her legs down, trapping them under his,

grabbed her arms, yanked her close to his body. "Didn't we go through this yesterday?" He kissed her lightly. "I'm a son-of-a-bitch." He lay on her, making sure she felt his hardness. "And you hate me," he drawled out. "Will you behave today or do I stop controlling myself around you?"

She didn't answer.

"Open your eyes, Diana. Always look me in the eyes. Every time you look away, I'll kiss you." He kissed her; she bit him. He laughed. "Are you planning on fighting like this when we make love?"

"You have making love and rape confused. I'll never make love with you."

"Whatever you want to call it, you'd better behave if you don't want to do it with me." He rolled away. "I had your clothes cleaned. They're hanging in the bathroom."

⁂

Diana settled in one of the ladder back chairs at the kitchen table. "Do you need help, Maria?"

"No thanks." She continued paging through the Betty Crocker cookbook Tony told her to select the menu from. "This is my job, you know. Will you be eating in the dining room with the others?"

"Too many men for me. How long have you been working here?"

"Six years, but for the Carter's, two weeks." She flipped the page. "Tony says he hates Mexican food."

Diana's mouth transformed into a sly grin. "How interesting."

"It's not a problem. I'll follow the directions in the cookbook."

"I'm sorry. I was talking about your working for the Carters. What about the rest of the staff?"

"In a way, we came with the house. Why?"

"Just wondering. How many speak English?"

"Me, Hector, some of the exterior guards and Tony's friends that came down with him. I hope you're feeling better today."

"I'm feeling much better at the moment. Thanks."

Tony walked in. Diana looked away, acting like he wasn't there. He crossed the room and knelt in front of her, placing his hands on her thighs for balance and to remind her to behave. "You have such beautiful eyes, darling. I missed them when I came into the room. I'll need a kiss to make up for my loss."

She narrowed her eyes on his, wanting to gouge them out. He had explained how the staff thought they were lovers. "Of course, darling." She smiled sweetly.

He stretched, kissing her. She opened up to him, allowing him to probe her mouth with his tongue. He moaned; she bit down.

He jerked back, holding his hand to his mouth. "Not so ruff, *love*. What will the staff think?" He wiped off the blood.

She innocently batted her eyes. "I'm sorry, *darling*. I didn't mean to embarrass you. Did you happen to see my bra. I searched high and low and thought maybe you were wearing it... again."

Maria unsuccessfully stifled a giggle.

Tony sucked air through his teeth. "Well, *love*. I know how confining you find them, so I threw it away. I also took the liberty to fix your list."

She frowned. "What do you mean by fix my list?"

"I removed bras, jeans, T-shirts and replaced them with sundresses and teddies. I know how much you love easy access."

"You shouldn't have," she replied dryly.

Maria laughed. "Breakfast is ready."

He held his hand out to Diana.

"I'll eat in here."

He raised a brow. "Nonsense." He pulled her out of her seat, hugging her body into his. "Or would you like to shower." She stormed out of the room. He laughed, hunching his shoulders. "She's been acting so emotional lately. I don't know what it could be."

"Could there be a Tony Jr. in the works," Maria's happy voice chimed in. "I turned into an emotional roller coaster when I was pregnant."

He strolled out of the room. *Antonio Carter Jr. has a nice ring to it.*

❧❧❧

"Would you please pass the steak sauce?" Diana took the sauce from Tony and poured a little on her plate.

Baxter and Leon continued watching the two's sparring match.

She glanced up and saw then staring, again. "Would you two please stop staring at me?"

"Leave them alone, Diana."

"They're big boys and don't need you to fight their battles."

Baxter whispered in Tony's ear, "You did a great job breaking her, boss." Chuckling, he returned to the corner.

"Are you tired, darling?"

Diana didn't answer Tony, but continued cutting her steak. She wasn't his darling, and his men knew she wasn't there voluntarily.

Through clinched teeth, he said, "I'm speaking to you."

Diana stared into his whisky eyes so he couldn't accuse her of turning away. "Who is Yu? I had a friend from China named Yu." She looked around the dinning room. "He's not here." She pointed at his men. "Which one of y'all is Yu?"

Tony's lips thinned and eyes became cold. "Don't worry, love, you don't have to pretend around the boys. They won't tell Santiago." She didn't take the bait. "You were right, Baxter. She's a dynamo in bed."

"You liar!"

"You should have heard her. When I took her breast into my mouth, she begged for more. When I stopped to take a breath, she practically—"

"Stop it." She banged the table with her fists.

"Oh no, love. Let's get it all out. They can be trusted not to tell Santiago you came here willingly. We've been lovers for years."

"You bastard."

"No," he said calmly. "I'm the son-of-a-bitch who made you moan all morning long."

Snap.

One second she's sitting in the dining room experiencing the most humiliating moment in her life, setting aside the shower incident of the previous evening, the next she was penned on the floor, gasping for air and Tony was strangling her.

Baxter and Leon pulled him off her. "You can't do this."

Tony shook the men off. "Get out of here now."

"No, boss. We can't," Leon said with a gulp.

Tony straddled Diana, keeping her from moving away. "If you don't get the hell out of here now, you'll wish you were dead."

"You'll kill her."

"I'm not stupid. Get out and keep everyone away!"

Both men backed out of the room.

Diana drew in several deep breaths, readying for the fight.

He covered her body with his. "There's no freaking way I'm standing still while you try to kill me." He attempted to yank down her pants.

She fought him with all of her strength, keeping him from accomplishing his task. She was much stronger than he'd thought.

"It was an accident."

He gave up on her pants and held her hands above her head. "How the hell is your throwing a steak knife as hard as you can at my heart an accident?"

Coming from him, it sounded stupid. She laughed uncontrollably. The past two days were too much for her to handle. She'd snapped. "It was an accident the wood part hit you instead of the steel."

Her laugh was contagious. This whole Santiago business stressed him out, having him act out of sorts for the past few months. He rested his head on her shoulder. He'd said some pretty wild things. "We've got to stop this, Diana, or we'll kill each other."

"Then take me home."

"You know I can't." The smell of the lilac shampoo she'd used brought back memories of her in the shower. He traced her ear with his tongue, whispering, "We don't have to fight."

"I want to go home." She leaned her head to the side, closed her eyes, shut him out.

He kissed her neck while caressing her breast. "I'll make you feel so good you'll call this home."

"You make me feel filthy."

He stopped abruptly. He was no rapist and had no intention on starting today. "You'll behave or we'll make love. I'm tired of having to remind you to behave every time we enter the same room."

She studied him a few seconds. "What you want to do isn't called making love. You humiliate me at every turn, then expect me to sit and take it."

His eyes sparkled with humor. "If you'd behave, I wouldn't humiliate you. It's a vicious cycle you could stop."

"What do I have to do to stop the cycle?"

"As I tell you. We are supposed to be lovers, so you will treat me as such."

"I'm not sleeping with you."

"You will sleep with me. We won't have sex—or whatever you want to call it—unless you misbehave, but you will share a bed with me. We will share our meals together, shower together, and I will hold you all night."

"But." She paused.

"But what? I think I'm being quite generous considering in the past twenty-four hours you've tried to knee my balls into my throat, knock my brains out though my ear and murder me."

Memories of the pain she caused him brought a brief grin to her lips. "You killed my dog, beat my neighbor and kidnapped me. I believe I have a right to be angry."

"True, but I am the one in control. You do as I say."

"It's just." How much more embarrassment would she have to endure before Ashton rescued her? Tony didn't have a decent bone in his body for her to appeal to.

"What? Spit it out."

"It's already bad enough you humiliate me, but I'm starting my period. Having anyone in the shower with me is disgusting. I don't want to be touched during that time, and you're always threatening to force yourself on me. How can you expect me to *behave* when I have nothing to lose, including my dignity?"

He propped himself on his elbows. "You're joking right? You're not really starting your period?"

She pushed him away from her. "Yes, Tony. I'm starting my period. It happens every month about this time."

"Well how long does it last?"

"A week. Don't act like you don't know this stuff. It's embarrassing enough to be telling you. And so there is no misunderstanding, if you continue torturing me, I'll fight you tooth and nail. You leave me no alternatives."

"No wonder you've been acting so psycho."

"You're the one acting psycho. I'm fighting the only way I can."

He leaned back on his hands. "For the next week I won't touch you sexually, and you can shower by yourself. But you will stop disrespecting me. The first time you slip, we go back to the old way."

"What about when the week is over?"

"We'll cross that bridge when we come to it."

"What am I allowed to do?"

"You can go anywhere on the grounds, and do whatever you want. We'll eat our meals together and share a room."

Her brows rose.

"I don't want to rape you. I need to keep an eye on you. Do we have a deal?"

"It's a deal." *Ashton will have me out of here by then.*

CHAPTER NINETEEN

"**W**ould you like a drink, Agent Rogers?"

"No thanks, Mr. Carter, and please call me Leonard."

Robert Carter poured two brandies, placed one in front of Leonard, then took his seat. "In case you change your mind. So what's your role in this?"

Leonard shrugged. "I'm not sure. I was called in by my supervisor last night and told to act as mediator between you and Santiago Calderon," he lied. "I met with Calderon earlier today and now—"

"Mediator for what?"

Leonard hated being interrupted, and Carter seemed to be a pro at it. "Mr. Carter, things would go a lot easier if you'd allow me to finish my sentences."

Carter frowned at the sloppy agent. "When DEA comes into my establishment, I believe I have the right to ask why."

"I'm not denying that. I'm just attempting to give you the whole picture instead of a puzzle piece."

"Fine. Do it your way. Just be quick about it."

"First let me say I do not have any recording devices on me. You may search if you'd like. Everything I say in here is between us unless you want me to take it out."

Carter nodded his head for Leonard to continue. "Calderon called us yesterday, requesting our help in retrieving his godchild who was kidnapped. In exchange for our assistance, he's giving us information that will bring down your empire."

Leonard enjoyed watching Carter turn red. He looked like he would burst at the seams. Leonard picked up his drink, sniffed, drank a sip, stalling.

"I don't even know who his godchild is. Why didn't he go to the FBI for help? Kidnapping is a federal offense. And if he has some information on me, why hasn't he used it?"

"Let's be frank shall we. Calderon is head of the second largest drug cartel in the world. You run the sixth. Everyone knows you two have been in a cold war for years.

Since the death of Steven Warren, Calderon's turned up the heat. We have eye witnesses that say your son kidnapped his godchild. We were looking for her also," he tipped his drink toward Carter, "but you found her first. Calderon called us knowing we are already knowledgeable about you. We should be able to find his godchild faster than the FBI."

Leonard took another sip of his drink. "We don't want a war started on our streets, Mr. Carter. This case is being handled off the books, giving everyone more leeway, even if we have to forget about the files that contain your pipeline connections. My number one priority is to prevent a war."

"Let's say I know where she is. What will Calderon give for her safe return?"

"He refuses to use her as a bargaining chip. If you do not return her safely, he will give us the information Steven copied from your files and the war begins."

"Have you seen the files? How do I know he isn't lying?"

"He gave me a little preview."

"What do they contain?"

"You don't know what's in those files do you?" Leonard chuckled and shook his head.

"I can make it worth your while to cooperate with me."

"If Calderon finds out I've put his godchild in danger, he'll kill me."

"Five million."

"A dead man can't spend."

"Fifteen million for what's on the file." He held up a hand, stopping Leonard from commenting. "I assure you I will not harm his godchild."

"Give me two million now to think about it."

Carter slammed his glass on the table, spilling a portion of his drink. "That's absurd."

"Humph. Absurd is you thinking I believe you won't hurt his godchild. I want two million now and another eighteen million once I hand you a copy of the information."

"For twenty million I want more. I'll need you to stall

Santiago and the DEA."

"You want more, it'll cost you more."

"Why you greedy son-of-a-bitch."

"I'm not greedy, you're cheap." Carter's head whipped back in shock. Leonard continued, "You're a multi-billionaire whose ass is in the sling. I'm saving said ass, and you're squabbling over a few measly million. I'm crooked, but I'm not a murderer. You have his godchild. Once I give you the information, you can do damage control to protect your former contacts before the DEA acts, and her usefulness ends."

Carter crunched on ice to keep from exploding. He needed to know exactly which of his contacts were in danger. Depending on which contacts and how much information was on the file would determine how much damage control was needed. "Agent Rogers—"

"Please call me Leonard."

He ticked his teeth impatiently. "Leonard, you are incorrect when you say his godchild's usefulness ends once I obtain the information. I'll pay you thirty million to obtain a copy of the file. Ten million now and twenty when you deliver the package."

"I'll do it on one condition?"

"What?"

"The agent in me wants to know how she'll still be useful."

"Are you agreeing to the price?"

"If you tell me what I want to know."

"You're a manipulative asshole."

"Yeah, but I have what you want, so deal with it. Are you telling me or not?" He pointed his glass at Carter. "I want my ten million in cash."

"I don't have that kind of money lying around. I can transfer it to an account."

"That won't do. We know all of your accounts and mine are checked to ensure I'm not on the take."

"Open an account oversees."

"Hell, man. When's the last time you think I opened an account oversees. Shit. Like I'd know the first thing about it. Just give me the damn cash. Now answer the question."

"You're as bad as Tony and Santiago." He relaxed in his chair. "I need her to control Santiago. He's turning our cold war into an all out war. He doesn't take prisoners. He doesn't want my territory or money. He wants to ruin me and everything I've built. I took his godchild to stop him."

The fear fueling Carter's shaken voice intrigued Leonard. This tuff drug lord was used to having others do his dirty work for him. Carter thought he couldn't be touched. He panicked and took Diana. Now Santiago had slapped him with a reality check he couldn't cash. "What are you trying to accomplish? If you harm her, Santiago will do more than ruin you."

"I won't harm her. I wanted him to see he could be touched. I need to convince him to stop this war before it begins. I need to know exactly what is on those files."

"He won't let you off Scott free for this. He wants proof she isn't being harmed."

"Aren't you supposed to be negotiating? Negotiate! I wouldn't allow any harm to her. Like you, I don't wish to die any time soon. I'll have your proof by tomorrow."

"Let me put my negotiator hat on." He resituated himself in his seat. "What do you want from Santiago?"

"For him to leave me the hell alone! What kind of stupid assed question is that?"

Leonard laughed at himself. "You need to begin thinking about what you're willing to give in order to appease Calderon. I don't know how this feud of yours started, but he's powerful enough to put you under." He shrugged. "You can't say I'm sorry. This is way past the sorry stage. You aren't negotiating for his godchild's life, but yours."

"How long until you can copy of the files?"

"I've only seen Calderon once. He gave me a quick look then put it away. I'll need time to gain his trust. Once he becomes comfortable around me, I'll copy the information. He won't retaliate as long as she's safe. He hasn't asked, but I suggest you give him evidence daily of her condition. I can stall these negotiations and obtain the information for you."

"Sounds like we have a plan."

"Not until you give me my ten million."

CHAPTER TWENTY

Diana removed the chair from behind the bathroom door and set it in front of the mirror. Tony said she could shower alone, but she wouldn't take any chances.

She sat combing out her hair. Two days of her reprieve were gone and no sign of Ashton. She had taken pictures with Tony and shot video's in the study with printouts of the *New York Times* to prove the date.

Thinking Santiago was her only hope of being found, she sighed. She prayed Santiago wouldn't hurt Ashton or Leonard. She pushed her worries to the side. Santiago wasn't a monster. He'd reunite her with Ashton.

At least Oprah hadn't let her down. According to her show, your abductor thought of you as an object. If he thought of you as a person, he'd be less likely to harm you. She had to become a person to Tony. She looked to the ceiling, trying to figure out what show she actually saw that on. In the end, she decided it didn't really matter.

Being a friend to her kidnapper seemed insane, but it was working. *Oprah really has good guests. I may have to start watching her network regularly.*

"Diana, I'd like to take a bath tonight if you don't mind."

She was ready to give a smart reply such as, "What's wrong with one of the other three tubs in the house?" Instead, she sweetly replied, "I'm sorry. I lost track of time. I'll be right out." She quickly cleaned, then exited the bathroom.

Tony stopped her in the doorway, teasing, "Do I need to place the chair behind the door, or can I trust you to keep out."

"I'll try my hardest to resist the urge to knock down the door." She grabbed the chair and winked on her way out.

Day's weren't bad. They played, joked, and talked most of their time away. She often found herself wishing the day would never end. Nights were scary and couldn't pass fast enough. She was exhausted from only half sleeping and staying on guard. Tony slept in briefs and didn't care about showing his aroused state to her. He hadn't touched her sexually since the first morning, but the fear still lingered. In a way, she felt sorry for him. He'd cuddle her in his sleep, making her wonder what happened to make him so heartless.

Tony woke to an elbow in his gut. Diana was in the midst of another bad dream. He moved further away and waited for her to relax. The past few days she stirred emotions in him he didn't realize he had. She joked, laughed and teased him, seemingly forgetting how they'd met. Forgetting until she slept.

He pushed away his feelings of guilt. She could be having the dreams for any number of reasons. She wasn't afraid of him when she was awake. Something was definitely at the root of her fear, but it wasn't him.

Once she calmed, he kissed her lightly. "I have to go now. Try not to miss me too much." He left her alone.

"How much of this do I put in?" Diana cut the jalapeño in half.

"Roll it like you would a lemon before you juice it. Then dice it into tiny pieces and add to taste."

Diana stood at the large oval island in the center of the kitchen, chopping one of the peppers into tiny pieces. "I love guacamole. Thanks for teaching me how to make it, Maria." She stirred the pieces into the contents of the bowl, tasted. *Not hot enough*. She cut a second pepper in half, rolled then diced it into tiny pieces.

"What are you doing, darling?"

She didn't turn to greet Tony. "Cooking." She made a small divot in the guacamole and filled it with finely chopped pepper. Maria shot her the what-are-you-up-to eye. Diana winked and cut a third pepper in half.

"So I see. What?" he asked.

She grabbed a bag of tortia chips. "Guacamole. I've never made it before, but it's pretty good. Too bad you don't like Mexican food." She opened the bag.

He watched over her shoulder. She dipped a chip in the guacamole and ate. "Mmm, delicious. This'll be perfect later."

He turned her to face him. "Why later?"

She looked into his cheerful eyes. "Because the seasoning will have more time to mix." She turned away, grabbing the bag. "Just one more before I put it away."

"I want some."

"You can have some later. Now go away and let me create."

He snatched the bag of chips. "I'm not waiting. I want a taste now."

Feigning disgust, she yanked the bag from him, dipped a chip into the pepper-ridden portion of the guacamole then held it out to him.

"Feed me."

She lifted a brow. "If you insist. Open wide." He closed his eyes and opened his mouth. She placed the chip into his mouth, then applied slight pressure to his chin with her fingertip. "All done. What do you think?" She looked over her shoulder at Maria and flashed a grin.

He chewed. "This is good." He stopped chewing and turned red. "Hot, hot... Shit..." He waved his hands. "Get me some water."

Diana laughed. "*Quero leche por favor.*" Maria quickly followed her orders, then handed Diana the cup. "Drink this."

He grabbed the cup, guzzling until he realized what she'd handed him. "Shit, woman. I said water, not milk. Damn. Learn Spanish."

Everyone in the kitchen laughed, including Tony. He bobbed his head. She'd gotten the best of him this time. "So you think you're funny."

"Yep."

"Maria, may I have whatever burned the taste buds out of my mouth." She handed him a jalapeno. "Your turn."

Diana ran out the back door. No way would she eat one of those peppers. She ran across the yard, thinking they must have some sort of special soil in Mexico that made peppers extra hot.

"I'm catching and making you eat this whole pepper." He continued chasing her.

"Not in this lifetime, dragon breath." She cut sharply to the left, but he was much faster than her.

She fell to the ground. "I'm not eating."

He pinned her down, dangling the pepper over her nose. "Yes you are."

She clamped her mouth closed tight, shook her head vigorously. He tickled her. She knocked the pepper out of his hand.

"Now look what you've done." He lay on her. "I'm gonna get you for this."

Her mahogany eyes sparkled with mischief. "Not with that pepper." She rested her head back. He was truly a handsome man and sweet when he wasn't acting like a complete jerk.

He lowered his head, brushing his lips over hers. "Just one taste, Diana."

She turned her head to the side. How could he change so quickly? They were playing one second, and now he was on top of her, growing harder by the second. "You promised you wouldn't." There were two Tonies. The friendly, fun, loving one she liked, and his evil, sex-crazed twin who scared her.

He suckled along her neck, jawbone, ear. "Do you know how much I want you?"

Refusing to cry, she closed her eyes tightly. She wouldn't give him the satisfaction. "Why do you hate me?" She'd thought they were friends. How could she be so wrong about him and Ashton?

He kissed her lightly on the lips. "I don't hate you. I want to make love with you."

"You promised to leave me alone for a week. You promised." She loved Ashton, but had to face facts. She was nothing more than a case to him. She remembered the first rose he gave her. He'd known white roses were her favorite. He'd known her father was murdered. He'd known everything about her the whole time and used it to work his way into her life.

Tony rolled away from her. "Why don't you visit the dogs or something?"

Shaken, Diana leaned against the fence of the kennel.

"I'll never watch Oprah again."

Pablo laid his massive head in her lap.

"You're spoiling my dogs."

"Hola, Hector." She massaged the Rottwieler's massive neck. "I won't spoil them too awfully bad. Can I help do your rounds tonight?"

"Sure. Just no running this time." He handed her the dog brush.

Diana saw several trucks pulling onto the estate. "Do you know who they are?"

Hector turned to see whom she was talking about. "I'm suspecting the lawn guys. The old owners let the grounds fall to the way side a little."

"How long have they been working for Carter?"

"These are new guys. I hope they cut the grass, it's a disgrace."

"I'm a landscaper?"

"Really? I wouldn't have guessed it. You look more like a dog groomer." They both laughed. "I'm giving the dogs a bath today. Do you want to help?"

She watched the men unload the trucks. "I'd like to, but I want to see what's on those trucks. Can their bath wait until tomorrow?"

He held his hand out and helped her stand. "They've waited a month. I guess another day won't hurt."

"Great."

She brushed Pablo's fur, worried that Ashton had abandoned her just as her family had. He was DEA and had to know where the Carter hideouts were. She sighed. He'd chosen the DEA over her just as Santiago chose the drug world over her. She had to accept that Ashton wouldn't come to her rescue because he didn't care. Her only hope was contacting Santiago.

"Make it fast, Baxter. I need to check in." Tony watched Diana through the study window in the distance with the dogs. Her words were strong, but he had felt her tremble under him. Their first night when he'd made her tremble in the shower, it aroused him, but now it sickened him.

"You need to stop Diana from spending so much time

with the dogs."

"Hector isn't complaining."

"Hell, his hard-on for her is almost as bad as yours."

"Watch your mouth. She isn't hurting anything, and she isn't bugging us. Let her play with the stupid beast."

"She's turning them into pets."

He glanced over his shoulder at Baxter. "Is that all you wanted? If so, get the car ready." He hit speed dial on his cellphone. "I'm heading into town." Baxter stalked off.

"Hello, Dad. What's going on?"

Robert Carter updated him on his visit with agent Leonard Rogers.

"How do you know he won't double cross you with Santiago?"

"I recorded him taking the money. I have video and audio. I'll show him a copy to ensure he understands I mean business. He'd better get me the information."

"I have the perfect solution to our Diana problem."

"What?"

"I'll seduce her." He waited for his father to stop choking and laughing.

"What in the hell has come over you? She'll never sleep with you. You'd better not rape her."

"I've never raped a woman in my life, Dad. Can you say the same? Damn, I know what I'm doing. I just need more time." He watched her speak with the gardeners.

"How will you accomplish this, Tony? Drug her? Santiago's already mad enough. We can't give him a drugged out daughter."

"Did you even look at the pictures or videos I sent you of us dancing together? Those weren't staged, Dad."

"You're sleeping with her," Carter hissed.

"Dad."

"This is great," he threw out sarcastically. "Santiago acts like a dog in heat but will blow up once he finds out you're—"

For a change, Tony interrupted his father. "Would you please stop for a breath of air? The only way out of this mess is for you to give up everything to Santiago. I can work from the inside, eventually taking over Santiago's business."

"He already has people lined up, Tony. He won't allow a Carter to head his organization."

"He isn't like you, Dad. He doesn't hold me responsible for the crimes you've committed. I've been in the business my whole life. I can run things. His son's are dead. Once he realizes how happy I make Diana and he sees his grandson, he'll leave his organization to me." He'd always felt a strange kinship with Santiago.

"Why would she fall for you? You kidnapped her."

"Haven't you ever heard how hostages start empathizing with their captures? It's related to Stockholm syndrome. I don't understand all of the psychobabble, but it's true." He laughed reminiscing, "The first day we fought like cats and dogs, literally almost killing each other. Once we came to the understanding neither of us wants to be here, we decided to make the best of it."

"She's actually falling for you?"

"Yes, Dad. I need more time to—"

"Time for what?"

He released a sigh of exasperation and frustration. "For her to fall in love or lust. I have to convince her to marry me so Santiago will back off. Before I forget, I need books on the hostage psyche by tomorrow. I've already read everything I could find on the Internet. I'll look in town, but I don't think they'll have any in English."

"I'll have some flown down once we finish. You'll have to be careful with her. Santiago will kill you if you disrespect her."

"I know not to track dirty shoes into the house."

After a long pause, Carter finally said, "This may work. Things have been so tense since Steven's death. I shouldn't have let them kill him. I don't know what came over me. I've just always wanted to one up Santiago." After Carter found out Santiago was intimate with Tony's mother, he considered making her have a late term abortion, but decided keeping Santiago's son for himself would be the best revenge. When the baby was born with Santiago's whisky eyes, he had no doubt who Tony's father was.

"You got caught up."

"Do you really think you have a chance with Diana?"

"Yes I do. She's a fighter, Dad. Once we have her on our side, she won't permit Santiago to follow through with his revenge. We have nothing to lose."

"I've already ordered the agent to stall things. You do whatever's needed to convince her to switch camps." Now he'd have Santiago's son and godchild under his control.

CHAPTER TWENTY-ONE

"**Y**ou've been working harder than my paid employees," Mr. Guevara said.

Diana pulled a few weeds out of the back flower garden. "I love doing yard work. It's relaxing. Mr. Guevara, I have a tremendous favor to ask." She quickly scanned the area, making sure no one could overhear.

His whole face lit up when he smiled. "Ask away."

Already stooped down, she leaned forward, lowering her voice. "I'm not Tony Carter's fiancée. I'm the goddaughter of Santiago Calderon."

She understood the shock on his face. A Calderon wouldn't be caught dead in the camp of a Carter. "Tony kidnapped me and brought me here." She glanced over her shoulder, ensuring no unwanted listeners were around. "Would you please call my godfather and tell him where I am. He'll protect you and your family and pay you handsomely." She could feel herself rambling. "I'd ask one of the staff, but I can't reveal my true identity to them. Santiago thinks of me as his daughter..."

She pulled weeds faster to keep from becoming too upset to speak. "Please help me." She bit on her bottom lip, momentarily gazing into his eyes. "I'm afraid."

"Honey, I'm home. Let's go for a walk," Tony called.

Fighting the fear, she closed her eyes. "I'm almost done," she shakily answered. "Can I finish this first?" *Santiago, hurry.*

"Fifteen minutes, then meet me at the kennel." Tony stalked off.

"What's the number?" Guevara asked.

❧❧❧

"Hector, have you seen Tony?" Diana asked.

"He's around back. Boy you got filthy today, didn't you?"

Diana wasn't in a mood to joke but tried to sound upbeat. "I guess I am a tad bit dirty. See ya." She walked around the shed, wiping the dirt off her navy blue sun dress. "Tony?"

He stepped out of the shed. "Come a little closer. I won't bite." She inched closer. "I didn't mean to scare you this morning. I got carried away."

Diana stared into his eyes, so he couldn't accuse her of looking away. He abruptly turned away and walked toward the shed. She could swear she saw guilt in his eyes, but that didn't make sense. His apology also confused Diana. Why would he apologize? He didn't care who he hurt.

He held out a large wicker picnic basket. "Take this. I bought it for you today."

"What is it?"

He grinned. "A gift."

A Rottwieler puppy stuck its head out of the basket. The shock of the sudden movement made her almost drop the basket along with the puppy. "What's your plan, shoot him after I get attached to him?"

Tony narrowed his gaze on her. "I wouldn't do that?"

"Why not? You shot my last puppy."

He chewed on his inner jaw several seconds. "I stand corrected. If this mutt attacks me, I'll shoot his ass, too."

"Wolfgang was protecting me."

"He attached me, and I shot him. I can't take it back, Diana. I can't take back what I did this morning either. I'm trying to apologize, but nothing I do is good enough for you." He turned on his heels and stalked off.

Diana's eyes traveled from Tony to the puppy back to Tony. Her heart raced with excitement. *Thank you Oprah!* She took the puppy out of the basket, tossed the basket to the side, then ran after Tony with the puppy in hand. "Tony, Tony, wait up. Please."

She grabbed his arm. He wouldn't slow down. "I'm sorry." He continued. "I said I'm sorry." He didn't stop. She rushed in front of him, mocking, "I'm trying to apologize, but nothing I do is good enough for you." She softened. "Please forgive me. I've been scared all day and took it out on you. I don't want to fight." She held out her hand to him. "Let's take the puppy for a walk."

He smiled, showing a perfect set of teeth against tanned skin. "I have something else for you." He reached in his pocket, pulled out a key and dropped it in her hand.

"It's the only key to your room. I'll sleep in my own room."

She wanted to hug Oprah, but she wasn't around so she settled for hugging Tony.

He held her a little tighter. No trembling. He rested his head on hers. "When I was in town, I bought all of the English DVDs. Do you want to watch one tonight after dinner?" She contorted her face. "Okay, so they only had three."

"Sure. Let's go in." She pulled him along. "I want to show you what I did today."

Leonard spread the photos across the coffee table in front of Ashton in chronological order. "Do you see what I see?"

Ashton took another look at the pictures. "Tony holding Diana's hand." He ground his teeth. "Tony dancing with Diana." He loosened his collar. "Tony hugging Diana from behind."

"Come on." Leonard said, voice filled with excitement. "Santiago, what about you?" The pictures were more than enough. He didn't want to show the videos again.

Santiago sucked air through his teeth. "I've already seen enough."

"Aw man, Ashton. I know you see it," Leonard pleaded.

"Hell yeah. I see that bastard holding my woman!"

Santiago chuckled. "You two are worse than me and Steven."

Leonard kicked at the table in frustration. "Dammit, man. I'm the insane one, and you're the sensible one. I don't like this role reversal shit." He snatched up all of the pictures. "I'll make you see this, even if it kills you."

He slammed down the first picture, then tapped on the coffee table with his index finger. "Excluding Diana and Tony, what do you see?"

Ashton leaned over and glanced at the picture. "A study."

"What are Diana and Tony doing?"

"He's holding her hand," he bit out.

"Great. Now that wasn't so damn difficult was it? Tell me about the room then them each time please." He set down the second picture. "What do you see?"

"They're still in the study and they're dancing."

Leonard set down the last picture.

"I don't see how this is helping," Ashton said. Leonard pointed at the photo. "They're still in the study, but this time he's hugging her."

Disgusted, Leonard plopped back. "Is that really all you see?" He stared at Ashton. "I'm not letting you off this easily. What's different about the room in the third picture compared to the others."

This time ignoring Diana and Tony, Ashton examined the photos closer. "The room has flowers in it." He did a double take of the pictures. "And Diana is holding a flower in the last photo."

Leonard smiled. "It's about time. Damn, I didn't think you'd ever get it. She's been telling us where she is. She must not have known they were taking the first photo. But in the second tape what dance would you say they are doing, Santiago? Even without audio, I'd say it was some salsa thing. She's saying she's left the states. I'd suspect Mexico since we're dealing with Carter."

He set the final photo on top. "Do you think Tony lost his mind and decided to order flowers for the study, or do you think Diana did it? What kind of flower is she holding?"

Santiago and Ashton scrutinized the photo. "I don't know. Some sort of lily," Ashton said.

"That's right. Lilies and roses are her specialties. I took this picture to this botanist over at the college and asked her where these grow naturally. She said they are indigenous to southern Mexico." He chuckled, thinking about how slick Diana was and how much trouble Ashton would be in if he ever crossed her.

"Most of the flowers in the room are from southern Mexico. To us they look like your every day, run of the mill flowers, but to the trained eye they're a message."

"Good work, Leonard. Do you know Spanish, Ashton?"

"Sí," Ashton replied.

Leonard laughed. "See what?"

"Stop playing, Leonard." Santiago turned to Ashton.

"You'll have to go in alone. We'll contact you once we've pen pointed her."

"I'll catch the next flight out." He nodded at Leonard. "Thanks, man." He left to make arrangements.

"You're really good at this," Santiago said to Leonard. "You can work for me when we're all done with this mess."

"I think I'll pass. I get into enough trouble as it is, and Ashton needs me to watch his back." Leonard kicked off his shoes. "Did you have time to set up my account?"

"All you need to do is sign and fax the forms, then you'll be ten million richer." Santiago helped Leonard hide the bribery money he received from Carter.

"I'll have five million more tomorrow. That bastard had the audacity to try and blackmail me." Santiago's brows rose. "He recorded me accepting the ten million and said he'd show you if he thought I was double crossing him."

Santiago shook his head. "So why is he giving you more money."

"I reminded the asshole I'm the only chance he has at collecting that files. Hell, I already have ten million. I could disappear and leave his ass hanging in the breeze."

"So you made him pay you more money."

"Hell yeah."

CHAPTER TWENTY-TWO

Diana set her puppy on the bed, then knelt beside him plotting. "We have to get rid of Leon and Baxter. Leon should be easy. He's as stupid as a post, but Baxter will be difficult."

She rolled the puppy over. "Mommy's little Niko like's his tummy rubbed, doesn't he. Where did I put your leash? One more potty run, then it's time for you to go to bed." She grabbed his leash off the nightstand and headed downstairs.

She listened to Baxter complain about her to Tony before she entered the study. "Good evening, gentlemen. I didn't mean to interrupt anything." She shot Baxter a toothy grin. "Tony, do you have a jacket I can borrow? It's sprinkling outside, and Niko needs a potty break."

"Leon, take Niko to the kennel," Tony ordered.

Though she wanted to slap Leon for staring at her breasts, her face softened. "Thanks, but I want Niko to sleep inside. This is his first day away from home, and he's probably scared. I just want to take him for a short walk."

She scanned the room and spotted a windbreaker on the back of a chair. "Can I use that one?"

"That's mine."

"Can I use your jacket, Baxter? I'll throw it in the dryer when I come inside."

He tossed the jacket at her. "Don't get any dog smell on it."

Diana watched Niko chase raindrops. She'd noticed Leon hitting on all of the female staff. If she played her cards right, she'd have him and Tony arguing in no time, then bye-bye Leon.

"Hey, Diana."

Deep in thought, she didn't hear Leon's call.

"Dy-ann-na."

Half startled, she whipped her head around. "You scared the life out of me, Leon. What? Niko, here boy."

"I need to speak with you. Hurry up."

Ready to tell him off, she calmed and rethought. This

could be her chance. "You have my undivided attention."

He took a tiny cellphone out of his front pants pocket. "Do you want to call Santiago?"

Excited, she held out her hand.

He put the phone back into his pocket. "After you sleep with me tonight."

"Okay, but let me call him now."

He chuckled. "I'm not as stupid as people think, Diana. You can't call until after." He caressed her face. "Tony will never know how Santiago found you."

His touch made her sick, but she played the innocent role. "How do I know this isn't a trick? Why would you help me?"

"I'm not helping you. Santiago will find you sooner or later. I might as well get mine while I have the chance. Don't you want to go home?"

"Yes but," she glanced away then back into his blankn blue eyes, "everyone has lied to me since I've arrived. How do I know Tony isn't trying to trick me? I promise, if you let me use the phone now, I'll sleep with you tonight and every night until Santiago comes for me."

"Every night?" She shook her head, hoping the jerk was stupid enough to believe her. "Sex first. I'm not tricking you."

"I can't trust you. Show some good faith, and let me call now." She held out the key to her room. "We can trade. The key for the phone."

He shook his head. "I'll give you the phone to keep after we have sex."

"You win." She walked Niko into the house, dried him with a towel, watched Leon strut into the study then followed. "I can't believe you'd try to trick me, Tony. I thought we came to an agreement."

Tony lifted his head from the magazine. "What are you talking about?"

Diana pointed at Leon. "You had Leon try to set me up with a cellphone. You're trying to make Maria's death my fault. Did you already kill her?"

He stood quickly and rounded the desk. "What in the hell are you talking about? Maria left hours ago. What's wrong with you?"

"I don't understand why, Tony. It doesn't make sense." She ran her hands through her hair. "Why would you do this?"

He held her by the shoulders. "Stop. Take a breath. Tell me what the hell you're talking about."

She stopped, drew in a deep breath, exhaled slowly. "Leon said if I sleep with him he'll let me call Santiago. You said if I try to call out, you would kill Maria. I want to know why you had Leon proposition me."

He targeted his killer stare on Leon.

"She's lying, Tony. I... I didn't."

She approached Leon, poking him in the chest with her index finger. "Is this part of the plan? Did he tell you to ditch the phone before you came in here so I'd look like a fool if I called out your sick game? Is that it, Leon?"

Tony pulled out his gun. "Empty your pockets, Leon. I said no phones on the premises."

"Tony, I don't know why you're perpetrating. You lied to me again." She ran out, grabbing Niko on the way. She wasn't proud of what she'd done, but this was for her own survival.

Leon held out his hands. "I made the offer, but I had no intentions on allowing her to make the call. I swear, Tony. You know I'd never double cross you."

"Give me the phone." Leon handed him the phone. "I should kill you for this shit."

Leon vigorously shook his head. "I swear, Tony. I wouldn't."

"I know you wouldn't let her contact Santiago. I should kill you for trying to take what's mine. Get your shit and return to Texas, you horny bastard." Leon rushed out of the room. "Can you believe this shit?" He tossed the phone on the desk.

"No I don't. She set him up," stated Baxter.

"He made the offer, not her. She came to me with it." If Leon messed things up for him, he'd kill him. He fumbled through the books on Stockholm syndrome his father had sent from Mexico City.

He needed to show her he wasn't the barbarian she thought he was. He needed to be the man she wanted. She accepted Santiago and would accept him also.

"You should send for more help," Baxter suggested.

He placed the books in the bottom drawer of the desk along with Leon's phone. "I have to go. I'll see you tomorrow." Tony left Baxter standing there.

Diana folded a blanket and set it on the floor for Niko. "Sleep tight little puppy." Worried about Leon, she bit on her inner jaw. He was a jerk, but she didn't want to cause his murder.

She dressed for bed and covered herself. *Tony won't kill him.* She chewed her nails. *If I got him killed.* She tried to shake off the feelings of guilt. *I shouldn't have been so dramatic. Oh please don't kill him, Tony.*

She stopped fretting at the sound of a knock at her door. "Who is it?"

"Tony. May I come in?"

"Come in. It's unlocked." She combed her fingers through her hair.

Tony stopped to see Niko on the way to her bed. He stooped down and rubbed the puppy behind his ears. "Tell your mommy I didn't do it this time. Make her believe me."

He looked over his shoulder at her. She caught the innocence in his eyes. He and Niko made such a cute picture. She smiled her approval.

"I should have thought of this days ago." He sat on the edge of the bed. "I really didn't try to set you up, Diana. I had nothing to do with Leon's proposition. You were right to be weary, but not of me. He wouldn't have let you call Santiago. I sent him to Texas. There are too many beautiful senoritas around here for him."

Her heart heaved from relief. She should have known he wouldn't actually hurt Leon. He'd changed since they'd first met. Or was her original assessment incorrect? She'd been wrong about Ashton. Her heart sank. She wished she could turn her love for Ashton off. She repeated in her head, *Ashton never wanted you. You were his case.*

She pushed thoughts of Ashton to the back of her mind and focused on the key to her freedom, becoming Tony's friend. "I knew something wasn't right. I'm sorry I thought it was you. I've just been on edge since... Well, you know." Tony had given her the key to her room, after all. He couldn't be all bad.

He toyed with her hair. She didn't flinch, back away, or cringe. "How would you like to take a trip into town tomorrow? We can do whatever you want except contact Santiago."

She wanted to stay at the estate in case Santiago came for her, but didn't want to draw attention to her plans. "Sounds great. Do you speak any Spanish?"

"No. But I know how to speak money. We'll be fine."

She leaned against the headboard. "Your mother was Mexican, you lived here most of your life, but you don't speak Spanish. How did that happen?"

He took her hand into his.

She forced herself not to pull away. *I need to continue becoming a part of his life, his confidant, so he'll help me if Santiago can't find me.*

"My parents didn't get along very well. My dad, as you know is white, married my mother as part of a business deal. He didn't want her, and he hates Mexico. He considers it backwards and didn't want me learning about my Mexican heritage. Our servants were American. Our everything was American. We just lived here."

Ready to sleep, she scooted under the light cover. Becoming Tony's best friend would have to wait until tomorrow. "Interesting. What time are we leaving?"

"Nine. Should I lock the door on my way out?"

"Do I need for you to lock the door?"

His face lit up with amusement. "No. About tomorrow. I won't hurt you, but if you try to escape, I'll kill whoever's in my way. Do you understand? Don't test me."

"I won't. Tony..." She hesitated. Asking her question wouldn't work to her advantage, but she wanted to know. "You really didn't mean to scare me this morning, did you?"

He lovingly brushed her face with the back of his hand. "No I didn't mean to." He paused. "I'm sorry about Steven." He shrugged. "About all of this. If I had a choice, you could go home. But I don't."

"Do you always do as your father says?" she asked quietly, hoping an argument wouldn't ensue. She needed him to choose to do the right thing. She needed him to choose her.

"He's all I have. You still love Santiago though you know what he is. I don't agree with my dad on his tactics, but he's my father. If it were my choice, he'd retire from the life and give Santiago control." He fiddled with the blanket edge.

Diana heard the sincerity in his voice. He'd actually opened up to her. She took his hand into hers and caressed it, thinking his life had been no better than hers. "You don't want to betray your father. I don't blame you. But Santiago will kill him. I've already lost my father to all of this. I don't want you to lose yours."

He stroked her hair behind her ear. "It's no use. I've spoken with him about his retiring and my running our interest for Santiago. He won't listen. He doesn't want to leave the business. His Al Capone ways don't work anymore. You can't go around strong-arming and blackmailing people into submission and expect them not to fight back. He hasn't changed with the times."

"When I get home, I'll talk to Santiago for you. I'll explain the situation. Santiago isn't a monster. He's a businessman. He'd rather have your cooperation than war. If it's a war, Santiago will win, and your father will be dead in the end. It isn't worth it."

"I've kept you up too long. We have a busy day tomorrow." He tucked in the sides of the blanket. "Goodnight, Diana." He kissed her forehead. He had studying to do.

CHAPTER TWENTY-THREE

As Diana entered the kitchen, the smell of fried chicken made her mouth water. "When will dinner be finished?"

Maria turned the chicken. "You sure like to eat, don't you? Ten minutes. You look like you had a good time in town today."

She pulled a stool to the island. "Oh yes. We had a ball. I bought you a gift." She took out a small rectangular box. "Actually, Tony bought it because I don't have any money, but you get my meaning." She set the gift on the island. "I'll leave it here for you."

"You shouldn't have."

"Don't get all water eyed on me. I love to eat, and you're a great cook. This is my way of saying thanks for feeding me."

"What the hell's taking so long for dinner, Maria?"

Startled by the sudden shouting, Diana jumped. "Shoot, Baxter. What's wrong with you?"

He directed his anger from Maria to Diana. "Shut the hell up, bitch. I'm not in the mood for you today."

Ready to fight the war of words, she hopped off the stool. "Who the hell you calling bitch? I got your bitch."

Maria stepped between the two. "It's all right, Diana." She held Diana's hand while speaking to Baxter. "I'll serve dinner in the dining room in fifteen minutes. If you would like to take a piece of chicken now to hold you over, there is some on the counter." She motioned over to the chicken she'd already cooked.

He growled and reached for the chicken.

"At least use a napkin. I don't want him touching the food I'm eating. He might have the cooties or anything."

Maria snickered under her breath. "Don't worry, Diana. Yours is from the next batch."

Baxter shook the chicken breast at Diana. "You think you have the upper hand, don't you?" He bit into the chicken.

Diana stepped around Maria, put her hands on her hips and rotated her neck to ensure he understood she wasn't taking his crap. "I think you sound like a jealous bitch chasing after a cheating man. What are you, on the down low or something?"

His fist was swift, but not swift enough. Maria screamed for Tony. Diana sidestepped his blow and kicked him in the rear with her powerful leg. Baxter thumped to the ground. She grabbed a butcher knife. "I'm tired of your shit, Baxter. Come on with it, big boy."

Maria ran to the kitchen door. "Tony, come quick! They'll kill each other."

Baxter rose and assumed a defensive stance. "You think you can take me on."

"I told you what I think you son-of-a—"

"Diana, Baxter!" Tony grabbed the knife from Diana. "What the hell happened?"

"I hate him." She ran out the room.

Maria picked the chicken up off the floor, praying to blend into the room and Tony would forget she spoke English.

"What the hell happened, Baxter?"

"Why the hell did you take her to town? Do you know what could have happened? Anyone could have seen you. If Santiago finds out she's here, we aren't protected. You need more men."

Tony glanced over at Maria who was taking out the second batch of chicken, seemingly ignoring them. "Diana and I will take care of Santiago *if* he comes. I'm not making her stay cooped up on the estate."

Maria placed paper towels over the chicken to soak the excess grease. Hector and Maria had speculated what was going on between Diana and Tony. They thought the couple had a Romeo and Juliet relationship, which was why Tony brought Diana to Mexico to hide.

"Just stay away from Diana and everything will work out," Tony said.

"That's what she wants."

Tony slammed the knife onto the kitchen island. "I won't stand by while you continually harass her, Baxter. If you can't do as I say, carry your ass to California. Maria, would you please fix two plates." She nodded.

"You're pussy whipped. Think with the head on top of

your shoulders for a few minutes."

"I advise you to shut the hell up now. Diana is mine." He thumped his chest. "I know what the hell I'm doing and don't need your advise. Either do as I say, or get to steppin'."

Feeling more confident, Maria handed Tony two plates and drinks on a tray. Tony would protect Diana, and the baby Maria suspected Diana carried, from Baxter.

"Thanks." He turned and stalked out of the room.

Diana stepped out of the shower to dry herself. Period over, she felt fresh again. The day had gone so wonderfully until Baxter. *What a jerk. And he made me miss dinner. I can't stand him.* She dropped the towel, opting for a brush. "I need a haircut and a retouch." She stared into the mirror. Her thick, dark hair dipped well past her shoulders. *Maybe I'll try a short crop this time.* After grooming herself, she changed into her nightclothes and cleaned her mess.

To her surprise, when she exited the bathroom, Tony was sitting at a card table with dinner waiting. She couldn't help but grin. He could be so thoughtful when he wanted. The more she thought about it, the more he reminded her of Santiago.

"It's a little cold, but I think it will do. Come. Eat with me."

She fastened her red silk thigh-high robe, then sat across from him. "Thanks. I'm starving."

"Baxter can be a real ass at times, but he's good at his job. I've told him to steer clear of you." He watched her as she devoured the chicken, macaroni and cheese and string beans. "Have you ever missed a meal?"

"I can't help it. I have a large appetite," she said without missing a bite.

"I'm not putting you down. It's a good thing you eat like a horse." They both laughed. "Hell. If you didn't, you'd whittle away to nothing. You must have a fast metabolism." They finished their dinner, then adjourned in the sitting area of her suite.

"I had a great time today, Tony. Thanks." She drew her legs up on the couch.

"I'll have to start being nice more often if you'll keep thanking me. I could get spoiled." He stroked her hair behind her ear. "Uh, Diana." He paused. "I was wondering if... if you have anyone back in San Diego waiting for you? Besides Santiago."

Tickled by the new shy Tony, she wondered if he showed anyone else his sensitive side. She doubted it. That he'd reveal so much of himself made her feel special. Her heart warmed; they'd become true friends. Oprah's show didn't say how to handle this scenario. "Are you asking me if I have a boyfriend?"

"I guess so. I assume you do. You're a great catch." He stopped rambling, leaned his head on the couch and closed his eyes to miss the amusement she must be showing in her face.

"I thought I had a fiancé, but I don't know anymore."

"Why not anymore?"

"I fell in love with a man, then found out it was all a lie. He used me to catch your father and Santiago."

Tony straightened. "Why that son-of-a-bitch. I'll kick his ass for you."

She laughed internally at his protectiveness. "Are you trying to make me thank you again?" She pressed him back gently, then rested her head on his shoulder. Having a real friend wouldn't be too bad.

"Did he work for the government or something?"

"DEA. Santiago found out and told me. This man had asked me to marry him and everything. When I confronted him with the truth, he said he was after Carter and he loved me. I don't know if he was lying about being after Carter. How can I believe anything he says or said?"

"You can't trust those sneaky bastards."

"I know." She sighed. "But I still love him. At least I love who I thought he was." She shook her head. "I don't know what I feel anymore. Since my father died, I've been on an emotional roller-coaster."

"I've never lied to you."

"No you haven't." Emotionally drained, she snuggled closer.

"The first morning." He didn't want to bring up unpleasant thoughts, but they needed to work through this. "You thought I was him, didn't you?"

"Yes," she replied softly.

"I'm sorry about the way I've acted. I don't know. I'm not good at apologizing. When I'm angry I act before I think."

"I feel like a complete idiot for being taken in by him. Was I only a case?" She wiped away her tears with the back of her hand. "I guess I needed someone after my father was killed and didn't want to see the truth." He held her closely, comforting. "I know the truth now, but I can't let go of how I feel for him. What's wrong with me?"

Tony stroked her hair. "What's his name? I'll take care of everything for you?"

"You sound like Santiago."

He chuckled. "He's my hero. Now give me the name."

"I don't think so. I can't have the men in my life taking after people who piss me off."

He raised a brow. "I'm a man in your life?" He grinned. "So tell me how you ended up being half Colombian but growing up in New York."

"Actually, Steven is half Colombian half African-American, but that's neither here or there. He met my mom when he and Santiago were expanding their base in New York." She continued telling him about her family tree late into the night.

Baxter sat across from Diana and Tony, glaring at the two as they slept in each other's arms. "Tony, get up and call your father."

Tony opened his eyes slowly. Diana lay in his arms on the couch in the sitting area. "I'm not ready," he whispered. With Diana in his arms, he may never be ready. "Take the phone and make the call yourself." She'd fallen asleep in his arms. He reveled in the feeling of triumph.

"You have to at least send a picture. Get up."

Tony caressed Diana's back and thighs as she stretched awake on top of him. "You're smashing me," he said as he held her close. "But I don't mind."

Baxter jumped up suddenly and startled Diana to full alertness. "I'm getting out of here." He stalked off.

"He needs to lighten up."

"What was he doing in here?" Diana asked.

"It's time to send a picture to Dad. Have any ideas on poses?"

"How about by the dog kennel? I want to show Santiago Niko."

CHAPTER TWENTY-FOUR

Hector took Niko from Diana. "I don't trust Baxter. He's been sneaking around all morning. You should tell Tony to send that trouble maker away." He put Niko in his pen.

She grabbed a broom to help clean. "I can't tell Tony to do anything. He has to see it on his own."

"See what on his own?" Baxter interrupted.

They both turned toward Baxter. "I wasn't talking to you." Diana swept the dust and poop from the corner of the kennel toward Baxter.

"If you were talking about Tony, you were talking to me."

"Don't start with me. I told you yesterday you aren't my boss." She pointed the handle of the broom at him. "Go harass someone else. Don't you have some candy to steal from a baby or something?"

"You two are awfully cozy in here. I don't think Tony will like it."

"Since I don't care what you think, you can take your opinion back to hell when you go." She heard the lawnmowers and became excited. Hopefully, Mr. Guevara had good news for her. She placed the broom on the rack. "I'll talk to you later, Hector." She felt Tony had become her friend, but she didn't trust her judgment. As of late, her mind was jumbled. At times she didn't know if Tony was one of the bad or good guys.

She walked across the lawn. Her thoughts scared her. She'd never been unsure of herself before, and now unsure was all she ever was. "Hello, Mr. Guevara." The only thing she was sure of was she needed to get off the emotional roller coaster she'd been riding before she lost herself.

❧❧❧❧❧❧

"Maria, have you seen Diana?" Tony asked.

"I believe she's with the dogs. Do you want me to send someone for her?"

One of the lawn men walked into the kitchen through the back door with a box of fresh cut flowers.

Tony didn't like the looks of him. "Who the hell are

you?"

"*No hablo Ingles.*"

Maria intervened. "Mr. Guevara must have sent him up with Diana's flowers. She wanted fresh ones for the house. I'll help him."

Tony walked out. "That's one big black, mean assed Mexican there."

⸙❀⸙❀⸙❀⸙

Ashton took the last set of flowers into the study as ordered by Maria. He could see Tony and a large white male arguing in the middle of the yard.

This is the room the photos were taken in. He searched through the drawers for what he didn't know. He needed a clue into how they'd treated Diana, and this room was his best bet.

What the heck? He set the books on the desk. They were all on the psychology of a hostage. Some pages were highlighted, others marked. *The bastard even took notes.* He tossed the books in the drawer, opting to read Tony's journal on how he would brainwash and manipulate Diana. *She doesn't stand a chance. I have to get her out today.*

He stared out the window. Tony was heading for Diana. "I'll kill him."

⸙❀⸙❀⸙❀⸙

"Your godfather has sent help, but we'll need two more days. Can you hold out?"

Diana continued digging weeds out of the side flower garden. "If I can steer clear of Baxter, I should be fine. Why can't I leave today, Mr. Guevara?"

"Santiago's man needs to check out the compound and plan your escape. He also needed to be sure you knew when he's making his move so you'd be ready."

"Thank you for doing this." She tossed a few dandelions in her pile of weeds.

"You look mind weary. This'll all be over in a few days."

"I've been so confused lately I can't tell a dandelion from a butter cup."

"Diana!"

Fear gripped her heart. Tony hadn't been this angry in

days. She looked around into his eyes and saw rage. "Yes, Tony."

"Come with me."

She brought her head back forward, closed her eyes tight. "Can I finish pulling the weeds first?"

He grabbed her arm and dragged her along. "How could you?"

Tony pushed Diana into the tool shed. "I can't believe this crap." He slammed the door.

She shook her head, shying away. "What, Tony? I don't know what you're talking about."

He backed her against the wall. "You know exactly what I'm talking about. I can't believe I..." he trailed off.

She peered into his incensed eyes, trying to find the Tony who brought her Niko, who confided in her, who made her laugh all day long. "You're scaring me." All she saw was fury.

"Tell me the truth, Diana."

"I've never lied to you."

He pressed her against the wall with his body. "Are you still on your period?"

She cocked her head to the side. "N-no."

"I want to make love now." He nuzzled her neck.

"You said I have a week."

He stiffened. "Is that what you told Hector? How could you sleep with Hector?"

"I'm not. I swear. Why would you think I am?"

"So you're saying Baxter is lying on you? Why would he lie, Diana?"

She pushed away from him. "I don't know, Tony. Why on Earth would *Baxter* lie?" Hearing Baxter's name, she knew she'd been set up. Tony had better not be stupid enough to choose a jerk like Baxter over her. If he did, she'd never forgive him.

"Shit." He kicked the working bench. "That bastard lied, didn't he?" She wouldn't look at him. "Let's not go back to your pretending I don't exist." He reached for her hand. "He's lying, isn't he?"

She stepped away from his touch. "I thought we were friends. I thought you cared." Truly hurt, she trailed off, wondering why no one ever chose her.

"He said he saw you two."

She continued backing away. "Knowing he hates me, you believed him, no questions asked." She turned away. "Why do you act like you care about me?"

He reached forward, pulling her close. "I'm sorry, Diana." She didn't move or acknowledge him. "I didn't just take his word for it." He maneuvered her to face him. "Without thinking, I allowed my jealousy to speak. I know you aren't interested in Hector."

"Can I go back to the yard now?" He sounded sincere, but she didn't know what to believe. Ashton had become her friend but had ulterior motives. If Tony were tricking her into believing he was her friend, why would he do things to anger her? Nothing made sense anymore.

He hugged her close. "You can let that mangy mutt chew my favorite pair of shoes for my being such an ass."

She grinned. "I'm still mad at you." She had teased him about all the care he put into his shoes.

"You can slap me around."

She shook her head. "Nah. You'd get pleasure out of my slapping you."

"I was wrong, Diana. I'm new at this stuff." He held her hands, resting his forehead on hers. "I've never been able to trust anyone in my life. Not even my father. Then you came along."

"I'm sorry about the way you grew up, but you can't keep taking it out on me." *Like I did with Ashton.* She backed away.

"I know." He paused to gather his thoughts. "How about this? I go the extra mile to make sure I don't allow my past to interfere with our future, and you stop letting your relationship with the agent interfere."

He stopped her before she had the chance to comment. "He is an agent, Diana. I know this hurts you, but he didn't love you. He was using you."

Everything Tony said made sense, but she wasn't ready to accept she could be so wrong or Ashton could be so cruel.

"I can't stand to see you holding back because of your misguided loyalty for him. You know I'm speaking the truth. That's why it hurts so much."

"He loved me," she said with a conviction she didn't feel.

"His job was to win you over. My father has been in contact with Santiago daily. He hasn't mentioned anything about a fiancé. He's moved onto his next case because he's blown his cover."

"Maybe I started out a case, but he changed his mind and really fell in love with me."

"He didn't tell you who he was. He wasn't planning on telling you."

"He was afraid I'd be mad or wouldn't believe him. He was about to resign."

"All lies, love. He didn't tell you because he didn't want to blow his cover. Why hadn't he already resigned if he was actually giving up the life? Hell, he could have resigned. You'd of never known."

"But I heard it in his voice. Felt it in my heart."

"That was his job, Diana. He knew everything about you when you met. He manipulated you at every turn until you fell in love with him because he needed you to catch Santiago and my father."

Memories of Ashton's face lighting up when he saw the jump drive filled her mind. Now she realized he had agreed to leave her alone so easily because he was in a hurry to examine the content. "He was only using me."

"I'm afraid so."

She examined Tony. He'd turned out to be a nice person after all. She laughed at herself. How had this kidnapper turned out to be her only real friend? "Thanks, Tony."

He cocked his head to the side. "For what?" He grinned. "Accusing you of sleeping with Hector?"

"For always telling the truth, even when I don't want to hear it. I love Santiago, but he only tells me what he wants me to know. Half-truths have been the story of my life. I'm tired of being manipulated. I'm so tired."

He ducked his head, hoping she didn't see his guilt. When he first set out to seduce her it was to manipulate her, but now he actually loved her. He pushed the guilty feelings to the side. "You know how I feel about you don't you?" She'd never find out the truth of his original intent.

She released an anxiety laugh. "It's one of those truths you tell me I don't want to hear."

He took her hands into his. "I may get mad and show my ass from time to time, but I do love you. You know everything about me. I'm not hiding anything. I don't have any ulterior motives."

She looked away.

"What's wrong?"

"How do I know you aren't using me? You want to run Santiago's empire."

"When Santiago finds out how I feel about you, he'll want to kill me. He won't believe my feelings for you. He'll think I'm using you to work my way into his organization. My being a Carter is a huge mark against me. My pursuing you will make things harder on me."

"I don't want to live in the drug world, Tony. We can be friends, but nothing more."

"I'm not saying we have to marry. All I'm asking is for you to stop using this agent against me. He was doing his job. I'm being me. You see me the good, the bad, and the ass. I'm not holding anything back. He was holding back from you. Let whatever happens happen."

"I'm heading to the yard. Working with the earth helps clear my head."

"And what a pretty head it is."

She walked out laughing. "You are such a flirt."

"I do my best to please."

Diana took her time strolling back to Mr. Guevara. She could identify with Tony. They both grew up captives of sorts. She felt sorry for him. At least she hadn't been raised in a country where she didn't know the language or culture and wasn't allowed to learn it. He had to feel so isolated.

According to Tony, his father claimed he was protecting him from the drug world, but Diana didn't believe it. If Robert Carter had wanted to protect his son, he wouldn't have inducted him into their family business when Tony was only thirteen. That's one thing she could credit Steven and Santiago with—they always sheltered her from their illegal lifestyle.

Tony was a victim of circumstances, just as she was.

Both of their fathers chose the drug life over them. Both of their lives had been filled with lies and half-truths from the people that supposedly loved them. Both of them were stuck in Mexico because of their families. Both needed someone to honestly be on their side.

A chill went down her spine. When Santiago came for her, his men would shoot Tony at first sight. *What have I done?* She couldn't tell Tony that Santiago was coming for her or he'd think she'd been using him. She scanned the grounds for Mr. Guevara.

CHAPTER TWENTY-FIVE

"**L**isten up you son-of-a-bitch. You almost ruined things for me." Tony leaned against the study window and watched the men manicuring the yard. He smiled when he spotted Diana and Mr. Guevara in the distance. "I'm sending you away."

"What the hell are you doing?" Baxter asked. "You can't manage her alone."

"I didn't ask for your approval. I've won her trust, but I can't risk her ex-fiancé coming back into the picture. She's in love with the bastard. I've got her convinced she was only a case to him. I need you to remove him from the picture permanently, just in case he actually loves her."

"Are you sure he's DEA?"

"Yeah. So be careful. I also need the location of Santiago."

"I'm on it."

"Don't fail me again. Next time you pay with your life. I'll bet the lawyer Ashton Powell, who lives across the street from her, is the guy. That asshole Barns should have told me he was DEA. Eliminate his stupid ass, too."

"Maybe I should stay until re-enforcements arrive. If she escapes, you'll be up shit creek."

"I can handle Diana. You're mission is to get rid of her fiancé agent and Barns. I'm giving you seventy two hours. The clock began ticking fifteen minutes ago." Tony left the room with Baxter close behind.

Ashton heard more than enough. He sat on his haunches in the closet and waited a few minutes to ensure both men were gone. *I need to scout the grounds, count guards and figure a way to sneak Diana out today.*

"I'll try to find your godfather's man. Maybe we can sneak you out today."

Diana quickly scanned the area. No one else was around. "I'll be fine." She knelt next to Mr. Guevara.

"What's wrong?"

"I don't want anyone hurt. Tony isn't like I thought."

"I saw your face, Diana."

She resumed planting flowers. "Sometimes he gets angry, but don't we all. He wouldn't hurt me. I think if I speak with him he'll take me to Santiago, and no one will be hurt."

"You're afraid of him."

"I can handle Tony. It's his henchman Baxter who's the problem. He goes out of his way to start fights with me."

"Like I said, we'll return in two days. If you convince Tony to release you earlier, great." He looked over her shoulder. "Here he comes."

Niko jumped on Diana, attempting to lick her. She placed him on his back, rubbed his belly. "How's my little baby boy?"

"I was just about to take him in the house for a shoe party. Do you want to come and watch?"

A devilish grin tipped her lips. "Do I get to choose the pair? Thanks for letting me help, Mr. Guevara. In case I don't see you again before you leave, have a great day."

Tony led her and the puppy around the house. "I think he should pay you."

"I love doing yard work." They entered the house through the kitchen.

"Get that dog out of the kitchen," Maria ordered.

"I want to give him a little midmorning snack," Diana said.

"Give it to him in the kennel. I've told you not to bring him through here."

"Yes ma'am." Diana hit Tony for laughing at her.

He took the leash from her and handed it to one of his men out back. "Take Niko to his pen."

"He was on the floor." Diana washed her hands. "It's not like he's a cat or something."

"He's a filthy, furry animal. Unless we're cooking him, I don't want him in the kitchen."

"That's nasty, and he isn't filthy, but I'll keep him out. I'd hate to see him on my dinner plate."

Maria laughed. "Good girl. How are you feeling these days?"

Tony playfully wrapped his arms around Diana's waist, drawing her into his body. "She's feeling great." He turned her in his arms. "I have a surprise for you."

"Please tell me you don't want me to guess." She always liked his surprises. First he gave her Niko and the key to her room. Then he personally planted white rose bushes on either side of the front porch steps.

"Of course not. It's upstairs."

She followed him upstairs into her room. "I'll be spoiled fooling around with you."

He kissed her cheek lightly. "You're onto me. I'm spoiling you for everyone else. Now take a seat. I'll be right back." He closed the door.

She settled in the overstuffed chair in the sitting area. He sat on the table directly in front of her. "Baxter is a real asshole."

Her laughter filled the room. She grabbed her stomach. "Oh my gosh." She tried to catch her breath. "Knowledge is your gift. Thanks, but I already knew."

He grinned. "I thought you'd like to hear me say it. I've sent him back to the states."

She stopped laughing. "Now we're talking about my kind of gift!"

After she calmed, he said, "Diana, what do I need to do for you to come to me?" He reached forward and caressed her face with his hands. "I'll work things out with Santiago."

"It's not Santiago. I don't agree with the drug life, Tony. Plus, I'm not in a good place right now emotionally. I'm fresh out of a relationship. In all honesty, I'm not ready to start a new one." She shook her head, momentarily peeking into his eyes. "He really had me fooled."

"I'm not him."

"I know, but I don't know what to believe."

"Look at me. Come on, look into my eyes." He waited. "Much better. I am not an agent. I do not have ulterior motives. I love you." She turned her head away. "Diana, don't shut me out.

"Santiago already wants to kill me for kidnapping you. My father will want to kill me once I tell him I'm in love with you. My being in love with you will not help me in any way shape or fashion. My love for you complicates my life exponentially."

The sincerity in his voice touched her. "I won't let Santiago harm you."

"So you're gonna protect me from the big bad Santiago?"

"Let's go to him together. I'll make him understand, but you have to make your father step off."

He sat on the chair with her, then rested his forehead on hers. "You don't have to protect me, Diana. I'll take you to Santiago tomorrow." He closed his eyes, gently rubbing his nose against her cheek. "I want to take you back."

Glad the feud would end without bloodshed, she rested her head on his shoulder. She laughed inside, thinking Tony turned out to be more trustworthy than Ashton, and she'd fallen in love with the wrong man. She couldn't deny her feelings for Ashton if she wanted to. She hoped with time her heart wouldn't ache so much.

Tony's light brushing of her lips with his eased her out of her pity party. Gentle. How could he be so gentle and kind? She gazed into his eyes and didn't see the Tony people feared: she saw her friend, the man she identified with, the man who understood her needs, the man who chose her over everything and everyone else.

He took her bottom lip into his mouth, lightly teased with his teeth, released. "My feelings are real, Diana. Do you believe me?" He traced her jawbone with feather kisses.

She closed her eyes, wanting to be taken away. "Yes."

He circled her breasts with his finger until they both showed their peaks. "I love you, Diana. Believe me."

Feeling passions warmth fill her body, she nodded. Ashton held back because he didn't love her. She couldn't see it before because of the blinds of love. Now his deceit rang out as clear as day. To Ashton she was only a means to an end. She was his job.

Tony loved her for her. Tony would give his all to her. Tony protected her from Baxter. Tony would go against his father. Tony would take her to Santiago. Why couldn't she be in love with him instead of Ashton?

She shook her head. Love gets you into trouble. Her

mother loved Steven, and he broke her heart. Her dad loved her mother, and she broke his heart. Santiago broke women's hearts every day of the week. Ashton used her love to move ahead in his career. Love was a fantasy for the hopelessly romantic.

He suckled the breast he admired so, coaxing a moan out of her. She'd been so distracted she didn't notice him lower the straps of her sundress. She leaned back, enjoying the physical pleasure he gave.

He stood, pulling her along with him. "So beautiful. Let me look at you." She allowed her dress to slowly slide down her body, finally dropping it to the floor. His eyes followed the dress on its descent, enjoying every glorious inch. "Do you mind if I lick my lips?" he teased as he wrapped his arms around her.

Embarrassed, she laid her head on his shoulder. He lifted her chin. "Can I lick your lips?" Before she could answer, he covered her mouth with his, working, hoping, praying, she'd open up to him.

Purely physical, yet delicious. She stopped her train of thought because she wasn't being fair. She'd never allow herself to love again, but it wasn't purely physical. He was strong, handsome, kind, and most importantly her true friend. He didn't lie to or manipulate her. He was always real whether pissing her off, scaring her, or making her laugh. Tony was always Tony, and the only person she could depend on totally and completely. Not even Santiago would confide his all with her. No one had until Tony.

He slipped out of his shirt, then took a condom out of his back pocket and unfastened his pants. It was Diana's turn to enjoy the view. Liking her eyeing him, he stripped, first tossing his beloved shoes to the side, then his pants, socks, and for the grand finally, his briefs. With a twirl of his hands, he reached over pulling her against his chest.

As he led her into the bedroom he donned his condom, then laid her on the bed. He traced her lips with his finger. "Full lips." Dropped his finger to her chest, circling. "Full breasts." He slowly slipped his finger into her soft, wet heat. "Let me fill you, love."

She closed her eyes, forced away thoughts of Ashton and allowed the joy of Tony to take over. He was so attentive to her every need. Feeling him removing her panties, she opened her eyes.

An overwhelming need for acceptance had overtaken her. She needed someone to want her. Her father chose the drug world then death over her. Her siblings didn't want her. Santiago loved, but didn't understand her. Ashton chose the DEA. Only Tony accepted, wanted, understood and chose her. Tony would be there for her. Tony would do anything for and protect her.

He kissed her. "I love you, Diana." She lifted her head to reach his lips and show him she needed him. He entered her and pumped slow and gently.

Diana couldn't take her mind off how Ashton had made her feel. She'd never felt anything so glorious. Her mind spun around in turmoil. How could she fall for Ashton's lies? She looked into Tony's eyes and her own actions made her feel ill. *What's wrong with me?*

"Come on, baby." He pumped harder.

Disgusted with herself, her eyes filled with tears. She'd just ruined her first real friendship. He'd never believe she wasn't using him.

He closed his eyes. "That's it, baby." He stroked as deep and hard as he could. He hit his climax, then lay beside her.

"Damn, girl. You're killing me." He patted his chest with her hand as he lay breathless beside her. "You about gave me a heart attack." He rolled over and cupped her into his body. "I've never made a woman shed tears before. Making love shouldn't feel so good."

Mind weary and guilt ridden, she didn't know what to say. Tony was her only true friend and she'd... She was so confused she wasn't sure what she'd done, but she knew she regretted sleeping with him and leading him on. She didn't know what had come over her. "I'm exhausted."

He dragged her into the restroom. "While you nap, I'll make our travel arrangements and find some ID for you." They waited for the water to heat.

She covered herself with her short silk robe. She wanted to shower alone, but wasn't sure how to explain and apologize. She searched for a way around hurting him. "Why don't we take the jet?" She wanted his friendship, but couldn't continue leading him on. Afraid he'd think she'd used him to escape, she massaged her temples.

"I don't want my dad to know what I'm up to or he'll try to stop me. We need to reach Santiago before I confront my dad." He placed his hand under the water, testing the temperature. "It's perfect."

They both stepped into the shower.

She decided to put off telling Tony she wasn't interested in a romantic relationship with him until they reached Santiago's for two reasons: she knew he'd be hurt, and she wanted to make sure he was out of harms way. "Your father wouldn't really kill you would he?" If she told him her feelings, he wouldn't go to Santiago's and the war would continue.

Tony laughed hard and loud. "Don't worry. He'd never hurt me. He'll just try to change my mind."

CHAPTER TWENTY-SIX

"What the hell are you still doing here?"

"I had to pack," Baxter said.

Tony cursed under his breath. He'd wanted to rush out but couldn't until Baxter left. "Well you have your shit. Go kill those bastards." Standing at the edge of the porch, he scanned the grounds for Guevara.

Baxter watched the big black Mexican pull weeds out of the front flower garden. "You sure you don't want me to stick around a few days until help arrives. English speaking help."

"I don't need help. I can handle Diana myself."

"You can't watch her twenty-four seven. Where is she now? How do you know she isn't trying to make the great escape?"

Thinking about making love with Diana made Tony flush. "She's asleep." He glanced toward her room.

Baxter's mouth dropped wide open. "You're fucking her, aren't you?"

Ready to fight, Tony turned on Baxter. "Watch your mouth."

"How the hell did you break her? Through those books of yours?"

"As a matter of fact, those books you dogged me out about helped considerably." He looked at her window.

"And now you're screwing her brains out. Damn, she's one fine piece of ass."

"I told you to watch your mouth," Tony snapped. "I didn't break her. That was my original mistake. I've learned to bend along with her. Once she accepted me, I guided what direction she'd bend. I control what way she goes."

"But how?"

"She's been dicked around her whole life by everyone she loves. I don't think anyone has ever told her the truth. Not the whole truth anyway. Granted, they were all trying to protect her in one way or another, but I've used it against them. Now she sees their omissions as lies and betrayals. I always tell her the whole truth." He shrugged. "Or at least she thinks I do. I've become her confidant, lover and thanks to you, her protector." He momentarily gazed toward her window. After she fell in love with him, he'd tell her the whole truth.

"I was part of some stupid plan. You should have told me. Hell, I thought you were switching sides."

"I couldn't take the chance on you over acting." He smirked. "Your natural jacked up attitude was perfect. Your fights with her and anger with me for defending her were genuine. That's what I needed her to see to accept me as her protector."

"So now my usefulness is over, and it's back to California Baxter?"

"Damn, Baxter, Diana's right. You do sound like a jealous bitch. I don't have to explain myself to you."

"If you'd tell me what the hell is going on, I wouldn't ask so many questions? I don't give a damn who you fu... take to bed, or how often. All I care about is ensuring Carter interests are taken care of. You've been in my way."

"I am the Carter interest."

He stepped up to Tony. "Well you could have fooled me you pussy whipped mother. You let her trick you into sending Leon away. Now you're sending me away. I'm not jealous of her. I'm doing my job."

Tony pulled out his piece. "I suggest you step off." Baxter backed away. "You actually think I don't know she set the stupid bastard up. Hell, I thought it was cute. Why the hell else do you think I didn't kill his ass. I turned the tables by showing her my gentle side. He was my opening." He put away his gun.

"When I took her into the city," he paused raising a brow, "without your permission or knowledge, she confided in me." He didn't feel a need to tell Baxter he'd done just as much confiding. "She became close to me. I was there for her as no one had ever been. I listened to her, helped her organize her thoughts as I wanted them. I leaned all of her needs and set out to fill them. I prove day after day she can trust me, and I will never betray her. I tell her I love—"

"What are you trying to do?"

Tony clinched his teeth. "If you interrupt me one more time, I'll stop explaining." He turned away. "Forget it. You wouldn't understand anyway." He sat on the railing of the porch. "She believes I'm her everything and desperately in love with her." It was easy to convince her that his love was genuine because it was.

"In her mind I've saved her from my father, you and the agent. I'm the only one who gives her total and complete honesty. I'm the one who supplies all of her needs. I'm the one who makes love to her. I'm the one who will return her to Santiago." He glanced over his shoulder at her window.

"You can't be serious. Santiago will kill you on general principle."

"She won't allow him to hurt her husband." He smirked at the shocked look on Baxter's face. "That's right. I'll convince her to marry me before I take her to Santiago. She'll think it's the only way to save me. I've protected her from everything. She'll do the same for me. She's the key to unlocking his organization."

"Wife? This is crazy. She's actually in love with you?"

"Unfortunately, she's still in love with that agent, which is why I need you to wipe his ass out of the picture. I can't chance him showing up and ruining my plans."

"Santiago may have already taken care of him for you. You know he doesn't play when it comes to Diana."

"I don't want any ghost coming back to haunt my ass. Make sure he's permanently wiped out. I'll handle Diana. Once we're married, Santiago will back off."

"I guess you have everything under control after all."

"Of course I do." Tony spotted Hector approaching with Niko. "I have work to do. Get the hell out of here."

"I'm on my way." He descended the stairs, heading for the car with his bags.

"Hector." Tony waved for Hector to come to him.

Hector released Niko's leash. The puppy ran for Tony. Tony met them halfway, then stooped down and rubbed his belly. "You're supposed to be viscous." He stood, speaking with Hector. "Have you seen Guevara?"

"Who?"

"The head gardener."

He shook his head. "I haven't seen him. Do you want me to find him for you?"

"Nah, don't worry about it. I'll find him myself. What are you doing with Niko?"

"Searching for Diana. It's time for his lunch."

His eyes traveled from Hector, to her window, back at Hector. "You can feed him this time. She's asleep."

"I know this isn't my place, but you'd better marry her soon. I'm sure Santiago is worried out of his mind. The sooner you two confront him, the easier it will be on the both of you."

Stunned beyond belief, Tony stopped scanning the yard for Guevara. "You know who Diana is?"

"It wasn't difficult to figure out. Santiago and your father must be kicking the can. Whatever you're planning, I suggest you do it soon."

Grinning at his new ally, he admitted, "We left California kind of fast. Do you know where I can obtain Diana some ID around here?"

Hector rested his hands on his hips, trying to remember. "I used to know someone. I may still have his number in the kennel."

Tony pulled out his cellphone and handed it to Hector. "Would you make arrangements for me? We need to travel freely. Let me know where to go and what I need to take with me."

"I'll handle it for you. Give me fifteen minutes." Hector took Niko's leash and headed for the kennel.

Tony glanced at Diana's window, then walked up to the large black Mexican that was weeding the front flower garden. "Excuse me." No answer. The man tossed a few weeds into a pile. Tony tapped him on the shoulder. "Excuse me."

The man continued snatching weeds as if he didn't hear Tony's words or feel his tap.

Tony cleared his throat loudly. "Excuse me."

The man grumbled under his breath as he yanked the weeds and threw them at the weed pile.

"Hell, man, I know you hear me."

He rose quickly, turning angrily on Tony. "*No—hablo—Ingles,*" he roared slowly and clearly.

Tony didn't scare easily, but damn. This was one intimidating, scary son-of-a-gun. He backed away slightly, hands up. "Relax, big boy. I'm just trying to find Guevara."

The man ground his teeth.

"You're in the wrong line of work. Dondé... um dondé es Guevara? Or something like that. Shit."

The man rolled his eyes, pointed to the side of the house, then knelt and tortured more weeds.

"Gracias." Tony headed for the side of the house. "That is one mean mother." He rounded the corner. "Mr. Guevara, could I speak with you a minute please?"

Guevara wiped his filthy hands on his dark blue pants as he stood. "What can I do for you?"

"Before you leave today, would you speak with Diana about how she wants the grounds? I should have asked her before you started, but didn't think of it."

"You're the boss."

"The big black Mexican out front pulling weeds, he didn't come with you the other day, did he?"

Guevara fidgeted with his working gloves. "No, senior. Is there a problem?"

"I just think pulling weeds is a waste of his talents. How long has he been working for you? How well do you know him?"

He hesitated before answering, "He's my nephew."

"I'm not trying to interfere in your family business, but he's a time bomb. He should work for me. I'll put his anger to use. He'll make good money."

"What would he have to do?"

"You know the business I'm in. We'll need to work on his English." Tony laughed. "And teach him I'm not the enemy."

"I'll speak with him."

"I'm heading for town, but I'd like to know if he agrees. Would you bring him by again tomorrow? I'll speak with him after you explain what I want. I'll need you to translate for me."

"We'll return, but he has his own mind."

"I could tell. I'll convince him to work for me. Let's say we meet for breakfast. Maria serves at eight sharp."

Guevara knelt beside Ashton. "He's headed into town."

Burning with hate and rage, Ashton glared into Guevara's eyes. It took everything he had to keep from strangling the life out of Tony. He had to regain control before he could rescue Diana.

"Who is she to you?"

"She's my fiancée." Ashton snatched off his work gloves. "He's really done a mind job on her. I don't know how I'll save her."

"We have to rescue her first. You can work on her emotional scars after she's safe."

He rubbed his temples with his fingers. "In a way, I'm guiltier than Tony." He tore a few weeds apart. "I was a DEA agent working the Carter case when Diana and I met. She was supposed to be my in." An anxiety laugh escaped him. "I wasn't pretending with her. I actually love her. I didn't see myself as manipulating her. I thought I could love her and still do my job. I separated the two." He tossed his gloves to the side. "But there is no separation. Using her to capture Carter and Santiago was my job. She gave me her all, but I held back. I put my job before the most important part of my life."

"Who told her you're DEA?"

"I swear I planned on telling her, but Santiago told her first. I knew in my heart she'd forgive me. She'd recognize my love for her was genuine. Then Tony kidnapped her. He took her in her most vulnerable time and..." he trailed off, thinking he'd done the same thing when her father had died. "I'm worse than Tony."

"No you're not. You made a mistake." He stretched his arms out wide. "A huge mistake, but a mistake. Put Diana first. Love her. Give her your all."

"Thanks, Guevara. I didn't know love was this strong."

"I'll bring my truck around the side of the house. We can hide her in the camper."

"I hope she'll come with us. He's really worked her over good."

"You'll find a way. Let's do this. Tony said he's heading into San Cristobal, so we have at least a four hour head start."

CHAPTER TWENTY-SEVEN

Tortured is how Diana looked, lying there asleep gripping her pillow. She inhaled deeply. "Ashton." Her grip on the pillow relaxed.

"I'm so sorry." Ashton caressed her face, wiping away the tears that fell. "I love you, Diana." Gently kissing her ear, he continued whispering his love for her until she woke.

Eyes filled with disorientation, Diana backed away. "I'm in Mexico?"

"I've come for you." He held out his hand, hoping she'd accept it. "We need to leave."

She frowned. "Ashton? Why are you here?" She wiped the sleep out of her eyes.

He eased his way into her comfort zone, praying she wouldn't back away. "I've come to take you to Santiago."

She fell off the opposite side of the bed in retreat. "Liar, you're tricking me." He crossed the bed to help her up. She kicked at him. "Go away. Go away." She drew her legs into her body, rested her head on her knees. "You want to use me. Your cover's blown. I won't let you use me anymore."

Unsure how to proceed, he lowered his head. "I did use you, Diana. I apologize." No excuses, only the whole truth would do. He sat on the floor a few feet in front of her, leaning against the bed for support. "I tried to separate my feelings for you and my job, but I cheated on you both. I didn't realize what I was doing until it was too late."

"You want to use me to bring down Santiago. I'm your means to an end. I'm your case."

"You're my love." He slowly held out his hand. "Please come with me. It isn't safe for you here."

"Leave me alone, Ashton. I'm perfectly safe. I'm done being a fool for love."

"Tony will return shortly."

"He would never hurt me," she snapped. "Unlike you, he loves me. Go back to your beloved agency." She turned her back to him. "Leave me alone."

"I don't work for the agency. I quit."

She glared over her shoulder with a raised brow. "Oh, and I'm supposed to believe everything you say. You must think I'm stupid."

How to convince her to believe in his love for her was the million-dollar question. "I've never tricked or manipulated you."

"You knew who I was from day one. You convinced me you loved me when you were actually after that stupid jump drive."

"That's not so, Diana."

"It is! Now you're lying to me again. You got your information and Carter. Now you're after Santiago."

"I quit the agency and went to Santiago for help."

She shook her head. "You're lying to me. He'd never help you. Why are you doing this?"

"Leonard and I are working with Santiago. I love you." He inched closer. "I was in the area when Mr. Guevara called Santiago." And Closer.

"Why were you in the area?" she quietly asked.

Still Closer. "The videos, baby. You are so smart." Only a few inches away.

She raised her brows. "You saw my clues?"

Sinking deep into her big brown, expressive eyes he admitted, "All I saw was you. Leonard pointed out the clues you left." He gently combed her hair with his fingers. "All there is, is you."

She lowered her head. "I don't know. I'm so confused."

He drew her close to his body, rocking her. "It's all right. Come with me. I'll take you to Santiago and leave you alone to think."

She snuggled into him sniffling. "I'm so tired. I can't organize my thoughts."

"I know, but we have to leave. He'll be back soon."

She pulled away. "I'm not leaving with you. Tony's taking me to Santiago tomorrow. I know he isn't lying. I know he loves me, but you." She shook her head. "You're an agent. You'd say anything for your case."

"The only lie I ever told you was a lie of omission."

"A pretty big lie of omission, Ashton. I don't even know your real name."

"Ashton Powell. I'm Ashton, the man you love. The man who loves you."

"Tony loves me. He'll take me to Santiago so I can think. I can't think straight around you. Just leave. I won't tell him you were here. Let Santiago know I'll be home tomorrow."

"Diana, he isn't taking you home tomorrow. I overheard him speaking with Baxter."

"How dare you!" She reached for her sandals. "Go to hell, Ashton." She slipped her shoes on. "He'd never lie to me. He isn't you. Go back to your agency."

He followed her out of the room. "Come to the study with me. Give me five minutes. Then I'll leave if you'd like."

She poked him in the chest. "For what? More of your lies? No thanks. I'll pass."

"If I were you, I wouldn't believe me either, but there's something I must show you. Please, Diana. Five minutes, then I'll leave. I swear on my sister's grave."

"Fine." She stalked off to the study with him close behind. "Talk fast." She stopped in the center of the room then folded her arms over her chest.

He sat at the desk and sorted through the items in the bottom drawer. He'd hoped he wouldn't have to do this. "Come here. I want to show you something."

She studied him for a while before finally crossing over to him. "You have four minutes twenty-eight seconds." She knelt on the floor beside him.

He took the books out, handing them to her. "I found these when I was snooping earlier." He set the journal on the desk.

She opened the first book, *The Kidnapped Mind.* "These could be his father's."

He watched as she skimmed the sections of the books Tony had marked. After a few minutes, she tossed the books to the side. "He wouldn't do this. There must be an explanation."

"Tony's been manipulating you to infiltrate Santiago's régime."

"No! He wouldn't betray me. Those are his father's."

He handed her the journal. "I know I'm causing you more pain, but you need to know." She read the journal. "It's all in here," Ashton said in calm, hushed tones. "His plan. The notes he took from the books, his objectives, observations and even his progress."

He pointed to the section where Tony had detailed what each man in her life had given her and what was missing from each relationship then had the nerve to write a list of everything she'd been missing and titled it his to do list.

He wiped the tears from her eyes. "You didn't stand a chance."

She tore the journal apart, tossing the pages all over the room. Once she finished destroying the journal, she took after the books: ripping, shredding and throwing. Ashton stood close to the door, guarding for intruders until she fell to the floor in a heap of tears.

He crossed the room and knelt before her. "I love you, Diana." He pulled her into his arms and allowed her to cry. "Let it all out, just let it all out." He continued rocking her until she calmed.

"Ashton."

"Yes," he whispered.

"I need to know something. Please don't lie to me. I can't take it." She paused. "Do you love me?"

He rested his forehead on hers. "Love is close, but not strong enough to describe what I feel for you. I'm so sorry to have caused you to doubt me. I should have told you sooner about my agency ties, but I was afraid you wouldn't believe me."

She held onto him tightly.

"I hate to interrupt, but we need to leave." Both spun around and saw Guevara. "Didn't mean to startle you. I have the truck ready, and the coast is clear."

Ashton helped Diana stand. "We're on our way."

"I'll be waiting outside," Mr. Guevara said on his way out.

Ashton hugged Diana. "I do love you." He'd take her to Santiago and give her time to clear her mind.

CHAPTER TWENTY-EIGHT

"**M**aria, where's Diana?" Tony set his packages on the kitchen table.

"I haven't seen her since lunch. She grabbed a few sandwiches and headed to the kennel."

"Come over and see what I bought for her." He arranged the white roses in a vase, then pulled out a small rectangular box from one of the bags and opened it.

Maria's breath caught. "It's beautiful." She lifted the ruby and diamond choker out of its case. "She'll love these." She placed them back into their box.

"Wait until you see the dress. This seamstress lady is coming by tomorrow to make sure it fits right. I'm taking my baby out in style." He handed her the box with the matching earrings. "Hide them for me. I want to surprise her with them."

"So when's the wedding?"

He laughed. "You too, Maria. Dang, Hector already got on me this morning."

"Well?"

"When she says yes. We're taking a trip around the country starting tomorrow. By the time we return, we'll be man and wife."

"Now that you've gotten rid of Baxter, I think things around here won't be so tense. He used to pick fights with Diana."

"That's why his ass had to go." He gathered the rawhide he'd bought. "This should keep Niko out of the kitchen for a while." He headed out the back door for the kennel.

"Hector, where's Diana?"

"I don't know. She came for Niko a few hours ago. I haven't seen her since."

"Did you see the big black Mexican who came in with the gardener?" Hector nodded. "He'll be working for me. Could you help him learn some English? I'd ask Maria, but he might scare the poor woman to death."

Hector chuckled. "Sure."

"I'll send him down in the morning. If you see Diana, tell her I'm home." He walked the grounds, searching for Diana. *I'll bet she's been in the house laid up watching DVD's all this time.* He entered the house and skipped up steps to her room.

"Hey, lovely lady." He searched her room. "So you want to play do you? A little hide and go get it perhaps."

He looked through all of the upstairs rooms, then the kitchen. "Maria, has Diana come in here?"

She glanced at the clock. "I'm afraid not, and dinner was ready a half hour ago. I'm starting to worry."

"Well hell. She has to be here somewhere. Oh shit." He hit himself in the head for being such an idiot. "I'll bet she's in the study listening to the stereo. I gave her a collection of Santana CDs." He headed for the study.

No music. No dancing. No sound at all. Nervous energy set his hair on ends. "Diana?" Maybe she was reading. He stepped into the room. The study was a complete mess. He picked up one of the pages of his journal.

"No," he gasped. All of his books were ripped to shreds. His heart pounded. "No, no, no." He picked up the pieces of his journal. "Maria," he called. He had to find Diana and explain. "Maria," he yelled. He had to make her understand. "Maria!"

Maria saw the destruction in the study and froze. "Oh my God. What happened?"

"She's gone. Shit, shit, shit! Did Guevara come in here to see Diana?"

Maria set the chair upright. "He asked where she was right before he left. Do you think she left with him?" She picked paper off the floor.

"I'm afraid so." He kicked the waste can across the room. "Would you please help me make some calls? I don't know if his people speak English."

"I'll make the calls?"

Tony handed her his phone. "How could I have been so stupid?" he mumbled to himself. "Arrogant stupid son-of-a-bitch." He tapped on the window. Harder. Harder. Smash. He'd punched the window.

"What are you doing, Tony?" She grabbed his hand

and picked out the tiny shards of glass. "Don't do this to yourself. We'll find her. Let's clean your hand then head to Guevara's shop. I left a message on his answering machine."

"I love Diana."

"I know." She looked around at the mess. "What was in those papers?"

"I've wanted Diana since the first time I saw her. Before I fell in love with her, I'd planned on seducing her. I wrote my plans."

"And she found them."

He motioned around the room. "I'm afraid so."

Tony opened the car door for Maria. "Thanks for coming with me." He looked across the parking lot toward the large tool shed. "I don't see Guevara."

"It's late. He might be inside." She followed him into the small shop where she did the speaking in Spanish.

"Hello, gentlemen. Is Mr. Guevara in?"

"No, ma'am. He left a few hours ago."

"Did he have a young lady with him? Her name is Diana." Tony's ears perked up when he heard Diana's name.

"Yes, ma'am. She had a little puppy with her." He pointed to the ground.

Maria smiled at Tony. "Yes that's her. Do you know where I can reach Mr. Guevara?" She motioned to Tony. "We need to find Diana."

"He sent her out with the new guy. Rico, what's the new guy's name?"

"You mean the big black guy or the puny guy?" Rico asked.

"The black one."

"I think his name is Jose. He's Guevara's nephew."

Maria interrupted the two. "Do you know where Jose and Diana were headed?"

"I'm not sure, but I overheard them talking about Guatemala."

Tony understood. "Shit, shit, shit!"

Diana hadn't spoken a word since they left Guevara's.

They'd crossed the border into Guatemala over an hour ago. She felt Ashton watching her, but couldn't bring herself to look into his eyes. She kept her face forward, squinting to see into the darkness ahead, thinking.

Ashton hadn't told her of his agency ties because he feared she wouldn't believe him, just as she hadn't told Tony of her feelings because she thought he wouldn't believe her. But Tony had been the one manipulating her, lying—not Ashton. She smoothed her hand over her face. *What am I going to do?*

"Storms seem to be rolling in. I hope we make it before the rains start," Ashton commented.

Silence.

"Why don't you take my phone and call Santiago? I should have called him myself instead of having Mr. Guevara call him. I was in too big of a rush." She shook her head, turned away and stared out the passenger window. He rested his hand on her lap. "Are you sure you don't want to speak with him?"

"I'm not ready yet. Can it wait until we arrive in Barillas?" He tried so hard and deserved better than her, she thought.

"We've already passed Barillas. We aren't stopping until Coban. We're halfway there."

Ashton sounded worried, but she was glad they hadn't stopped. They were on a narrow, dark road surrounded by woods with at least thirty miles ahead and thirty miles behind them. She could barely hear the thunder of the approaching storm over the truck's engine. "Do you think the truck will make it to Corban? It's sounding kind of clunky."

He smiled. "Clunky?"

Niko woke, climbed into Diana's lap, then scratched on the window. "I believe someone needs a potty break. Could we pull over for a few minutes?"

"I think our clunky engine could use a break. It sounds like it wants to overheat. I'll call Santiago and check in." He maneuvered the truck over to the side of the dirt road. Diana and Niko hopped out.

"Stay close," he said.

Diana stood in the line of the headlights with Niko.

Ashton acted like everything was fine, but she felt guilty and filthy. She'd actually believed Tony. How could she be so stupid? And how would she tell Ashton she'd made love with Tony. She couldn't forgive herself. How could she expect Ashton to forgive her?

Niko finished his business. She carried him to the truck. "What's wrong?"

Ashton hit at the steering wheel. "This raggedy thing won't start, and the phone isn't getting a signal." He motioned behind her. "I don't want to go out there because it's about to storm, but we can't stay here. Tony may have people following."

"Do you think he would have them come this deep into Guatemala? He doesn't even know what city we're heading to, and this is a back road."

"No, but I don't want to chance it. If he knows you left with Guevara, he could find out what our vehicle is. He could have lookouts."

Thunder clapped in the distance. "I'm not afraid of a little rain. Let's go." She opened her door to leave.

"Wait a second, baby." He caught her by the hand. They were jolted by the charge between them. He brought her hand to his heart. "If it were just me, I'd go out on my own, but I don't want you out there. A major storm is brewing." He pointed to the woods. "It's pitch black, and we don't know how far away we are from the next house."

He reached under the seat for his fanny pack, holster and flashlight. "I'm not prepared. I was in such a rush, I didn't stop and think." He put on his jacket to cover his holstered gun.

"I can walk. Let's try to find a farmhouse. Maybe if we follow along the road."

"Love, if we follow along the road, we might as well wait in the truck."

She flushed. "Tony could ride up behind us, couldn't he?" He nodded. She looked out the window into the darkness. "Then let's walk into the woods and over one of these hills. We can walk until we reach a farm, plantation or something."

Disgusted with himself, he said, "We don't have a choice but leave the road, love." He continued calling her love to soak into her head that she was his love—his only love.

"I'm not complaining. Let's go. What's the problem?"

"I'm worried about you."

She frowned. "Me. Why? I exercise all day. I'm in excellent shape."

"Yes you are, but the terrain is rough and your feet..."

She twiddled her toes on her sandaled feet. "We don't have a choice. I'll survive."

"I shouldn't have brought you out here. We should have stopped in Barillas." He stroked his hand along her jawbone. "I don't know what to do." He wasn't referring to their stranded status.

"Thanks, Ashton."

His face scrunched up. "For what?"

"For saying you don't know. For not holding back."

"I make lots of mistakes. Want to hear some more?" He winked.

"How about you tell them to me out there." She stepped out of the old pickup. "I'll carry Niko for a tad bit. He's tired."

Ashton rounded the truck. "Hand me Niko. Now get on my back."

"I'm too heavy for you."

"Don't argue with me, Diana. After I'm tired, you can walk."

"Do you promise to tell me when you're tired?"

"I promise."

Approximately two miles later, it was drizzling and Ashton had slowed down considerably.

"I don't know about you, but my legs hurt," she lied, knowing he'd continue until he dropped. "Would you let me down? Thanks." She took Niko from him. "Do you need a break?"

"Not really. If you want to stop, we can."

"I can keep going." She set Niko on the ground.

He held his hand out for her. She didn't take it. He stood still, waiting. He noticed she'd been acting afraid of his touch. It was time to start working her out of it.

She twisted her lips. "Do you want the flashlight?" She held out the flashlight.

Sorry for his part in her pain, he gently took the flashlight and her hand, then led her deeper into the woods. "If I'm moving to fast say something."

After a few hundred yards, she relaxed her grip, just as after a mile on his back, she'd begun to relax.

Her hair was all wet and ragged, hanging down past her shoulders, white sundress soaked and dirty, shoes beyond repair, feet filthy. Their eyes met and held. She was the most beautiful person he'd ever seen.

Diana felt the flash between them also, but couldn't bring herself to act upon it. The physical exertion of walking helped to clear her mind. She knew he loved her as much as she loved him. There was only one problem. She'd betrayed him. Once he found out, he'd never forgive her, just as he never forgave his ex-wife. Eventually she'd have to tell him. "I'm feeling gypped," she teased.

His brilliant white smile lit up the night. "Oh really. Tell me about it." He held her hand to his heart. She was his love. He'd do whatever it took to help her heal.

She boldly stepped forward and declared, "We've been walking for miles, lost in the mountainous jungles of Guatemala."

He chuckled at her antics. Technically, he didn't think they were in the jungle or mountains.

"It's dark. We have no food. I don't think it'll ever stop raining." She aimed the flashlight at the surrounding trees and underbrush. "According to the books, there should be a convenient cave and fruit trees nearby. We should have passed several of them by now."

Still tickled, he pulled her into his chest and held her tight. She would return to him. He released her. "I have a little something for you. Take a seat." According to the books they should also be making love, but he would have to wait.

He sat in front of her cross-legged and took Niko's leash from her. "First I have to take care of the baby." He took a few beef jerky strips out of his pocket and set them on the ground for the puppy. Ready to eat, Niko ripped and tore at the meat.

"Now it's time to feed my baby." He winked at her, took the flashlight and disappeared into the woods, appearing a few seconds later with a mango.

Her head tilted to the side. "Where did you find that?"

He hesitated before answering, "Maria's kitchen. I had it in my fanny pack." Her smile encouraged him. "You didn't think I actually found a mango tree did you? I don't even know what a mango tree looks like." He took out his pocketknife.

Instead of cutting the mango in half, he pealed a portion, then cut off a strip. "Open wide." She looked at him like he'd lost his mind. He rubbed the mango strip on her bottom lip. "Let me feed you."

She lowered her gaze into her lap. "I can feed myself, Ashton."

"I know. I want to." She eventually opened and ate the strip. He kept the portion his fingers touched, throwing it to the side.

The sorrow, regret and shame reflecting in her eyes told the whole story. He sliced another strip of mango, fed it to her, then tossed the portion he'd touched away. "Give it time, love. I wish I had the magic to wipe your pain away. But there is none." He continued feeding her.

Her eyes welled up with tears. "I don't want anymore. You eat."

"I'll get us out of this."

"I know you will." He reached over to caress her face. "Please don't," she said. "I'm filthy."

He touched her chin and lifted her gaze to meet his. "So am I, love." It all fell into place. Why hadn't he figured it out sooner? Well, he knew the answer. He'd been concentrating on getting her as far away from Tony as possible.

She closed her eyes and lowered her head. "You don't understand." She shook her head, but her damp hair stuck to her shoulders.

He pulled her into his arms, rocking, refusing to allow her to shy away. "I understand that because of my stupidity, the woman I love is afraid of my touch."

She shook her head into his chest stammering, "It... it's not that. I'm not... afraid of your touch... I don't... deserve your touch."

His heart sunk. "Don't do this to yourself. None of this

was your fault."

"But I..." she trailed off, inhaled deeply, sat up straight, peered into his eyes. "I'm filthy."

He dropped his head back and allowed raindrops to fall freely on his face. "My grandmother once told me something about rain I didn't understand until now."

He lifted her face for the rain to clean away her tears. "The rain is one of God's ways of cleansing." She closed her eyes, allowing the rain to fall on her face.

He wiped the stray hairs from her face. "My mother never allowed us to play in the rain. When we'd go down south to visit Granny, she'd practically throw us out in it."

Diana put his soft voice and words in the background, and brought her troubles to the foreground. The cool mist did feel glorious. So freeing.

The rain stopped. He pulled her into his arms. "You're all clean now."

"I'll never be all clean again. You see. I gave myself to Tony freely." She looked into his eyes, fearing the rejections she knew she'd find. "I let him touch me. I let him. I wanted him to."

"You didn't let him. He raped you," he replied calmly.

She knew she couldn't see through the blur of tears, and he couldn't see through his denial. "He didn't rape me, Ashton. I wanted to."

"He took away your choice."

She shook her head; he just didn't understand.

"He raped your mind, which is far worse than raping your body. The body heals quickly, but the mind..." He paused. "You didn't read the whole journal. I did. Please believe me. You didn't have a choice. You were under his complete control."

Choking on her words, she asked, "How could I have allowed him to take control of my mind?"

"You didn't allow anything. Though we all react to situations differently, the human psyche is somewhat predictable. He took advantage of the situation and manipulated you to do his will. Given your background, you didn't have a chance or choice."

"I feel like such an idiot." She pulled away. "How could I have been so fooled? I must have wanted him."

"No, Diana." He held her close. "I won't permit you to blame yourself. You've done nothing wrong. It's my fault you were so vulnerable." He rocked her. "It's my fault we weren't in New York when Tony kidnapped you. I knew you were in danger and should have protected you. If you must blame someone, blame the ones who are responsible: Tony, Santiago, Carter, and me."

"But you didn't do anything wrong."

"Yes I did." He combed her soaked hair behind her ears with his fingers. "I love you more than I thought humanly possible. You've forgiven me for the unforgivable. Why won't you forgive yourself for being human?"

She hugged him tightly, releasing her guilty feelings. "I was so scared, Ashton. I didn't want him to hurt me. I thought he wouldn't hurt me if I became his friend."

"Didn't we watch that rerun of Oprah together?"

Her lips turned up into his chest. "Yeah. I wish I'd seen one on Stockholm syndrome. When we get home, I want to buy those books Tony had. I need to read them."

Niko barked into the woods. Ashton took out his nine millimeter.

"Niko. Come here now," she forcefully whispered. Instead of obeying her, he ran deeper into the woods. She took after the puppy. Ashton followed close behind.

CHAPTER TWENTY-NINE

"**D**iana, wait." Ashton followed her through the brush, up a hill, then came to an abrupt stop to keep from tripping into her. "Don't ever run away like that again. You know about dogs. He won't go far."

"Stop fussing and look." She pointed behind her.

Niko continued running across a field of tall grass, weeds and foxtails toward a chicken coop. Ashton grinned. "I can't give you a cave, but what about a farmhouse?" He held his hand out to her. "Niko, get back here now!" The puppy stopped in his tracks, turned around and headed back to Ashton's position.

They walked toward the small farmhouse hand in hand. Though drenched and in danger, the stroll to the farmhouse put her in mind of their nightly walks back in San Diego. She was past ready to return home. "What time is it?"

He pulled his sleeve off his watch. "One thirty-six."

"Someone's gonna be mad at us. Do you have any cash?" She tied Niko to the porch.

"A bit." He knocked on the door. After a few minutes, the door creaked open.

In Spanish he said, "I apologize for knocking on your door so late, but my wife and I are stranded. Our truck gave out a few miles away." He took out fifty dollars. By the looks of the run down house, the owner could use the money. "May we please use your phone?" He held out the cash.

The older woman cracked the door open a little wider. She looked from the dripping Diana to Ashton. "Please come in," she replied in Spanish. They both followed her in.

"I don't have a phone, but you're welcome to stay the night. My grandson will take you to a phone in the morning."

"Thank you so much." He held out the money.

"I won't take your money. If one of my children were stranded, I'd hope someone would take them in."

"I'm Ashton Powell. This is my wife Diana."

"Pleased to meet you both. I'm Lucia Alvarez. Are you hungry?" She led them into the kitchen. "I don't have much, but you're welcome to what I have."

"Diana, do you want to eat?" he asked in English.

"No thanks. I'm not hungry. Could I have a piece of bread for Niko?"

"I'm sorry. I didn't realize your wife doesn't speak Spanish." Lucia switched to English. "The best my English may not be, but manage we will." She handed Diana a few slices of bread.

"Thank you so much for taking us in. You're very kind." Diana left the room to feed Niko.

Switching back to Spanish, Lucia said, "Your wife is very beautiful inside and out." She opened the refrigerator and took out her leftover roast. "I could hear her stomach growling." Ashton watched as she prepared a sandwich. "Give this to her."

"Please take this money. You're being so kind. If I had been smart, I would have stopped in town and had to pay for a room and dinner."

She made a second sandwich for him. "It's not very often I have the opportunity to give. Now stop fussing and allow me." She handed him a sandwich.

His eyes filled with amusement. "This is the second time I've been accused of fussing in ten minutes. I guess I must fuss." He followed her to the front of the house.

"I'm old and tired. At the back of the kitchen is the guest room. The bed is made and there's fresh linen in the bathroom. I'll see you in the morning. Say goodnight to Diana for me."

"Goodnight, Mrs. Alvarez. Thanks again."

"Please call me Lucia. Goodnight, Ashton."

❧❧❧

"How could you take her food, Ashton?"

"I didn't have a choice, and you'd better eat every bite. I don't know when we'll eat again."

"This is good, but she can't afford to feed us." She took another bite. "Let's leave some money behind in the kitchen somewhere. When we get home, I'll send her money to thank her for her troubles."

Diana finished her sandwich, then went into the bathroom to take a shower. Ashton lay on the bed awaiting his turn. The door to the bathroom wouldn't close fully. After a few tries, Diana gave in and stripped, oblivious to or not caring he watched.

Ashton turned his head. Watching Diana undress was not what she needed. She needed him to keep his libido in check. The condoms in his fanny pack would have to remain there. The shower started. He could imagine her washing herself. *Shoot.* He rose quickly and headed for the kitchen.

He stopped in the doorway. "Excuse me. I didn't realize anyone was up. I just came in for a glass of ice water."

Lucia took a cup out of the cabinet for him. "I trust you're finding everything."

"Yes, ma'am. Thank you." He filled his cup with ice. "Goodnight again."

"Didn't you forget your water?"

"I guess ice water is better with water, isn't it. Do you have a T-shirt Diana can use for night clothes?" He filled the glass with tap water.

"I'll be right back." She returned a short time later with a wife beater. "This belongs to my grandson. I'm sure he won't mind."

"Thanks." He returned to their room, hoping she was done so he could take an ice cold shower.

"Finished already." He set the glass of ice water on the nightstand.

Diana lay in the bed covered with a sheet. "I went as fast as I could."

Fighting to ignore the outline of her body, he handed her the tank top. "You can put this on if you'd like." He kissed her on the forehead, then went into the bathroom, relieved she hadn't uncovered herself before he left the room. *How on Earth will I stay away from her?*

⁂

It's amazing what one can see through three inches of open door. Diana turned away to keep from intruding on Ashton's privacy. Why had he barely touched her since they arrived at the small farmhouse? She believed he loved her, but her sleeping with Tony must have put him off. She didn't blame him. She wouldn't want Tony's leftovers either. She tossed the tank top to the side and went to sleep.

❧❧❧

Diana looked exhausted. Ashton would rather her sleep be exhausted than tortured any day of the week. This was nothing a few hours of rest wouldn't clear up.

She cuddled into him, inhaled deeply then released a sighed Ashton and relaxed.

"I'm here." He'd stayed away from her for six months, so why was this so difficult? Now she needed him to be in control, but all he wanted to do was lose control.

❧❧❧

Diana woke, cupped in Ashton's loving embrace. "Ashton, are you awake?"

He pulled her closer to his body. "I am now. Did you need something, love."

"It's just... Never mind. I'm sorry I woke you."

"Look at me." She turned in his arms. "You aren't alone, Diana. I'm here for you. If I could take the pain away and feel it for you, I would—but I can't. If I could straighten everything out in your mind for you, I would—but I can't. All I can do is be here and pray I'm doing enough."

Ashamed of his lustful feelings, he closed his eyes. She needed his support, yet thoughts of taking her bottom lip into his mouth had flooded his mind.

"Would you please tell me what you're thinking, Ashton? I don't want to be protected by omission."

"Trust me, love. You don't want to know."

"But I do. It's Tony isn't it?" she whispered.

He rested his arm on her waist. "Have you ever wanted something so bad you could taste it? It was within your reach, but you weren't allowed to touch it."

After a little thought, she replied, "My mother's white roses. I could smell them from the porch and wanted to touch them. We weren't allowed within two feet. They looked so soft, beautiful and delicate."

"You are my white rose." His eyes opened long enough to show her they blazed with passion and wanting.

"I won't touch you, baby. I promise. You don't have to be afraid. I'll take you to Santiago and leave you alone to think."

"But what if I want to be touched?"

He slid a hand along the curve of her waist and over her hips, effectively knocking out all notions she had of him not wanting her. "I would die a very happy man."

"How do you do that?" she moaned, soaking in the passion filled sensations of his touch.

"Do what?" He closed in, kissing her lightly and sucked in her lower lip before she could answer. This was not good. He needed to stop, but couldn't find the will power. She was his and there were no obstacles. No secrets, work, Santiago, family, or Tony. He could give himself to her completely. He reached for and removed a condom from his fanny pack, then protected them both.

She forgot her own question when he caressed and suckled her breasts. He said he didn't have magic, but he was wrong. He definitely had the magic touch whenever he touched her.

He blazed a path of kisses to her ear whispering, "I don't want to stop, Diana, but I will if you want me to."

She lifted herself slightly, kissing his eyelids, nose and finally mouth. "If you stop, I will be the one to die, and I won't be happy."

"I don't want to be the cause of your death." He kissed, taking in all of her while giving of himself completely. This is how things should have been for them from the beginning.

One second she was riding the waves of passion from his kisses and fondling, the next she found herself groaning, drenched in orgasmic rapture.

"You sound so beautiful. You are so beautiful." His hand traced her breast, traveled down her abdomen to her waist and inner thigh taunting and teasing her senses into frenzy. How could this be? She'd already hit her climax. She knew her body. It was time for him to come to completion.

He covered her body with his. "What's going on in your pretty little head?" He entered her slowly, savoring the feel of first penetration. "Umm," they moaned simultaneously.

Stroke after glorious stroke rattled everything Diana thought she knew about her body. Pleasure filled waves rolled through her. Each so wonderful, so powerful, so Ashton.

Every time she peaked validated she was perfect for him. No woman had ever been able to keep up with him. He'd never have to rush with her. He could give her his all, and she'd be his all.

He bit his bottom lip to keep from yelling out. This was like nothing he'd ever experienced. His hearing became muddled and his sight cloudy. She was under him yet in and around him at the same time. She cried out as their climaxes pushed them together into the secret place where souls have the ability to combine. They were one.

CHAPTER THIRTY

"**J**uan will drive you into the city."

"Would you please let me show my appreciation, Lucia?" Diana asked.

"Stop arguing with your elders." She glanced over her shoulder. Ashton and Juan were standing with the puppy beside Juan's old pickup. "You have a good man. Don't keep him waiting."

"All right. All right. I'll go." She hugged Lucia then joined the others.

"How far is it, Ashton?"

He climbed into the truck and took the center seat. "An hour or so. Use some muscle closing the door."

She heaved the door closed with a loud bang. "Was that good enough for ya?"

He kissed her. "I love you."

She leaned on his shoulder, totally happy for the first time in her life.

He turned to Juan, speaking in Spanish. "Thanks for the ride. I hope you won't be stubborn like your grandmother. Please take payment for your hospitality."

"She'd kill me. I don't mind. I don't go into town very often. Your wife is very beautiful."

He glanced over at Diana and smiled. "Yes she is, isn't she?"

"You two are being so rude," she teased. She understood enough to know he'd complemented her. "Could I have your phone? I'm hoping to get a signal, so I can call Santiago." She held out her hand.

Ashton laughed and handed her the phone. A few minutes later, Diana interrupted their conversation. "I'm sorry, but would you please tell Juan that Santiago wants to speak with him."

"He wants to speak to Juan?"

"Yes." She handed Ashton the phone.

Ashton explained to Juan, handed him the phone then turned to Diana. "What was that about?"

"I told Santiago how Lucia helped us and wouldn't

take any payment. He'll make sure they're taken care of."

"Did he say anything about Guevara?"

"He and his family made it to Colombia." Thoughts of Tony plagued her mind. Was everything he said a lie? How could he act so well? She stared out the window, thinking she'd been right to believe in Ashton. If she'd of trusted her own heart, she would have saved herself a lot of heartache.

Juan handed Ashton the phone. "Her father is a very scary man."

"He can be at times."

"He said he's giving us a million dollars, and we don't have a choice but take it. Are they really rich?"

"Most definitely. Take the money, Juan. What your grandmother did for us is priceless. You have no idea how tired and hungry we were. She took us in no questions asked and fed us the last of her food. You don't find people like her very often."

"How did she end up having a Colombian father, but can't speak Spanish?"

"She was raised by her mother in the states."

Juan nodded his head.

Ashton whispered into Diana's ear, "Penny for your thoughts." He reached around, brushed her jawbone with his knuckle.

"When I had indisputable evidence you used me, I couldn't stop loving you." She turned into his stroking hand, loving his touch. "I tried not to. I had all of these reasons not to, but I did." She rested her head on his shoulder.

"Before I met you I'd already started falling in love with you."

She turned to him wide eyed.

He pressed her head to his shoulder. "I'd read your letters to Steven and admired the strong, devoted woman I saw. You wrote to him every week though he never replied. Did he ever contact you?"

She shook her head. "He didn't want to give away my location or identity. And he was my father. Of course I kept in contact with him."

"You'd be surprised at how many children don't keep in contact with parents who aren't in jail. Let alone those who are. You're a very loyal person. I've always been attracted to your loyalty." He took her hand into his. "I'm sorry about my role in this. I thought I could do my job without falling in love with you. I didn't want to. I fought against love. I'm glad I lost." He kissed her fingertips. "How did Tony learn so much about you so quickly?"

"I was trying to become his friend, so he wouldn't hurt me. It worked. One day we went into town and ended up talking the day away. Every time I opened up, he'd share a piece of himself. I think he was telling the truth. It all seemed so real. I don't know anymore. I just felt like something changed for Tony and me when we opened up to each other. Like we had a bond or something. We could identify with each other. Does that make sense?"

"You love him, don't you? Not in love, but love the friend he became. Now you feel guilty about your feelings." She nodded into his shoulder as the truck lumped and bumped along the uneven, weedy path.

He leaned his head on hers, reluctantly admitting, "He kept glancing at the house."

"Excuse me?"

"Yesterday. He kept looking to your bedroom window. I was so angry with him because," he trailed off.

Choked up, saying, "Because I gave myself to him."

He caressed her face, sinking deep into her sorrowful eyes to make sure she understood. "You did not give yourself to Tony. You gave yourself to me. The man you love." She relaxed. "I hated him because he looked toward the house with longing. I could see he'd fallen in love with you. I was jealous because he had the good sense to give you what I wanted to give, but wouldn't because of my job. He was trying to take what was mine. I hated him for it." He shook his head. "Tony and I are alike in so many ways. I won't lie and say I like your having any sort of feelings for him, but I do understand them. If I had my choice, I wouldn't share you with anyone. Including Santiago."

She grinned, relieved she wasn't totally out of her mind. "Greedy."

He feather kissed her ear, whispering, "With you, you bet I am. In loving you, never again."

CHAPTER THIRTY-ONE

"**W**hat took you so long to get here?"

Refusing to be rushed, Leonard sat in a chair and propped his feet on Carter's desk. "I'm not on call for you. Do you have the rest of my money ready?"

Carter stood abruptly. "You have the information? Why didn't you tell me? There's been a change in plans. Diana escaped."

"Why would I care about Diana escaping? I have a copy of the jump drive for you. After you transfer the money to my account, I'll give you your precious package."

Carter rounded the desk, dragging an office chair along with him. Leonard sat face to face with Carter, giving him his full attention. "I have tried to have Santiago assassinated several times, but he's heavily protected."

Leonard walked over to the wet bar. "I don't see what this has to do with me."

"I'll pay you thirty million to kill Santiago."

He stared at Carter. "Are you crazy? I wouldn't make it out alive. Thanks to you, I'm already a rich man, and I plan on living to spend it."

"You don't have to shoot him." Carter approached Leonard. "Poison him. I need him dead, and I need him dead quick. Once Diana's safe, he'll take his revenge out on me."

"Why me?"

"Because you're on the inside now. You can slip something into his food or a drink. You'd be long gone before anyone knew he was murdered and didn't die from a heart attack."

"You haven't even paid me for the jump drive yet."

"You'll get your money," Carter snapped.

"Damn skippy I will. The question is when?"

"Give me the drive, and I'll transfer the money. I'll pay you sixty million to kill Santiago for me."

Leonard's brows rose. "Sixty million. That's sounding pretty damn good to me. Let's settle this other business first, then we can discuss our next group project. You owe me twenty million."

"Not without the drive." He held out his hand.

Leonard walked past Carter toward the door. "You taped and tried to blackmail me. I don't trust your ass. I have the jump drive tucked safely at my place." He opened the door. "You and I'll collect it. You can skim through to ensure I'm not cheating you, then you transfer the money over to my account, and I give you the drive."

"Let's do this." They left the office together.

Diana pulled free of Ashton's grip. He turned from the hotel clerk, asking, "Where are you going?"

She motioned across the lobby. "The gift shop."

"Stay close." He handed Niko's leash to the hotel clerk to have the puppy kenneled.

Diana rolled her eyes and continued onward. She hoped the gift shop carried clothing. A quick scan revealed tons of T-shirts and shorts but no underclothes. She pulled a few pairs of shorts off the shelves. At least they had an under lining in them they could substitute for underclothes.

"Hey sexy lady." Ashton drew her into his body.

Diana set her purchases on the counter. "Did you mean to say sexy lady or starving lady?"

"I'm taking care of both. I've already ordered room service." He paid for her purchases with his credit card.

You can't go wrong with eggs, bacon, and hash browns. "I was dying." Diana took a sip of her hot chocolate. "There's only one thing I love doing more than eating."

He licked the excess chocolate from her lips. "What would that be? Working in the yard."

She tasted his coffee by taking his tongue into her mouth. Delicious. "Actually, yard work is tied with eating."

Her shocked squeal as he carried her to the bed made him laugh. "Talking about eating has made me hungry again." He set her on the bed, ravishing her with his eyes.

Ashton wasn't the only one enjoying a feast. Diana lifted his shirt then threw it to the side, revealing his powerful chest. Her fingers glided over the ripples of his abdomen, along his pectorals, over his shoulders until she found her arms wrapped around his neck. "Me too."

"Stand a second." As she stood, he slipped her sundress off her shoulders. "I can't imagine staying away from you. How did I do it?"

His tiny nibbles along her neck made her so weak in the knees that he had to help her lay on the bed before she fell.

"I was never a breast man," he suckled her nipple knowing how much it drove her wild, "until I met you." He took one of her breast fully into his mouth, worked her into a manic state, then released her.

He only stepped away momentarily to take of his pants and briefs and protect them, but to Diana it felt like a lifetime. She knew what would come next and could hardly wait.

Covering her with his embrace, he cocooned her in his masculine scent, his warmth, his tender touch, his love all working wonders to heal her soul.

"I love you so much, Ashton."

His heart smiled. "You've made me a better man, Diana." He entered her slowly. "You are my everything." He kissed her, probing every succulent inch of her mouth while continuing to stroke.

Simply put, she could eat him up. Her first climax was a nice, light, shiver filled quake that placed her senses on full alert.

She gazed into his deep-brown, passionate eyes. He was hers. Her heart smiled. He rolled them over placing her on top. She wasn't sure what to do.

"You've never been on top before, have you?" She shook her head. He held onto her waist and showed her how to stroke. "You'll like this."

She learned quickly and soon stroked without his guidance. He now had second thoughts about this position. With her powerful legs and abdominal muscles, her strokes held him captive. For the first time in his life, he had a hard time holding onto his control. She hit another climax and almost sent him over the edge.

She kissed him lightly on the chest. His hands gripped her waist keeping her from moving so slowly: taunting, teasing, pleasuring him. It was too much. His eyes rolled back in his head. "I'm about to explode, love."

"That's the point," she whispered over his mouth, brushing his lips with hers.

He couldn't take it anymore. He rolled them both over and stroked like every one was his last. She cried out, loving this harder version. The sound of flesh pounding flesh filled the room. The sound of their screams when they climaxed together filled the hotel. The sounds of their souls joining as one filled the heavens.

Drifting into sleep, Ashton cupped Diana into his body.

Diana's stomach growled. "I'm hungry."

He tightened his grip slightly. "I'm sorry, but I need to reenergize before I can feed you again." He lifted himself, kissing her ear, then relaxed his grip.

"I'm talking about food, Ashton."

"We just ate."

She removed his arm, stepped out of the bed then headed for the bathroom. "You reenergize your way. I'll reenergize mine."

A few minutes later, she was showered and dressed in a new T-shirt and matching shorts. "I'll bring something back for you."

He grabbed her wrist and brought her left ring finger to his mouth. "We need to fix this." He kissed her ring finger. "Let me shower, then we can go together."

"I already have a slight hunger headache. I'll hold us a table and order our food. I saw a La Cocina two doors down. The one in Mexico was great."

"I'll meet you there in twenty minutes."

⚜⚜⚜

"Grab a seat anywhere. I need to boot my system." Leonard opened his laptop. "Do you want a drink or something? I have beer in the frig."

Carter hunched over the coffee table and stared at the computer screen. "No thanks."

"Well I'm thirsty." He set a CD he'd made from part of the jump drive on the table. "When it finishes booting up, go ahead and look at the CD." He left Carter alone.

As Leonard stepped into the kitchen, he nodded at Santiago.

"Did you have a difficult time convincing him to leave without his bodyguards?" Santiago whispered.

Leonard opened the refrigerator. "For some fool reason, he trusts me." He took out a beer, offering one to Santiago who declined. "By the way. I'm supposed to kill you for sixty million."

"Stupid bastard. What's he doing now?"

"Looking at the CD." He glugged down the beer. Belched. "Ah, now that's good stuff."

"Let me know after he's transferred the twenty million into your account."

Leonard nodded on his way out. "So how much damage control are you in for?" He sat next to Carter.

"A hell of a lot. I changed my distribution routes years ago, but I'm still up shit creek. Where is the rest of the information?"

He took the jump drive out of his pocket and placed it on the table.

Carter shook his head. "You had it on you all the time."

"Hell yeah. I don't trust anyone." He gave Carter a quick view of the jump drive's full contents, then connected to the Internet. "Now would you kindly transfer my payment?" He pushed the laptop toward Carter.

"Do you think about anything besides getting paid?" He began the transfer of monies from his account to Leonard's.

"Getting paid and getting laid are my top two priorities at this point in my life. Why?"

Carter laughed. "While I'm in here, are you taking care of Santiago for me or not. I'll give you half now and half after his funeral."

"I'll do it, but then I'm retiring, so don't ask for anything else."

"Quitting while you're ahead sounds like a good plan." Carter finished the transaction, then turned the laptop toward Leonard and waited.

"You deposited too much. I'm not a cheat." There was an additional twenty million in the account.

"Think of it as a bonus. Like you said, I'm a multibillionaire."

Leonard turned off the laptop. "I'm not stupid. I'll take the money."

"When will you handle Santiago?"

Leonard sat back on the couch. "My mother always told me there's no time like the present." He paused. "Santiago, would you come in here please?"

Carter reached for his gun as he stood. "Shit!" Leonard had taken his gun before allowing him into the house. "You son-of-a-bitch. I'll have you killed."

Leonard stood, drew his piece and pointed it at Carter. "Shut the hell up before you piss me off. Shit, if it were up to me, your ass would already be dead."

Santiago motioned for Leonard to calm. "I promised Ashton to keep you out of trouble. I'll take that." Santiago took the jump drive off the table and placed it in his briefcase. "Have a seat, Carter. We have business to discuss."

"I'm not discussing shit with you."

"Fine with me. I agree with Leonard and don't give a damn if you live or die. The only reason you aren't dead is because Diana asked me not to kill you. But since you refuse to come to an agreement," he shrugged, "I'll tell my baby girl I tried." He leaned back in the chair. "I don't know why she wants to plead your case." He shook his head. "My baby girl's too kind hearted."

Carter cursed under his breath as he sat on the couch. "How much is he paying you?"

Leonard smiled and took his seat. "Absolutely nothing. You're the stupid, mindless ass who kidnapped my brother's fiancée. There was no way in hell I would allow you to get away with that shit."

CHAPTER THIRTY-TWO

"**Y**ou won't believe who I saw go into the restaurant across the street."

"I'm in no mood for games, Baxter."

"Diana."

"Is she alone?" Baxter nodded.

"Stay here." Tony rushed out.

Tony watched Diana eating salsa and chips. He didn't wish to frighten her. He inhaled a deep cleansing breath, released it slowly.

"Hello, Diana." He sat across from her.

Eyes tearing, she choked. "A chip," she hacked, "down the wrong way." She grabbed for the glass of water setting on the table.

He raised her hands above her head, patted her back. "This is what the maid used to do to me." She stopped choking. He retook his seat. "I wasn't trying to scare you."

She pursed her lips. "What do you want, Tony?" She waved him off. "Never mind. I don't care what you want. Just go away. Santiago's sending a plane for me."

He scanned the room. There was only one other couple around, and they were seated on the other side of the restaurant. "I love you, Diana. I'm sorry you found the journal."

"You're sorry I found out you're a liar."

He reached his hand over the table, but she didn't take it. "In the beginning I was trying to seduce you. I was trying to manipulate you, but things changed for us. Come on, Diana. You know more about me than anyone. I opened myself to you because I love you."

She pointed a salsa covered chip at him. "When I said the same thing about Ashton, you told me if he loved me he would have revealed the whole truth. Are you saying the same goes for Ashton? Or are you a special case? Only you can deceive in the beginning then have a change of heart." She popped the chip into her mouth.

He held up his hands with a fat grin plastered across

his face. "Honestly. I thought he loved you. But damn, this Ashton guy was my competition. Why the hell would I say something that would make you hold onto his love?"

Stifling a laugh, she smiled. "What should I do with you, Tony?"

"Make love with me. Marry me."

She held her hand out to him. "Please stop." He took her hand. "You know I'm in love with Ashton. Even if I weren't, we could never be a couple."

He leaned back in his chair moaning, "Please don't give me the 'I love you, but I'm not in love with you' talk."

"I do love you, Tony, but I don't want the drug life. I've held resentment in my heart my whole life because the drug world kept me from my father and godfather. I was also mad at them for choosing a life of crime over me. Since spending so much time with you, I understand them better. They didn't choose the life over me. That was my view. Now I understand things from their view. The life became part of who they are. They were protecting me the only way they knew. They loved me. Santiago loves me.

"To you there is nothing wrong with the drug life. You believe you can protect me, but I don't think it's right. I don't want to have to hide my children. I don't want the government chasing after me because my husband is a drug lord. I don't want to worry about if you have been put in jail or murdered. I don't want the guilt of ruining all of those lives. It's hard enough being Santiago's goddaughter. There's no way I could marry into the life. I won't ask for trouble. I don't want it."

He released her hand. "I've grown a lot since meeting you. I'm not even mad." He chuckled. "The old me would be blowing his top right now."

"I do love you, Tony. I'll worry about you constantly." Her eyes teared up. "I wish you and Santiago would give up the life. I don't want to lose either of you."

Touched she'd actually shed tears for him, he said, "I love the life, Diana. You don't have to worry about me. I can take care of myself. I'm as mean as Santiago. Nothing ever happens to the mean ones."

Her gaze fell to her chips. "I know you're not ready. I'll still talk to Santiago."

"I'll go to him with you."

"I don't think that's such a good idea. You see Ashton—"

Baxter cleared his throat. "Look who took a crash course in English."

Both startled, they saw Baxter standing behind Ashton.

Reflex. Tony whipped out his nine millimeter and pointed it at Ashton's gut so the couple across the diner wouldn't see.

"Tony." Diana stood slowly. "This is Ashton."

Shit shit shit. Tony saw the anguish in her eyes and put his piece away, but continued glaring at Ashton.

Under his breath Baxter hissed, "What the hell are you doing? I won't allow this bitch to keep us from taking care of business."

"I told you to watch your mouth. I know what the hell I'm doing, Baxter. I don't need your advice."

"How did she escape in the first place? If I remember correctly, you said you had the situation under control. I work for Robert Carter, not you. Having this big mother here is a threat. His ass dies today. Now take your bit... woman and get out of here."

Tony gazed into Diana's eyes. "You know I love you, don't you? Do you love me?"

She gazed into Tony's eyes, making sure Baxter saw. "Yes, I love you."

He turned to Baxter saying, "Hell no. I'll do the shit myself. I want to know his ass is dead."

"Damn man, what the hell you got between your legs to—" Seeing Tony's face, he stopped abruptly. "I'll take her to the room."

Baxter reached for Diana's arm. Tony knocked his arm aside. "No. She doesn't leave my sight."

"But, Tony."

"Allow me to explain something, Baxter. If you so much as accidentally brush Diana, my father will lose his most loyal employee." He held his arm out for Diana. "Now let's take care of this."

❦❦❦

Ashton didn't want Diana to see him die. She'd been

there when Steven died. It almost destroyed her. He stared out the window of the car as they drove into the back woods. She loved Tony, but she was in love with him. He knew this in his heart. She wanted to save him, but didn't know how.

They were out in the middle of nowhere. How could he save her? At least save her psyche. Tony loved her and would take her to Santiago. He looked over at Baxter; he had an itchy trigger finger. Tony continued driving.

Ashton wished he could see Diana's face. He leaned forward, whispering, "I'm sorry, Diana, but I still work for the DEA."

Everyone could hear him, but no one else spoke. "I couldn't let Santiago go free. This was too big of a bust for me."

"What do you think this is," Tony snapped. "*True Fucking Confessions*? Shut the hell up." He pulled over.

"I don't even like Diana, but that was jacked up. Why the hell would you relieve your guilty assed conscious like that? You played her for a fool."

"Enough, Baxter," Tony said. "Let's do this." They all exited the car.

Ashton gazed into Diana's eyes. They contained the same emotionless stare as when they took Steven away to be executed. "Tony, at least leave Diana in the car. She shouldn't see this."

"Get into the car, Diana." She followed Tony's orders.

"Hell no! She might run away."

"Let's go." Tony took out his nine millimeter and walked the short distance across the field into the woods. Baxter had no choice but follow with Ashton.

Once in the foliage, Baxter pointed his gun at Ashton's temple and instructed him to kneel.

"Any last request?" Tony asked Ashton.

⚬⟡⟿⟬⟡⟿⟬⟡⚬

Diana's prayers were interrupted by a hollow shot. She prayed her trust in Tony wasn't misplaced. Seeing movement in the woods, she peeked up. "Ashton!" She ran out of the car to him and jumped into his arms.

He held her tightly, kissing and caressing her. "I'm all right, baby. I'm all right."

Tony brought up the rear. "I hate to break up this love fest, but we need to leave." Diana released Ashton and latched onto Tony.

He held her in his embrace, loving her with all his heart. He stroked her hair gently, knowing she was right. He wouldn't endanger her or ask her to live in the drug world. His eyes locked on Ashton's with the, "If you ever hurt her again, I'll kill you" look.

Ashton gave a single nod of understanding. "Tony's right. We need to leave."

"It's time to contact my father. He must be scared shitless." Tony led the way to the car. "Knowing him, he'll try to have Santiago killed. *Again.*"

CHAPTER THIRTY-THREE

"**W**ould you answer the damn thing?" Leonard snapped.

Carter reluctantly took his cellphone from his waistband, answering, "What do you want?"

"I'm fucking happy to hear from you also. Damn, Dad."

"I can't speak right now."

Leonard snatched the phone. "Who is this?"

"Who the hell are you, and why the fuck do you have my dad's phone?"

"I have a hell of a lot more than your daddy's precious phone you son of—"

Santiago took the phone from Leonard, stating more than asking, "It's Tony isn't it."

Leonard rolled his eyes. "Yeah."

Santiago explained to Tony they had his father.

"Santiago, it's me," Diana said

Thinking he'd played his trump card too soon, his heart raced. "What are you doing with him, Pepita? You're supposed to be with Ashton."

"Give me a second, and I'll tell you everything. Do you have a speaker phone where you're at? You all sound distorted."

He asked Leonard, then replied, "Yes. What's going on, baby?"

"Give me the number. We'll call you right back." Leonard gave her the number.

⟬⟭⟬⟭⟬⟭

Tony, Ashton, and Diana gathered around the speakerphone they'd bought in anticipation of this call. "How will your father react?" Diana asked.

"I told you, he'll want to kill me." Tony looked at the phone number, inhaled deeply then dialed. "Might as well get the execution over with."

"Hello."

"Leonard, this is Ashton. Turn on the speakerphone. Would you make sure Carter and Santiago are in earshot?" They heard a click.

"Pepita."

Diana spoke. "Santiago. I'm safe, but for how long? Because of you and Carter, I've been a captive my whole life. I'm tired of it. We're gonna settle this whole thing once and for all."

"How do I now Tony isn't forcing you into this?"

"You know I'd die before I'd—"

Santiago interrupted saying, "You don't need to finish. You're as bad as your father. So what do you want, Tony?" He couldn't stand Robert Carter, but always liked Tony.

"Diana and I have come up with a plan we believe will suit both families. Dad, are you there?"

"I'm here," he grumbled.

"Look, Dad. It's time for you to retire. I'll run our territory."

"What are you saying, Tony?"

"You know I can run things. I've earned it. Now step aside and allow me. You always say you're holding on for me. I don't need you to hold it for me anymore."

"And what will you do about assholes like Santiago who try to encroach? You don't have the balls to do what needs to be done."

Tony turned red with anger. Diana jumped in before Tony could reply. "How dare you, you sorry sack of crap. Tony does all of your dirty work while you sit back and hide in your office ordering people around because you don't have to balls to take care of business yourself. You are a self-centered bully, and it's time for you to quit before Tony gets killed covering your tracks. He'll make enough mistakes of his own and can't afford to cover yours."

"Who do you think you're talking to, little girl? I'll—"

Diana cut him off. "You won't do anything but hire someone to come after me because you're too big a coward to come at me yourself." Ashton reached for her. "Stop, Ashton." She pulled away. "It's about time someone told this jerk off. Tony is your son. Your only child, and you have done nothing but use him and put him down his whole life. Steven wouldn't win any father of the year awards, but at least he made sure I was safe. He would have never asked me to clean a mess he made. Yet you do it time and time again then have the audacity to attack Tony's manhood. From the looks of things, you don't even know what a man is."

"Pepita, enough."

"Don't stop me now, Santiago. I'm on a roll."

"I know, Pepita, but we need to finish this business."

"Fine. Tony."

"You know I can run the territory, Dad. I practically run it now. I don't think I'll have to worry about Santiago encroaching on our territory because I suggest we join the two territories."

"Hell, Tony. Why are you giving away all I've worked for? Is she that good in bed?"

They heard a smack, crash and yell of agony through the line. "What's going on over there?" Diana asked.

"Everything's fine. Leonard just punched Carter, knocking him out of his chair. I think his nose is broken, but he'll live."

Tony laughed. "Thanks, Leonard. I think I'll like you."

"Wha-what the hell are you saying, Tony? How can you side with them?"

"I'm not, Dad."

"Santiago, what do you think?" Diana asked. "I know you've been grooming Hugo, but he's almost as old as you."

"I'm not old," Santiago dryly replied.

"You're a lot older than me. I think you should give Tony a chance. I love Hugo and all, but you have him as number two because you had no other candidates. Now you do."

"I think Hugo wants out."

"This is the perfect time for you to expand your empire. You know this is good business."

Santiago had always suspected Tony was his son, but why would Carter raise his son? It just didn't add up. "If Carter steps down, I'm in." Tony may not be his son by blood, but with this alliance, Tony would become his son and he'd someday have the largest cartel in the world.

"I won't step down."

They heard Leonard say, "You can either step down voluntarily, or the position will be vacated due to your early demise." They heard the metallic click of a gun cocking back. "It's your choice. You said I was smart for quitting while I'm ahead. You need to do the same. Santiago may be a drug dealing son-of-a-bitch, but he's honorable. He'll do right by Tony."

"Are you sure you want to do this, Tony?"

"Yes, Dad."

"When he takes total control and kicks your ass out into the street, don't come running to me."

"I won't, Dad."

Diana released a sigh of relief. "Boy am I glad that's over with. Santiago, I don't want to return to the California yet. Can you meet us in Colombia?"

"Sure, baby. We'll finish negotiations in Colombia, Tony."

"And would you bring my identification. I left kind of abruptly and didn't have time to grab any." She kicked Tony under the table.

"What is going on between you, Tony and Ashton?"

"It's a long story. I'll tell you in private. Love you. I love you, too, Leonard. Thanks for helping Ashton find me."

Leonard laughed. "Damn, girl. You sure have a lot of love to throw around. I'll see you in Colombia."

"Santiago, hang up so I can call on your cellphone and tell you everything." She turned to Ashton. "Can I use your cellphone?" He handed her his phone.

"I'll be in the bathroom. I need some privacy." She left the two men alone.

"I'll see you in Colombia, Leonard. Stay out of trouble," Ashton jested.

"Hey, I resent that. I haven't killed anyone—lately. I can't say I didn't come close a few times though. Take care." They both disconnected.

Tony had never been so uncomfortable in his life. There had been a reason Ashton looked so enraged in Mexico. He'd heard everything Tony had said to Baxter and read the journal. Tony didn't blame Ashton for wanting to kill him. He'd want to do the same thing had the tables been turned.

"I don't know what to say. I truly hope you two are

happy."

"She loves you. I don't like it, but I guess I have to live with it." Ashton hunched his shoulders. "You saved my life. The least I can do is allow you're friendship to continue."

"She loves you. I couldn't let her lose you." He grinned. "Don't tell anyone I'm a softy. I have to protect my reputation. I'm off to my room." He rose from his seat and held out his hand.

They shook. "We're leaving after breakfast for the plane."

"I'll be ready." Tony headed for the door. "One last thing." He stood in the doorway. "She's really hurt about her good for nothing siblings. She needed them when Steven died and still needs a connection to her family."

Ashton smiled. "I'll work on it. Thanks."

A few minutes, later Diana came out of the bathroom. "Where's Tony."

"He'll meet us for breakfast." He led her to the bed where they cuddled. "I'll never let you out of my sight again."

She rested her head on his chest. "A little drastic, don't you think?"

In all seriousness he answered, "I don't think so."

"I was so afraid I might be wrong about Tony when he took you off."

"I really thought I would die, yet all I could think about was you. I didn't want you to suffer like you did..." he trailed off.

"When my father was murdered."

"I didn't mean to bring the memory back. I'm sorry."

"I have to face it. I love Tony but..." Lost in the thought, she hunched her shoulders.

"But what?"

"I'm grateful to him for saving your life. But today he killed a man. I hated Baxter, but I feel remorse. Tony won't give him a second thought. How can he be so caring with me one second, and a cold blooded killer the next?"

"I don't know. Santiago showed me his sensitive side whenever he dealt with you. I also saw his cruel side. The one that shot a man limb by limb without blinking." He inhaled deeply. "Leonard is so much like Santiago and

Tony."

"I'm glad he has you to keep him straight." She closed her eyes.

"In your records, it looks like you cut yourself off from Steven and Santiago when you were eighteen. Why?"

"I didn't understand what they were when I went to live with them. Once I did, I couldn't accept it, but my family had already disowned me. So when I was legal, I cut them off. I love Santiago so much, but I just can't..." She paused to compose herself. "When we're safe, I have to cut him out of my life again. Him and Tony. I can't support their lifestyle. I just pray they change." She kicked off her shoes then lay in the bed.

He kicked off his shoes and drew her into his body. "I've had more activity these past few weeks than I had my whole career. When we get to New York, I want to meet your family."

She faced him. "Santiago is my family."

"No, love." He kissed her lightly. "You also have two sisters a brother and lord knows how many nieces and nephews. You need to reconcile with your family."

"Why?"

"Because you want a relationship with them."

"Well they don't want one with me," she grumbled. "I tried for years to explain my side, but they wouldn't listen. Do you know how much it hurt every time I received a return to sender letter? They all changed their phone numbers, eventually obtaining unlisted ones. How much rejection should I subject myself to? I'm sorry, but I can't. I don't have the energy. Not now."

"I'll drop it until you're ready."

"Don't get your hopes up, Ashton. I refuse to try again. If they want me, they'll have to come to me."

CHAPTER THIRTY-FOUR

Two Months Later...

Diana woke first. She tried to escape Ashton's embrace; but as usual, he woke.

"Where do you think you're going?"

"I'm hungry and running late."

He kissed her lightly. "Are you sure you want to go alone?"

"I may be there all day. I have a few ideas on how I'd like to change his gravesite. Thanks though."

"I love you." He released her.

She kissed him. "I love you, too."

Leonard leaned back in his chair and glared at Ashton as he entered the kitchen. "Good morning."

Ashton nodded a good morning to Leonard and his older brother Brandon.

Brandon peeked over his paper, nodded, returned to the article.

"What's wrong with you, Leonard?" Ashton poured himself a cup of coffee.

"What kind of vitamins do you take?"

Ashton frowned. "I don't." He sat at the table and inhaled the rich aroma of the coffee. "Are you coming with us, Brandon?"

"Nah. You know how I hate drama."

"What do you eat before you go to bed?" Leonard asked.

Ashton cocked his head to the side. "Nothing, Leonard. Dang, what's wrong with you?"

Leonard took Ashton's cup of coffee. Upon careful examination, he saw nothing unusual about it. "Any special foods?"

"I don't know what's wrong with you, but I'm in no mood to listen to your craziness today. I have a lot on my mind. Are you ready to leave?"

"Do you wear boxers or briefs?"

Brandon laughed coffee out all over his newspaper. "I sense drama coming." He folded his paper neatly and set it on the table. "It's time for me to escape." He pushed away from the table, leaving the two friends alone.

"Let's go, Leonard."

Ashton pulled into the driveway of the large suburban house. "It's now or never."

"What additional exercises do you do?" Leonard asked. "You know, besides what we do at the gym."

"Would you please stop asking all of these stupid questions? We have business to handle." He opened his door.

"Wait a second. I only have one more."

"What?" Ashton snapped.

"How can you go so long?"

"Excuse me?"

Leonard shook his head and hunched his shoulders. "You and Diana go at it for hours at a time. I'm talking romance novel type shit." He trained his big blue eyes on Ashton. "What's your secret? Come on, we're brothers. You can tell me."

Ashton's eyes locked on Leonard. "You mean this inquisition has been about my stamina in bed?" He burst out in laughter. "You are out of your mind." He exited the car. Leonard followed him along the walk to the house.

"Well damn, man. I'm impressed. Hours. Come on. You have to admit it's a little out of the ordinary."

"Not hours."

"I timed you this morning."

"Liar." He rang the doorbell. "I hope this works."

Leonard shrugged. "We have nothing to lose. I can't believe you won't tell me."

"There's nothing to tell, Leonard. Now shelve this conversation. I'm already nervous enough without having to worry about what you'll say."

Leonard rang the bell. "But how can you go so long? It must be Diana's cooking."

Ashton chuckled. "You're half right. And it isn't I go so long. I just re-energize quickly."

They both stepped back as the door opened.

"Hello." Ronald nodded at the two men.

"Hello, I'm Ashton Powell, and this is my associate Leonard Rogers."

"I'm sorry it took so long." Ronald held out his hand to shake.

"Pleased to meet you, Mr. Johnson," Ashton said.

"Call me Ronald. My sisters are waiting in the study. I thought our father's estate was settled." They followed him into the study where he introduced them to his sisters.

Ashton and Leonard sat on the couch across from Diana's siblings. "First I must apologize," Ashton said. "I'm not here to settle your father's estate. I'm here about Diana. I'm sorry I deceived you, but I wanted to ensure you'd all show."

Jenny became enraged. "Diana? We haven't heard from her in years. What does she want?" She turned to her siblings. "She must be in jail. I knew she wouldn't turn out any good. Spoiled little brat. Who are you, her lawyer?"

Ronald placed his hand on his sister's lap, silencing her. "Excuse her outburst. We all had such high hopes for Diana."

"Oh really?" Leonard snorted. "Exactly what did you expect to happen when you turned your back on her?"

Ashton didn't want to continue the family feud. He was there to mend fences. "Please, Leonard, we aren't here for this."

Leonard slouched back on the couch. "Fine. Do it your way."

Jenny narrowed her eyes on Leonard. "We didn't turn our back on her. We showed her tough love."

He rolled his eyes, allowing them to settle on Jenny. "Maybe I should wait in the car. There's entirely too much ignorance, hate, stupidity and hypocrisy in this house for me." He shook his head mumbling, "Why did God waste such good looks on a shrew?" He smiled and winked.

"What are you here for?" Linda, the eldest of the three, asked.

"I'm her husband." All three's brows rose. "She's pregnant with our first child and misses her family. She needs you all."

Jenny stood. "After all of these years she comes

crawling back because... No, make that, she sends her husband crawling back to us. Damn, a fine man like you should have done better for himself. What a waste."

Leonard leaned forward, asking Ronald, "Has she always been like this?" He stood. "Come on, Ashton. Diana was right to stop trying."

Leonard watched his brother stand to leave, but his heart remained low. "Explain something to me," Leonard said as he waited beside Ashton. His gaze locked on Ronald, who seemed to be the most sensible of the lot. "This is a fine house. This is your childhood home, correct?"

Ronald nodded.

"Explain how your family could afford to live in this area, and did you all earn scholarships for college?"

Jenny spoke, chastising, "My father was a hard working man. He had honest employment, unlike the devil who spawned Diana."

Leonard's brow rose. "If you were so offended by the way Diana's father made his living, why did you allow him to pay for your college educations? Why didn't you sell this house after your father passed and donate the proceeds to charity? Why did each of you accept the trusts Steven had set up for each of you?"

She stomped her foot on the ground. "My father paid for—"

"Give me a break. Come down from your holier than thou throne for a few minutes into reality. Your father was a bus driver and your mother was a housewife. Steven paid for this house and all of your luxuries, and you know it. He even went a step further and ensured you good for nothings had the best educations and big fat checks waiting as graduation gifts. When your father became sick, you couldn't pretend your father was footing the bills anymore, so you turned on your baby sister when she needed you most."

Ronald held Jenny back, keeping her from interrupting. He'd been feeling guilty for years. He sighed. They all had felt the same. When his mother took ill then his father, they couldn't deal with it. They all needed to blame someone. Unfortunately, Santiago and Steven were easy targets. Diana was caught in the crossfire.

He understood his sisters' need to justify their actions, to cover for their guilt, but the time had come to heal their family.

Diana stood back and appreciated the work she'd done at Steven's gravesite.

"Hey, beautiful lady." Ashton wrapped his arms around her waist and massaged his babies.

She tilted her head back for a little kiss, then continued absorbing the beauty. She'd planted bulbs the previous fall. They had bloomed into a gorgeous red tulip tribute that spelled FATHER on a black tulip background. She'd also outlined the site with grape hyacinths. The arched trellis smelled sweet from miniature white roses.

"This is breathtaking, baby."

Feeling the loss of her father, she caressed Ashton's hand. "It'll look different each season."

He turned her in his arms. "Have I told you how amazing you are lately?"

She grinned into his chest. "Not lately."

"Hey, can a brother get a little love around here?" Leonard interrupted.

She opened her arms to him. "Always."

"Do you know what your man did to me this morning?"

"Kept you out of trouble," she teased.

"That's a given. Take a walk with me. " He turned her away from the grave. "We need to have a talk about sex."

Ashton slapped him on the head. Diana laughed.

"I'm just kidding. Let Ashton clean up this mess."

She walked off with Leonard. "What are you up to?"

He hunched his shoulders. "Who me? Nothin'. I'm putting a little something, something away for my godson. Ashton said you'd give me a hard time, but I'll give you a harder one if you don't allow me to do this."

"Okay, you win, and I'm planning on having a girl."

He raised a brow. "That was too easy."

"I'm in my first trimester of pregnancy, Leonard. I'm in no mood to argue. Why are we stalling?"

"I'm not stalling. Let's head back."

Diana's eyes narrowed at the site of people around her father's grave. Leonard smiled. "See. You made it too fancy. Now everyone will want their loved one's sites this nice."

Once they neared, Ashton took Diana's hand. "How was your walk?" He kissed her fingers.

"Leonard is up to something. I don't know what, but I know it's something."

The siblings turned. Diana froze as recognition dawned. "What are they doing here?" she asked Ashton.

He gently placed his hand in the small of her back. "For the same reason we're all here. To pay respect to Steven Warren, one of the few people who always put you first." He pushed her toward her sisters and brother.

"I'm sorry for everything, Diana," Ronald said. "Will you forgive us?"

Unable to comprehend, Diana stared. Linda walked over slowly, taking Diana's hands into her own. "I know we turned our backs on you." She pointed to her siblings. "We are truly sorry."

Jenny stepped forward. "Hey. I've always been a bitch. Hate me if you want. Hell, I deserve it after the way I've acted. But I'll always love you."

Leonard nudged Ashton whispering, "Now that's my kind of woman."

Feeling overwhelmed, Diana looked over her shoulder for Ashton. His slight smile soothed her heart. She turned to her siblings, opening her arms. Jenny was the first to grab Diana into a hug. The others followed quickly.

Leonard and Ashton finished cleaning the mess while the siblings continued their reunion.

"You're next man," Ashton said.

"I'm never getting married."

"That's what I used to think. Look at the way Jenny keeps sneaking peeks at you."

Leonard glanced up, and sure enough, Jenny quickly looked away. "She's cute and has good fight, but I'm allergic to marriage."

"Come and join us," Diana called.

A Word From The Author

I can't thank you enough for continuing on this writing journey with me. I originally wrote this title years ago, knowing publishing houses wouldn't want it because it's not a romance (though romantic) and it isn't street lit (though filled with drugs and death). Thanks to self-publishing, I have more freedom to do me.

I hope you enjoyed Ashton and Diana's story, and I look forward to writing the next adventure. No telling what I'll come up with next. I've been in a Sci-Fi mood lately, so don't be shocked if you see one from me in a few years.

Love you all,
Until the next book,

Deatri King-Bey

Titles By Deatri King-Bey

Romance
Beauty and the Beast
Broken Promises
Diamond in the Rough
Ebony Angel
Love's Desire
Santa's Helper (Write Brothers Series Book II)
Tell Her How You Feel (Write Brothers Series Book I)
The Other Realm
Trapped In Paradise
Whisper Something Sweet

Suspense
Black Widow and the Sandman (as L. L. Reaper)

Women's Fiction
Caught Up
Operation White Rose
Picture Perfect

Nonfiction
Become A Successful Author

Visit me online at:
http://www.BecomeASuccessfulAuthor.com
http://www.DeatriKingBey.com
http://www.LLReaper.com
http://www.Son4Sale.com

Until we meet again, keep reading and writing,
Deatri King-Bey